RESTORED HE...

Restorations

SUSAN ELIZABETH BALL

*To Cindy,
May God richly
bless you,
Susan Ball
1-7-11*

OakTara

WATERFORD, VIRGINIA

Restorations

Published in the U.S. by:
OakTara Publishers
P.O. Box 8
Waterford, VA 20197

Visit OakTara at
www.oaktara.com

Cover design by Kay Chin Bishop, www.kaybishop.carbonmade.com
Cover images © iStockphoto.com/bridge with reflection, rtlee; woman, Kemter
Author photo © 2010 Sarah Kittredge/Kitt Creative, Fredericksburg, Virginia

Copyright © 2010 by Susan Elizabeth Ball. All rights reserved.

Scripture taken from the HOLY BIBLE, NEW INTERNATIONAL VERSION®. NIV®. Copyright © 1973, 1978, 1984 by International Bible Society. Used by permission of Zondervan. All rights reserved.

ISBN: 978-1-60290-191-9

Restorations is a work of fiction. References to real people, events, establishments, organizations, or locales are intended only to provide a sense of authenticity and are used fictitiously. All other characters, incidents, and dialogue are drawn from the author's imagination.

⌘ ⌘ ⌘

To Steve,
With all my love.
I am so blessed
to have you in my life.

Acknowledgments

Thanks to my family and friends for their prayers and encouragement throughout this process. I am grateful to Writer's Edge Manuscript Services for the assistance they provide to new Christian writers and to the staff at OakTara who have worked with me on this book.

⌘ ⌘ ⌘

Create in me a pure heart, O God,
And renew a steadfast spirit within me.
Psalm 51:10

1

From her lounge chair strategically placed under the shade of a large oak tree, Karen looked up from the book she was reading and took stock of her family. Her husband, Jeff, frolicked in the lake with their youngest son, Kyle. Their middle son, Austin, had tired of the water and was playing Frisbee with a redheaded boy he had befriended. Trevor, the oldest, was trying to make small talk with a blonde in a tiny pink bikini. At twelve years of age, he had recently discovered girls and was wasting no time in getting to know the opposite sex better.

As Karen surveyed the scene, she felt a deep sense of contentment. It really doesn't get much better than this, she thought. A lovely spring day at the lake surrounded by those she loved best. Karen picked up the romance novel and continued her reading.

After a few minutes, Jeff brought Kyle to Karen and said that he was going to swim to the small island in the middle of the lake. Jeff was an excellent swimmer, and the short swim out to the island and back posed no serious challenge. Karen occupied herself with toweling Kyle off and changing him into shorts and a T-shirt. She began gathering up the wet towels and sunscreen. It was almost time to head for home. When she cast her gaze back to the lake, Jeff was about thirty feet from shore and struggling to keep his head above the water.

"Jeff! Hang on, Jeff! I'm coming." Karen's heart pounded in her chest as she raced to the dock and grabbed the life ring. She tossed it in Jeff's direction, but it fell short of his reach. She pulled on the rope until she could reach out and grab the ring and toss it again. Karen threw it over and over, as far as she could, but each time it landed a little bit short. Jeff was only able to get his fingertips on the ring once before it slipped from his grasp.

"Help us! Someone, please help us!" Karen yelled at the top of her *lungs as she continued to throw out the life preserver.*

A man and woman had been walking around the lake and heard Karen's screams. The woman called 911; the man joined Karen on the dock, offering his assistance. By this time, Jeff's head had disappeared in the murky water. The man dove in, but he didn't find Jeff.

The man and woman stayed with Karen and the children, as the rescue divers searched for Jeff's body. There was no hope now. Karen pulled her knees up to her chest and wrapped her arms around them. "You did everything you could," the woman told her.

"It wasn't enough." Karen sobbed and repeated over and over, "It wasn't enough. It wasn't enough...."

⌘ ⌘ ⌘

"It wasn't enough. It wasn't enough." Karen Harper's plaintive cries awakened her from her sleep. Her heart thundered in her chest. Her curly auburn hair was drenched with sweat. *What's happening?*

Bolting upright, she opened her eyes and tried to focus. The room was dark. She reached out until her hand found the nightstand. She felt around for the lamp and turned it on.

"A dream. I was only dreaming." Karen breathed deeply, trying to slow her racing heart. She closed her eyes again and shuddered. It seemed so very real. She could feel the warmth of the sun and the sand beneath her feet. She saw the panic on Jeff's face as he realized he was going under and the scared faces of her children. *Enough.* Her heart was racing again. She shook herself and tried to clear her mind of the horrible dream.

If asked, Karen would say that she never dreamed. She knew, of course, that everyone dreams, so certainly she must. But she could never recall having dreamed. Nightmares, however, were a different story. She could recall nightmares in vivid detail.

As she sat in her bed, trying to make sense of this nightmare, Karen recalled one from several years earlier. In that nightmare, Karen's extended family had gathered for a reunion. The children were playing ball and running around, while the adults sat in lawn chairs eating hamburgers and catching up on each others' lives. Suddenly, her father grabbed his chest and collapsed on the ground in front of her. She had crouched on the ground beside him and sobbed into his chest as he died.

Her sobs had awakened Jeff, who gently took her in his arms and stroked her head, whispering, "It was only a dream." It had seemed so real that it took several minutes before Jeff could convince Karen that her father had not suffered a heart attack. "Your family has never even had a reunion," Jeff had reminded her.

Even after all these years, she could visualize her father as he lay on the ground gasping for breath. Despite the fact that her father was still alive and well, Karen's pulse quickened anytime she thought of that nightmare.

This morning Jeff was not there to comfort and console. This nightmare, while not based on reality, was accurate in its conclusion. Jeff was dead. He had been for nearly two years. Karen had tried to rescue him and had failed miserably. For the first few months after his death, she had been haunted day and night by the horrible series of events surrounding Jeff's death. She had frequently awakened with a start, as she had this morning, frantic to save him.

Over and over, she had been plagued by questions for which she had no answers. "Could I have saved him if I'd tried harder? Is it my fault he's dead?" "If I had been a better wife, would Jeff still be alive?" As time passed, she had to set aside her constant thoughts of him. There was nothing she could do for him now, except raise his sons to be the men he wanted them to be. As a single mother to three young boys, Karen had no time for guilt or self-pity. She had to provide for her family.

The nightmares had eventually ceased. She hadn't dreamed of Jeff in—oh, how long was it now—maybe a year, perhaps a bit more. *I thought the nightmares were gone for good. I wonder why they came back now.* She pondered this as she lay in the bed she had shared with Jeff for sixteen years. Maybe it was because she was trying to move on and put the past behind her. She was making a new life for herself, one without Jeff in it. Perhaps subconsciously she didn't want to let him go.

Karen glanced at the alarm clock on the nightstand. It was almost five o'clock. No wonder it was so dark. Her body needed more rest, but

3

she knew it was useless to try. She would not be going back to sleep this morning. Still shaken and sweaty from the nightmare, she needed a shower.

Karen climbed from the queen-sized bed and headed for the bathroom. She paced around the small room as she waited for the water to warm up. When steam began to form on the mirror, she climbed in and allowed the water to gently massage her tensed muscles. The warm water felt so good. She stood under the spray until her fingers and toes shriveled. After toweling off and drying her hair, she pulled on a pair of plaid sleep pants—they had been Jeff's—and an oversized sweatshirt. She slipped her feet into the fuzzy blue slippers she kept beside the bed before heading downstairs.

Karen loved the 1960s Colonial-style house she had rented last summer. She would have preferred to purchase a home, but that was beyond her reach just now. When she sold the home she had shared with Jeff and moved to Fredericksburg, she had hoped the equity would be sufficient for her to put a downpayment on a home here. After discovering, however, that the housing market was much tighter here than in Chester, she felt fortunate to have found a rental she could afford.

Karen's only complaint was that the house was drafty and chilly on cold wintry mornings. It seemed particularly so this January morning, with the wind howling outside. Karen peeked out the kitchen window onto the deck. The large outdoor thermometer indicated that the temperature was 26 degrees.

"No snow," Karen said with a sigh, "but the windshield is sure to need defrosting." Karen was as bad as the kids when it came to wishing for snow. This was due, in part, to the fact that her compassionate boss allowed her the day off when school was canceled. A widower himself, he understood only too well the challenges Karen faced as a single parent.

Karen filled the teakettle with fresh, cold water and set it on the back burner of the stove. She selected her favorite mug from the cupboard and pulled a bag of English breakfast tea from the box in the pantry. While she waited for the water to boil, she unloaded the dishwasher. "If you've got time to lean, you've got time to clean," was

Karen's favorite mom-ism. It had been instilled in her by her own mother when she was growing up and reinforced by her first boss at The Hamburger Shack, where Karen had worked as a waitress throughout high school. Neither her mother nor her boss put up with anyone standing around idly while they worked. And they both found that there was always work to be done. As a single mother, Karen had found the "clean, don't lean" philosophy to be the key to her survival. If she wanted any leisure time, she had to take advantage of moments like this. She was amazed at how much she could accomplish by capturing otherwise wasted minutes.

She finished unloading the dishwasher before the water boiled, so she grabbed the broom to sweep up crumbs from last night's dinner. The whistle of the teakettle interrupted her work. She poured the steaming water into the mug and finished sweeping the kitchen and dining room while the tea steeped. After adding honey, she took her tea and yesterday's newspaper into the den, hoping to find some interesting article to divert her attention. Even though she would regret her abbreviated sleep later, Karen was thankful to have a few quiet moments by herself before beginning the activities of the day. She had long since learned that she had to allow herself some "me" time for sanity's sake.

"Family Home Lost in Fire" read the headline on the first page. Too depressing. She scanned the rest of the page. One article discussed potential solutions to the problems of overcrowded roads, another the dilemma of where to build yet another area high school as the region continued to grow, and a third compared snowfalls this year so far to predictions made by forecasters last fall. Finding nothing of interest in the first section, Karen pulled out the Region section. She was interested in a report on the results of the last year's standards of learning testing. It seemed that area school children had exceeded expectations. That was good news. Nothing else of interest caught her eye.

She laid the newspaper aside and sipped her tea. It had cooled to lukewarm. "Yuk." Karen popped it into the microwave to reheat it for a minute. While waiting, she pondered the question that plagued her nearly every morning. *What to have for dinner?* She went to the garage and surveyed the contents of her freezer. "Let's see. There's chicken breast, pork chops, and ground beef." She grabbed a frozen package of ground beef. *Tacos, it is.*

As she turned to walk back into the kitchen, a sudden, sharp pain radiated through her left foot. "Ouch." She grabbed her stubbed toe with both hands, dropping the frozen meat on her right foot. "Umph. Ouch." She released the left foot and reached for the now throbbing right one. If anyone had peeked through the garage window, they would have seen Karen hopping up and down, grabbing first one foot and then the other. That is, until she mistimed her hopping and wound up with both feet in the air. She landed with a thud on her bottom. Her head jerked backwards and banged on a chair, launching a pile of long-forgotten clothing into the air and unto her head. Karen had placed the boys' outgrown clothing on the chair last summer with the intention of delivering the items to Goodwill.

Karen sat on the floor, covered in clothing, massaging both feet. "I must look ridiculous," she said aloud. She giggled at the thought. The giggles turned into all-out laughter, which continued until tears ran down her face. The laughter released the tension she had been feeling. It also seemed to have soothed the pain in her feet. Karen wiped the tears and set about the task of picking up the far-flung articles of clothing. "What have we here? Why, it's one of the chairs from the flea market. I wonder where the other one is?"

She found the other chair on the far side of the garage behind Austin's bike. Karen had picked up the pair for next to nothing and had planned to strip them of their badly scratched finish and give them a new coat of stain. Fortunately, the upholstered seats were in good shape. When she purchased them, she had no real need for two more chairs, so they had been relegated to the garage. If she could find a table for the kitchen, they would come in handy. Of course, she would need more than two chairs. "A project would be good for me. This will be perfect." For now she would leave the chairs in the garage. She passed a hardware store every day on her way to and from work. She made a mental note to stop in soon and pick up the supplies she needed to begin the project.

She located the dropped package of ground beef and went back to the kitchen, where the microwave was beeping incessantly. She gave the tea a thirty-second warm-up, then took the cup back into the den. She still had a few more minutes before she needed to begin her day. Her gaze fell on the Bible gathering dust on the end table. There was a time when she faithfully attended church and began each day by spending a few minutes in God's Word. That seemed a lifetime ago. When had she laid aside those habits? *I guess after Jeff's death, I got busy and just didn't have the time.* She knew that this explanation was only partially true, like so many things she told herself concerning Jeff's death and the rocky time in their marriage that had preceded it.

Remembering the comfort the Bible had brought her in times past, Karen picked it up and flipped it open to Psalm 23: "The Lord is my Shepherd, I shall not be in want." She read the familiar passage. "He makes me lie down in green pastures, he leads me beside quiet waters, he restores my soul."

"He restores my soul." Karen read the words again, fully aware that it was no coincidence that she stumbled onto the chairs needing restoration just before reading this verse. Furniture restoration had been a hobby of Karen's for several years, although she hadn't worked on anything since Jeff's death. She wondered if there were similarities in the process God used to restore souls and the process she used to restore furniture. She would have to give that some thought.

After she finished reading the psalm and took a moment to pray—another habit that had fallen by the wayside in the past year or two—she felt more at peace than she had in recent memory.

2

Greg Marshall heard his front door open as he finished his breakfast. He glanced at the clock on the wall. Six o'clock sharp. Gretchen was right on time, as always. He knew she would hang up her coat, then head into the kitchen.

"I'm in here," he called out cheerfully.

"Good morning, Greg," his mother-in-law replied as she entered the kitchen. "I hope I'm not late; the car was iced up this morning and took longer to defrost then I had planned on." She set a large brown bag on the floor. Greg knew without asking what was in the bag.

"You're not late, but you know, Gretchen, that you wouldn't have to deal with frost on the car if you parked it in the garage. That's what the garage is for."

Gretchen rolled her eyes. "Why don't you suggest to Tom that he build a workshop in the backyard? Then he could clear a space for me to put the car in the garage." She pulled two plastic food containers out of the bag and placed them in the freezer.

Greg shook his head and gave up. Cindy's parents, Gretchen and Tom Sullivan, had argued over space in the garage for as long as he had known them, and he figured they weren't about to change their ways now.

"I made you a lasagna for tonight's dinner." Gretchen changed the subject as she pulled another container from the bag. She put this container into the refrigerator and placed an index card on the counter by the stove. "Cooking instructions."

"The instructions for the garlic bread are on the bag." She held up the loaf of frozen bread before adding it to the freezer. "You have plenty of frozen vegetables, so just pick one and heat it up. You'll have a nice dinner."

Gretchen had been helping out with children and bringing him frozen, home-cooked meals since his wife's death three years ago. He didn't know if they would have been able to manage without her help, and Tom's also.

"You are going to ruin my reputation as a starving widower who can't survive on his own cooking, if you keep this up. How am I ever going to get an eligible female to take pity on me?"

Greg was shocked to hear those words coming out of his own mouth. He hadn't been aware he was *in* the market for an "eligible female." He hoped he hadn't offended Gretchen. One look at her face assured him that he had not.

"Well, praise the Lord! It's about time you started dating again."

"Um, I'm not sure I'm ready to start dating yet." Greg shifted uncomfortably. "But I might start thinking about the possibility."

"What are you waiting for?" Gretchen seemed amused by Greg's discomfort. "Cindy wouldn't want you to spend the rest of your life brooding over her. And don't overlook the fact the girls are at an age where they really need a mother in their lives."

"I know, but I don't even know how to begin. I haven't dated in twenty years."

"You'll figure it out, with God's help. Robin and I will help, too." Robin Jennings was Gretchen's best friend. She was also Greg's receptionist. The two ladies loved to play matchmaker, though they referred to themselves as "relationship facilitators." Their usual method was to invite single people whom they considered compatible to their homes for Saturday dinner or Sunday lunch. The potential couples would be introduced and given ample opportunity to get to know each other as the hostess was occupied with putting the finishing touches on the meal. Often, the arranged meeting was all the interference that was needed. If the two were attracted, nature would run its course. The church membership included at least a dozen married couples whose romance began at one of the two ladies' dinner tables.

"Mrs. Clark's daughter Emily has just moved back to town. She's single." Gretchen's eyes had taken on the sparkle that told Greg she was working on a plan.

"Emily! She's practically a child."

"You haven't seen Emily in a long time. She's all grown up. She graduated from college a few years ago."

"Which makes her half my age. If, and when, I'm ready to start dating, I won't be dating women young enough to be my daughters."

"You're right, of course. We will look for more mature women."

"I think you and Robin need to stay out of it for now. I'll let you know if I want your help."

"Yes, of course. We won't forge ahead until we have your permission."

Greg knew Gretchen spoke the truth. As much as Gretchen and Robin loved seeing people find love and commitment, they were not busybodies. They never interfered without permission. When Greg was ready, they would happily arrange casual encounters with suitable companions.

Greg downed the last sip of coffee, kissed Gretchen on the cheek, and headed to the bathroom to brush his teeth.

Within a few minutes, he was backing his Lexus GX out of his tidy garage and heading for his office.

⌘⌘⌘

Tidewater Orthodontics was a quick five-minute drive from Greg's house in Artillery Ridge. He deliberately had chosen a site close to home so he didn't waste precious family time commuting to work. Certainly, he loved his work. It gave him a great sense of fulfillment to watch a patient's personal and emotional development as his or her teeth were realigned.

How many times had he watched a shy teenage girl blossom into a social butterfly as her teeth were straightened? Or witnessed the transformation of a gap-toothed timid boy into a confident young man? He knew, of course, that the changes in his patients were not due entirely to his efforts. It took up to two years for the orthodontic work to be completed, and his young patients matured greatly during that time. Still, his work contributed to their social growth, and he was enormously proud he could perform a service that helped so many people to feel better about themselves.

Greg worked long hours, opening early some days and staying late on others, to accommodate the busy school and work schedules of his patients. Yet, his family was his top priority. When work was over for the day, he was glad to leave it behind and head home to his precious daughters. He loved the way they still ran to greet him when he came home each evening. If only their mother were waiting for him as well. Cindy had always put aside whatever she was doing and met him at the door. Embracing her tightly, Greg would feel the cares of the day melt away. He loved her scent. The scent of her perfume mingled with the aromas of the meal she had prepared for dinner. He particularly loved baking days when she might smell of yeast or cinnamon and spices. Greg had never told anyone that he'd left the bottle of her favorite perfume, Paris Spring, on the dresser where she had kept it. Every few weeks during the first months of his widowerhood, he sprayed a bit on her pillow and breathed in her scent once more. The perfume had long since been used up and even the bottle no longer carried traces of its aroma, but having the bottle in sight helped keep the memory alive.

He had first laid eyes on Cindy in the dining hall at the University of Alabama. Greg was in his second year of dental school, and she was a junior majoring in elementary education. He was returning his meal ticket to his wallet when laughter exploded from across the room. His eyes scanned the mass of students until they lit on a blond coed doubled over in hysterics. His heart thumped wildly in his chest. He was attracted to a woman whose face he couldn't even see. He could, however, see long, slender legs and curvaceous hips. When she turned giving him a first glimpse of her face, he knew he was a lost man. How he ever got up the courage to walk over to her table and introduce himself, he would never know. That memory was a blur. Somehow he did, and she flashed him a big smile showing off a mouthful of perfect teeth. She claimed his heart and never returned it.

Cindy brought laughter and joy to Greg's life. Her playful nature balanced his tendency to be overly serious. She coaxed him away from his studies and taught him to relax and enjoy life to the fullest. They had married two years later. Cindy taught third grade and supported him through the four more years of dental school required for Greg to become an orthodontist. When Greg graduated, they decided to settle in Cindy's hometown in Virginia. They purchased a home, and Greg set up his practice. They had a wonderful life together, which was made even better by the birth of their twin daughters eleven years into the marriage.

They were approaching their seventeenth anniversary when "the accident" claimed Cindy's life. He was distraught, to be sure, when she died, but he didn't waste a single moment on anger or blaming God for taking her. She was God's child, and it was God's prerogative to take her home to Heaven at His discretion. Greg was thankful that he had been allowed to share his life with hers for as long as he did. If she'd only been his for one day, it would have the best day of his life, and he would have counted himself a blessed man.

Greg could hardly believe that Brittany and Bethany would be turning nine in a few short months. His girls were growing up too fast! How he wished Cindy could see them now. She would have been so proud of them. Both girls had taken Cindy's death hard, but they were strong and had allowed God to soothe their aching hearts.

They were so little when she died—not yet six. But Greg, with help from Gretchen and Tom, was making certain that they never forgot their mother. Pictures of Cindy were displayed in every room of the house, and Gretchen regaled them with tales of Cindy's adventures, and misadventures, as a child. Greg was thankful that they had purchased a video camera when Cindy was pregnant with the twins. He had recorded many hours of home videos. More than anything else, seeing their mother interacting with them on the TV screen kept their memories of her alive.

⌘ ⌘ ⌘

Reaching his office, Greg saw that Robin was already there. His receptionist made a habit of being the first one in the office in the morning. She liked to have the coffee brewing and the computer humming when Greg walked in. Robin believed that a steaming hot cup of coffee, along with a few moments spent in prayer, insured that the day got off to a proper start.

Greg stopped at her desk and asked about her family.

"They are doing wonderfully. Hannah is in her seventh month

already," Robin beamed. Hannah would make Robin a grandmother in early April, and that could not happen soon enough for Robin. "The doctor says she's doing great. The baby should arrive right around Easter."

"Well, let's pray for Hannah and the baby. Anything else we need to pray about?"

Robin filled Greg in on a couple prayer requests concerning two members of their church, Riverside Christian Fellowship, and a patient. Greg led Robin in a short prayer. The conversation and prayer lasted only a few minutes, but it was a marvelous beginning to their day. As they ended, the sound of front door opening notified them that Jenna, one of Greg's dental assistants, had arrived. It was time to get to cracking. The first patient was due in fifteen minutes.

3

The radio alarm clock blared the old Partridge Family hit, "C'mon, Get Happy!" Kevin Peterson felt anything but happy as he rolled over and pressed the snooze bar. *Why did I set the alarm for 7:00?* Kevin never went in to the Chevrolet dealership until noon on a weekday, except on the last day of the month. As he rubbed the sleep from his eyes and stretched, he remembered that today was the last day of the month. Tuesday, January 31st. The biggest car-buying day, thus far, of the young new year. But there was no need to jump right out of bed. He could doze a few more minutes.

When the alarm went off the second time at 7:15, Kevin climbed from the bed and headed to the shower. He was starting to feel happy at the thought of how many cars he might sell today. Kevin was a natural-born salesman. Nothing, well almost nothing, made him feel better than helping a customer find the right car for his needs and closing the deal. As Wilson Chevrolet's senior, and most successful, new car salesman, Kevin could make his own schedule. Nineteen years experience had given him much insight into the patterns ingrained in the car-buying decision. He scheduled his work hours to always be on the lot during the peak buying hours.

While Kevin's work schedule benefited his customers, and thus his sales, it created havoc with his personal life. Kevin preferred to take two days off at the beginning of the week, typically Monday and Tuesday, and to work from noon until closing time on weekdays. Saturday and Sunday were the major car buying days, so Kevin never took weekends off. He frequently worked all day on Saturday and from noon until 6 p.m. on Sunday. This had left plenty of time for his ex-wife Christine to meet other men and indulge in extra-marital affairs—he was aware of three. When he learned of her infidelities, he had filed for divorce and worked harder than ever to be a successful salesman.

⌘ ⌘ ⌘

As Kevin made the 20-minute commute from his home to the dealership on Route 1, he thought about his upcoming schedule. Kevin was a stickler for maintaining consistency and order in his life. He liked to have a plan and for everything to go according to the plan. He altered his work schedule only if a major event was occurring or if the change would benefit his sales volume. This week's change met both criteria. He was working Tuesday and would take next Sunday off to take advantage of shoppers looking for deals on the last day of the month and so he could watch the Super Bowl on Sunday. No one was going to be car shopping during the big game, and football was one of Kevin's three passions, outside of work. The other two were poker and golf.

As he contemplated his schedule further into February, he noted that Valentine's Day was two weeks away. For first time in years, he was looking forward to the day devoted to romance. Since Christine had moved out, more than two years ago, Kevin had ignored Valentine's Day. It was just another, albeit profitable, workday to him. Last year, he had convinced a desperate husband that a new Tahoe was the way back into his wife's heart. It was a small price to pay for getting caught in a passionate embrace with her best friend, and it had made Kevin's Valentine's Day more than tolerable.

This year, however, Kevin was in the throes of a new romance. He knew he wasn't in love with Karen, at least not yet, but he certainly was attracted to her. The attraction was more than purely physical; he enjoyed her company immensely. Kevin had met Karen in a chat room one night last summer. They quickly discovered that they were both thirty-ish and currently single. They had developed an instant rapport and conversed into the wee hours of the morning. Chatting with Karen online before bedtime became part of his regular routine. At first they had limited their discussions to safe and inconsequential subjects—whether the Redskins had a chance at winning the NFC East division next season, which beaches in the Outer Banks were the nicest, how depressing it was to be thirty-something and single. Gradually, their conversations took on a personal nature.

Kevin shared a wealth of personal information, telling her about his job at the Chevy dealership and his home near the Chancellorsville Battlefield. He confided in her that Christine had betrayed his love and broken his heart. He shared his passions for football, golf, and poker. Kevin loved the Redskins so much that he occasionally took a Sunday off from work to attend a game; he taped the rest and watched them after work. Monday night was poker with the boys. They played every Monday night; the only exception being when the Redskins played on Monday night. Then the guys all got together at Kevin's and watched the game on his 50-inch projection TV. Kevin liked to golf on Tuesdays. He had a membership at the Chancellorsville Golf and Country Club. Sometimes he played with a friend, but he was just as content to hit the ball around the course by himself. Due to his work and social schedule, he confined dating to Sunday and Tuesday nights. During football season, of course, Sunday dating took a back seat to football.

Karen was much more guarded about her personal life, but she did talk about the complications of being a single mom. She told him little about her husband, except that he was dead. She occasionally talked about the boys. Kevin learned that she had three sons and had a general idea of their ages, but she revealed very little about herself. Two months or so into their Internet friendship, she had left down her guard and mentioned that she lived in Virginia. When he pressed her, she confided that she lived in Stafford. Stafford! Kevin could hardly believe it. Stafford was the next county. Why, they were practically neighbors! Kevin decided then and there that fate had brought the two of them together.

He had asked to meet her. Karen was hesitant, and Kevin had the impression that she was seeing someone. He kept asking and she eventually relented. In late-October she agreed to meet him, just as friends, at a steakhouse in Central Park. They met on the Tuesday before Halloween. When she had walked into the restaurant and made eye contact with him, Kevin had been blown away.

He'd arrived early and secured a table with a clear view of the door so he could spy her the moment she walked in. She'd described herself somewhat and told him she would be wearing black slacks with a gray sweater.

He stood as she hesitantly approached the table. "Karen?"

"Yes. I hope you're Kevin." She held out her hand.

Kevin took her small hand in his own larger one and held it as his gaze took her in. She had auburn curls that framed her face. Kevin had always been partial to brunettes. Her beautiful green eyes shone when she smiled. She was more petite than he had expected, both in stature and dress size. Her stomach was remarkably flat, considering she had given birth three times, and he guessed her to be only a couple inches taller than five feet. While she certainly wasn't overweight, she was not overly thin. Kevin liked a woman with a little meat on her bones and some curves, and Karen definitely had curves in all the right places. Kevin hoped that Karen was as attracted to him as he was to her.

"Shall we sit?" Kevin pulled out a chair for Karen and held it as she sat down and scooted it closer to the table. He took his own seat across from her. He had considered momentarily taking the seat next to her, but he decided that might seem a bit forward. Additionally, sitting across from Karen afforded him a better view of her lovely face.

The waiter showed up at once and asked if they would like to order drinks before dinner.

Kevin, who had never acquired a taste for alcohol, decided to let Karen make the decision for them. "Would you like a glass of wine?" If she ordered a glass, he would also to make her feel comfortable.

"No. Thank you. I would like a glass of iced tea, sweetened."

Kevin indicated to the waiter that he also would like sweet tea.

"If you wanted wine…," Karen started to say, but Kevin cut her off. "I never drink the stuff. It's too expensive, and it doesn't taste good. I could never figure out why it's so popular."

"I agree," laughed Karen.

Kevin could see her visibly relax.

The waiter returned with the tea and took their orders.

Dinner had been comfortable. It helped that they were already friends. As the evening wore on, Kevin sensed that Karen found him as physically attractive as he found her.

"I love your eyes. They are so intense," she had told him, twice. When she reached over and brushed a stray strand of hair from his forehead, he felt his pulse quicken. He took it as a sign that she felt at ease with him. When dinner was over, he walked her to her car and asked her for a date—a real date. They'd been a couple ever since.

Kevin and Karen both lived busy lives. Between his work schedule and her family commitments, finding time to be together presented quite a challenge. They usually went out to dinner, and sometimes a movie, on Sunday evenings after Kevin was done at the dealership. Kevin knew he was smitten when he agreed to defer watching the taped Redskins-Lions game until Monday morning to go shopping with Karen on the Sunday before Christmas. Karen appreciated the sacrifice and rewarded him by making homemade cinnamon rolls when he came for dinner two nights later. Kevin didn't bother to mention that his favorite team was already out of the playoff picture at the time of his sacrifice.

Occasionally the couple met for breakfast on Friday mornings. Karen had invited him to have dinner at her home a few times. Those invitations were rare, as she didn't want to rush things with the boys. Karen had taken the boys to her parents' home in Chester for Thanksgiving and Christmas, so they had avoided awkward family situations over the holidays.

But Valentine's Day was different. It was a holiday with couples in mind. Fortunately, for Kevin, Valentine's Day fell on a Tuesday this year, so he wouldn't have to alter his normal work schedule. He would take Karen out for a nice, romantic dinner, of course. He'd already asked her to get a babysitter for the boys so they could have a leisurely dinner. At the next red light, he called Josh on his cell phone.

"What's the name of that fondue restaurant?"

"Fondue Extravaganza."

"Do you have the number?"

"No. Call information."

He picked up the small notebook he kept handy and wrote, "V.D. reservations—Fondue Extravaganza."

The restaurant was fairly new in town. Kevin remembered the women at the dealership being all in a dither when it had opened last summer.

"I can't wait to eat there," he had overheard Jan saying to Rhonda.

"I tried to get reservations for last Friday, but they were all booked up." Rhonda had answered back. "I called Tuesday to get reservations for this Friday. I made them, but I can't get in until 8:30."

"I'm so jealous," Jan had replied. "You'll have to tell me all about it."

Kevin had no real desire to eat at the restaurant. He considered fondue to be rather fussy; he put it in a class with petit fours and tiny sandwiches with no crust. The kinds of food women ate when they got together for luncheons and showers. But Josh said it was THE place in town to take a date.

"If you want to impress a woman, Fondue Extravaganza is the place to take her."

Josh had taken his wife for their anniversary last month and indicated, without sharing the private details, that his wife had indeed been very impressed and grateful. Josh was considered something of an expert on women among the salesmen at Wilson Chevrolet. He was forever picking up flowers or some trinket to surprise his wife. Kevin supposed that he knew what he was doing; Josh had been married, quite happily it seemed, for fourteen years.

Kevin felt certain that Karen would be impressed by his choice of restaurant; he also felt certain that she would be expecting more than a fancy dinner. She was looking for some form of commitment from him. Not marriage, at least not yet—both realized they were not ready to make that leap again. No, what Karen wanted, he knew, was more of Kevin's time and attention. He and Karen desperately needed time alone together to get to know each other more intimately.

If finding the time was difficult, finding the place was nearly impossible. Kevin's home was well outside of town to the west and hers, while closer, was east of the city. Kevin had calculated that if he drove from his house to hers and back again, he would be on the road more than an hour. And he would spend another hour to take her home at the end of the date. Her house afforded no opportunity for privacy with three children running around.

Karen's children posed another obstacle to their relationship. She didn't want to leave them with a sitter too often, and Kevin didn't want to spend too much time with the boys. He was the youngest child and had never had children of his own, so he wasn't quite sure of how to interact with them. If the relationship progressed, Karen would expect Kevin to take a bigger role in the boys' lives. The idea of being a father figure to three boys who really needed a male role model in their life scared Kevin more than a little. He'd make a concerted effort to get to know the boys better in the future. He would also work on the intimacy issue. But for now, he would concentrate on getting her an appropriate gift. A nice piece of jewelry ought to do it. As he pulled into the Chevy dealership, he made another note to himself, *Olde Towne Jewelry—gift for Karen.* He would take time to make the phone calls between customers; right now it was time to sell some cars.

4

Kyle, Karen's brown-haired, brown-eyed five-year-old, bounded down the stairs to the kitchen and stopped short as he smelled the sausage frying on the stove.

"Momma, you made breakfast?"

"Don't say it so incredulously. It's not like it's the first time I have made you breakfast." Karen feigned mock indignation at her son's words. She gave him a quick hug before she took the sausages from the frying pan and poured herself a cup of coffee. After her time of Bible reading and reflection, Karen had been energized by the prospect of a new project. She had decided she had plenty of time to fix the boys a proper breakfast. She liked to fix a "big" breakfast, as the boys called it, on weekends, but it had been quite some time since breakfast on a school day had been anything more than cold cereal, bagels, or toaster pastries.

"Oh, boy, French toast and sausage." Nine-year old Austin climbed onto the bar stool next to his brother. Austin looked more like Karen than the other two, with his light brown hair, green eyes, and freckles. But he had Jeff's nose and mouth.

"And hot chocolate. Real hot chocolate," Kyle added.

"Come on boys, give me a break. We have hot chocolate all the time, and I cook dinner for you every night," she responded good-naturedly.

"We don't have hot chocolate all the time before we go to school."

Well, that was certainly true. Karen set plates on the bar in front of the two youngest boys and poured them each a mug of steaming hot chocolate. She added some cold milk so they wouldn't burn their mouths.

"Anybody want marshmallows?" Karen reached into the cabinet for the bag of miniature marshmallows, wondering why she had even bothered to ask, as both boys shouted, "I do. I do."

Trevor soon joined his brothers; his appreciation for the hot breakfast was evidenced by the speed with which his food was consumed. Trevor was a high school freshman and the spitting image of his father. He had Jeff's thick, dark hair and brown eyes. He behaved like Jeff. Every mannerism and inflection of his voice reminded Karen of her late husband. As the self-appointed man of the house, Trevor tried to make up for their father's absence by watching out for the younger boys and teaching them the things Jeff should have; it was a lot of responsibility for a fourteen-year old to bear.

As they ate, Karen was pleased by how calm this morning seemed compared to the typical chaos as lunches were packed and cereal poured and quickly eaten. Karen had even made the boys' sandwiches while the sausage cooked. All that remained to be done was to put the dirty dishes in the dishwasher and have the boys brush their teeth. They might get out the door without Karen threatening to leave anyone behind.

⌘⌘⌘

Trevor's ride picked him up at 7:45, with plenty of time to arrive at the high school and make it to homeroom before the tardy bell sounded. The younger two were in elementary school, and their school day began at 8:15. Karen dropped them at the school and headed toward Tidewater Orthodontics, where she was employed as the business manager.

As she made the ten-minute drive across the Rappahannock River and down Route 2, Karen's eyes were drawn to the remains of last week's snow. Five inches had fallen, bringing a crisp, sparkling elegance to barren trees and transforming dead lawns into fluffy blankets of white powder. Karen had brewed a pot of coffee and sipped it while staring out the sliding glass door at the pristine landscape. She loved the purity of the freshly fallen snow when neither man nor animal had marred the surface with their prints. All too soon, her sons had donned their winter gear and trod every inch of the yard as they rolled the snow into balls for snowmen and for waging war on the neighborhood children. That snow was now a memory except for the ugly, black piles to be seen in every parking lot she passed. As cold as the temperatures had been, the piles wouldn't melt until spring, Karen forecasted.

Nearing the office, Karen switched her brain into work mode and the things she needed to accomplish today. It was the last day of the month, and as the business manager, she had invoices to print and mail, in addition to her normal responsibilities. It was a demanding job, but Karen was up to the challenge and thankful she had the education and the ability to support her family.

Jeff had left Karen a pile of debt and no insurance. She initially feared that she and the boys would be reduced to near-poverty, but she had managed to maintain a fairly comfortable standard of living for them. To be sure, she hadn't done it entirely on her own. Oak Hill Church, where she and Jeff had attended for more than a dozen years, had really come through in her time of need. The congregation had taken up a collection that covered the funeral expenses and paid off many of the other bills, giving Karen an almost-fresh start.

Before Trevor's birth, Karen had earned an associate's degree in business administration from John Tyler Community College. She had worked as a receptionist while in school and as an office assistant after graduating; both jobs were in Dr. Sherry Jernigan's pediatric practice. After Jeff's death, Dr. Jernigan had called and offered Karen a full-time position as her bookkeeper. Her earnings, combined with the Social Security payments the boys received due to their father's death, had been sufficient to meet their needs.

When Karen decided she needed a change of scenery and moved the family to Fredericksburg, Dr. Jernigan had kindly placed a call on Karen's behalf to her friend Greg Marshall. Dr. Marshall's business manager was expecting a baby and had decided to be a full-time mom. Dr. Marshall had hired Karen based on Dr. Jernigan's reference without even meeting her. Karen would always be grateful to both doctors.

⌘⌘⌘

Entering in the front door, Karen saw several patients in the waiting room.

"Good morning, Karen," Robin sang out from behind the reception window. Robin was always cheerful, and Karen made a point each morning to stop by her desk and chat for a minute or two before heading to her small office just down the hall.

"You look peaceful this morning," Robin continued.

"As opposed to my normal crazed-mother-running-late-for-work look." Karen poked fun at herself easily. "The morning got off to a good start." *Surprisingly so, particularly considering that the day had begun with a disturbing nightmare*. "I got up early and had a few minutes to myself and even made French toast for the boys for breakfast."

"I hope you spent a few minutes with God."

Robin made statements like this frequently; Karen usually mumbled some excuse about not having time and how hectic mornings were at her house. But this time Karen replied, "Actually, I did. I had forgotten how nice that could be."

Leaving Robin to ponder her comment, Karen headed to her desk. A pile of bills needing to be paid greeted her. As she sat down, her gaze fell on the pictures on her desk—she had several of the boys and one of Kevin sitting in the recliner in her den. She had taken that one the first time he had come to dinner. Jeff was in only one of the pictures. It was a picture she had taken of him and the boys on their last Christmas morning together.

Karen settled down to paying bills and worked steadily without interruption until lunchtime. Dr. Marshall closed the office for an hour at lunch. Karen usually brought her lunch to save money and ate in the small break room. As Robin also normally brought her lunch, they often ate together and were becoming good friends. Robin had only worked in the office since November when the former receptionist's Marine husband was transferred to Camp LeJeune, North Caroline. Robin had no need to work, but she had been friends with Greg for years and had agreed to fill in temporarily until he could find a permanent replacement. She had, however, found that she really enjoyed the job and decided to stay.

⌘⌘⌘

"So tell me, what prompted you to take time for devotions this morning?" Robin asked Karen as soon as they were seated at the round laminate table.

As Greg usually ate in his office and the other members of the staff, Greg's two dental assistants, ate lunch out frequently, the two ladies were typically the only ones in the break room. That was the case today.

"It sort of happened accidentally. I had a nightmare and was afraid to go back to sleep, so I got up early. As I was having a cup of tea, I decided to pick up the Bible."

"Good for you. It seems to have helped. You looked less frazzled when you came in today."

"Yes, I do feel less …*frazzled* is a good word for it. The extra time this morning made everything go more smoothly."

"You said you had a nightmare. Want to tell me about it?"

"Not really. Suffice to say it was about Jeff dying."

Karen seemed uncomfortable, so Robin decided not to press her for more information. Robin knew that Jeff, Karen's husband, had died a couple of years earlier. Other than that she knew almost nothing about him.

"You must miss him terribly." Robin sympathized with Karen's loss. Robin had been happily married to Chris for nearly thirty years. She could not imagine herself going on without him.

"Well, yes and no. There's a lot of things I miss about Jeff and, unfortunately, some I don't miss. I miss having a partner and a companion. I miss his smile and his easygoing nature. But I don't miss the man Jeff had become. And I certainly don't miss the fights."

"You and Jeff were having marital trouble?" Robin hoped she wasn't overstepping her boundaries.

"Yes, for quite some time before he…"

"Died." Robin supplied the word that Karen still had trouble saying.

"Yes." Karen took a deep breath. "The strain was nearly unbearable at times. It was difficult on the boys to see and hear us exchanging angry words. Don't get me wrong. Jeff was a great father. He loved the boys. And he was a great husband for a lot of years. But the last few years were different…difficult."

Robin nodded in understanding, although she had never experienced the type of that marital strife Karen was describing. "You have never talked much about Jeff. What was he like?"

Karen seemed lost in thought for a moment; then a tiny smile formed at the corners of her mouth. "I met Jeff before my senior year in high school. He was three years older than me. His younger brother Tommy was a friend of my brother. I met Jeff when he came by the house to pick up Chad. He was taking Chad and Tommy to a movie. He asked me if I wanted to go, too."

Karen paused to eat a bite of her lunch. "I climbed in the front seat with him. I couldn't believe I was riding in a car with Jeff Harper. I had fantasized about that moment since I first laid eyes on him my freshman year. Jeff was the star running back on the football team. All the girls dreamed of being Jeff's girl. He was strong and athletic and better looking than a guy has a right to be."

Robin chuckled but remained quiet. It was rare for Karen to open up about anything personal, and Robin did not want to interrupt the memory.

"Jeff was working in his father's construction business. He loved building things and working with his hands. He started helping his father on jobs in the summer when he was about eight or nine. He would pick up nails and scraps of lumber on job sites. As he got older, he learned to do carpentry work and how to frame a house. He loved going to work each day. Constructing houses was what he was born to do."

"It's wonderful that he got to do something he loved and work with his father."

"It was nice for both of them. They were best friends. They worked together during the week and on weekends they hunted and fished. Trevor is just like Jeff. As soon as Trevor could walk, he tagged along with the two of them wherever they went."

"How wonderful."

"Jeff was wonderful. I fell in love with him in the car that day. We got married as soon as I graduated."

"You were a young bride." Robin was thankful her own two

children hadn't rushed into marriage at such a young age. Hannah had waited to marry until she graduated from college; David was twenty-four and still single. Robin was hopeful he'd meet the right girl soon.

"Yes, I had just turned eighteen. But we were madly in love. Jeff was definitely ready to get married and have a family. He was already twenty-one and had been working for several years. Fortunately, we decided to not rush into having children. I was able to do two years at the local community college and work for a year before Trevor came along."

Karen stopped talking then and finished her sandwich.

Robin had learned more about Karen today than she had in all the three months they had worked together. She decided Karen had opened up enough for one day and turned the conversation to her excitement about becoming a grandmother.

5

When Karen got home her answering machine was blinking, indicating she had three messages. From Kevin, she assumed. He called frequently during the day, between customers, of course. He liked her to know that he was thinking of her. She dropped the mail on the card table that was supposed to serve as kitchen table but had become a catchall for backpacks, newspapers, and a variety of other miscellaneous items. She pushed the play button.

"Hey, Karen. Kev. Just wanted to remind you to get a sitter for Valentine's Day. I made reservation for a very romantic dinner. It's a surprise; don't ask. Our reservations are for 6:30; I want to have plenty of time after dinner for another surprise. Don't ask about that one, either. I'll pick you up at 6. Talk to ya later."

That kind of message made it worthwhile to have an answering machine. Karen loved surprises and wasn't sure what to expect from Kevin. While she wished he might be "the one," it was still too early in their relationship to be certain. She hoped, however, that he might be ready to prioritize their relationship above his work. Maybe that was the surprise.

It was good Kevin had called. Although he'd asked her out for Valentine's Day more than a week ago, Karen had yet to get a sitter, and it would be hard to find one. As she only had two weeks, she'd better make some phone calls tonight. She would be glad when the boys were old enough to stay by themselves. Trevor was already old enough, but she couldn't burden him with taking care of his younger brothers all evening, especially given the homework load he often had. Besides, she seemed to recall that he had been invited to a party that night. She made a mental note to ask him about that when he got home from school.

"Karen, remember me," the second message began. The familiar voice gave Karen pause. "It's your old friend Mike. I'm going to be in town on business on Friday, and I know you are off on Fridays, so I thought we could hook up, for old time's sake, you know. Let's meet for lunch. No pressure, just a friendly lunch between friends. We are still friends, aren't we? I'll call you later tonight. Can't wait to see you again."

Karen had thought that Mike Sloan was out of her life for good. She had no intention of meeting him for lunch, or anything else, and she would tell him so when he called back. Mike was one mistake Karen was not going to repeat.

The third message was from her brother. "Hi Karen, it's Chad. I wanted to let you know that I'll be coming to visit you on Saturday. If you had plans, change them. I won't take no for an answer. I'm bringing you a surprise. And I'm taking Trevor out for some guy time. I might even let you make me dinner."

A visit from Chad and another surprise! This must be my lucky day.

⌘⌘⌘

Karen turned her attention to dinner and helping the boys with their homework. While frying ground beef for tacos, she listened to Kyle read. She quizzed Austin on science terms for his test on Wednesday, as she diced tomatoes and shredded cheese. Kyle needed help with handwriting, but that would have to wait until after dinner.

Trevor arrived home just as Karen was stuffing the meat into the taco shells.

"Where have you been?"

"At Tim's house. He has a new X-box game."

"Wash up. Dinner's ready."

The family sat down at the table and bowed their heads for grace. Tonight grace would be more than just a routine. Instead of hurriedly rushing through, she took time to truly thank God for their food.

"Heavenly Father, we thank you for your provisions for our family. Bless us as we partake of this food. Thank you, amen." Karen prayed with true sincerity for the first time in a long time.

"Tell me about your day," Karen said to Trevor as she passed him the sour cream for his tacos.

There had been a time when Trevor had told her everything, but these days he never opened up much. "It was all right." That was Trevor's usual answer, which didn't mean that it was, in fact, all right. It only meant that he wasn't going to tell her if it wasn't.

"How'd you do on your Spanish test?"

"83."

"Is that a C?"

"Yes."

"Good."

"Not good, but okay."

"I got a star on my paper." Kyle was willing to share every detail of his day in kindergarten. How Karen missed the days when Trevor had been that small, and his whole world centered on her.

"You did, Kyle? That's great! I'll put it on the fridge after dinner."

Kyle beamed.

"I drew a dragon," Austin chimed in. "My teacher said I should write a story about it." Austin was the family artist and storyteller. Karen thought he might be an author when he grew up.

"You can put it on the fridge with my paper," Kyle told him.

The younger boys' chatter engaged Karen to the point that she nearly forgot about Chad's surprise.

"Uncle Chad is coming on Saturday," she announced suddenly.

The announcement was met with shouts of glee. Three years younger than Karen and still a bachelor, Chad epitomized "cool" as far as the boys were concerned. He loved all of the boys and had always made time to include them in his life. Since their father's death, he had taken a special interest in Trevor, knowing instinctively that the boy would need the extra attention.

"Is he bringing me a surprise?" Kyle loved surprises as much as his mother.

"I don't know. He said he's bringing ME a surprise."

"You. What about me?"

"You'll have to wait and see. Trevor, he wants to spend the day with you. He said you two needed some guy time."

Trevor didn't need to say anything; his big grin let Karen know how pleased he was with the news.

I wish Trevor could have a relationship like that with Kevin. Thinking of Kevin reminded Karen of Valentine's Day.

"By the way, what are your plans for Valentine's?"

"I'm going to a party at school. It's going to be in the gym. There's going to be food and a band and dancing." That was more words than Trevor had strung together in recent memory, clear evidence that he was excited about Chad's visit or the party. Maybe both.

"Do you have a ride?"

"Tim's mother is taking us and bringing us home. I assumed you would be out with what's his name."

"His name is Kevin."

"I don't like him. He's a jerk."

So much for Trevor having a good relationship with Kevin. Maybe when they get to know each better.

Karen decided to ignore Trevor's last remark. She was pleased that Trevor had two upcoming events to look forward to. Time with Chad would be good for him, as would the Valentine's party and dance. Trevor was still feeling like an outsider at school, although he did have a good friend in Tim, who lived a few doors down. Trevor had not wanted to move away from Chester and leave his friends just as he was entering high school, but Karen had believed a new start would be best for all of them.

The memories of Jeff's death were too painful in Chester. It was a small town, and everyone knew everyone else's business. The boys were reminded of their father and his death every day. And, as for herself, she would never be able to find someone new there.

6

Greg finished up with his last patient at 4:20. While he made a few notations on the chart, Robin set up the appointment for the patient's next visit, and Jenna, one of his two dental assistants, cleaned the dental instruments and put them in the sterilizer. Katie, his other assistant, took the chart when Greg had finished and gave it to Robin to file. Within a few minutes, the office was put in order, and the four of them all walked out together.

"It feels a bit nippy," Robin commented as she unlocked her car. "I heard that they are calling for snow on Thursday."

"I hope so," replied Jenna. "I love snow."

With that they all headed out. Greg glanced at the clock on his dashboard. "4:40. With any luck, I'll have that lasagna in the oven by 5:00," he calculated.

As Greg pulled into the driveway, Brittany and Bethany raced across the next-door neighbor's yard to greet him. They had spied him from Mrs. Warren's window as he had turned the corner onto Calvary Lane.

Greg thanked Mrs. Warren, gathered up the girls' belongings, and hurried to his own house.

"Girls, hang up your coats and get started on your homework. I'll start dinner," Greg called out as they entered the house. Greg picked up the instructions Gretchen had left beside the stove. "Preheat the oven to 350." He reached over and turned the oven on. He was starving and didn't want to waste a single minute; the sandwich Katie had picked up for him at lunch had not filled him up, and it had been five hours since lunch.

"Bake lasagna for 40 minutes, then remove foil and bake for 10 more minutes."

It seemed so simple and yet, without the instructions, he knew he would be lost. Although Gretchen had brought Greg dozens of lasagnas, he supposed, over the last couple of years, she always left instructions on the counter. She knew him well enough to know that he could never remember the baking instructions from one time to the next time. He was grateful she didn't make a big deal of it.

"Thank you, Heavenly Father, for the love and care Cindy's parents have shown me and the girls. I'd be lost without them and You."

It frustrated Greg that, despite being a well-educated, intelligent man, he was almost totally useless in the kitchen. With quite some effort, he had learned to manage breakfast for the girls on weekends. He considered pancakes and scrambled eggs to be his specialties. He was only able to make a decent cup of coffee because Gretchen and Tom had bought him a fancy coffee pot last Christmas. The pot brewed only one cup at a time and all Greg had to do was slip in a pre-measured coffee pod and press start.

The oven light indicated that it was hot. Greg slid the baking pan into the oven and noted that it should be ready at a quarter to 6. He slipped a pod of decaffeinated hazel nut coffee into the pot and considered what vegetable to fix with the lasagna and garlic bread.

I could use a wife. The thought popped unbidden into his brain.

Now, where did that come from? He shook his head. *Am I ready for a wife?* He made a plan to spend some time talking to the Lord about that tonight after the girls were in bed. Right now, he needed to check on them and make sure their homework was getting done.

⌘⌘⌘

Kevin Peterson hopped in his car at 9:30. He was feeling tired but contented as he left the dealership. He turned onto Route 3, passed the mall area, and headed out of town toward Culpeper. He wanted to call Karen on his cell phone, but he knew there were several pockets of weak signal out this way. He would wait until he got home. He had good news to share with her, although he would not reveal some of his accomplishments until later.

During a lull between customers around ten o'clock, Kevin had

33

called his friend Donnie, who managed the Holiday Inn in Central Park. Kevin had sold Donnie a Malibu in his early days in the business. Every few years, Donnie came back in and traded up for something new and more expensive. His latest acquisition, a green Avalanche, was three years old, and Donnie was thinking it might be time to trade up. He had recently test driven a Corvette. Kevin and Donnie had become good friends over the years, and Donnie had been a source of support when Kevin went through his divorce.

"Hey, buddy. It's Kevin Peterson," he began. "I was wondering what you have going on over there on Valentine's Day."

"We're having a party in the ballroom. The band's pretty good. You should come on by. There's a small cover charge, but you know I waive it for my good friends."

"Thanks. I think I might come by. I wouldn't mind doing a little slow dancing."

"You got a date this year?"

"I do. Her name is Karen. I've been seeing her for a few months."

"Glad to hear it, my friend. You've needed a woman in your life for the longest time. Bring her on by. I can't wait to meet her."

After hanging up with Donnie, Kevin had called information and gotten the number for Fondue Extravaganza.

On the third ring, a hostess answered the phone in a pleasant voice, "Fondue Extravaganza, how may I help you?"

"I would like to make reservations for Valentine's Day dinner."

"Name?"

"Peterson."

"How many in your party?"

"Two."

"Have you been to Fondue Extravaganza before?"

"Never."

"How did you hear about the restaurant?"

"From a friend. He highly recommended it as a great place for a romantic evening."

"Wonderful." The hostess sounded quite pleased with that information. " Your friend is absolutely correct. There are a few things you need to know. First, we only serve fondue. Don't come here planning to order a steak and baked potato."

"Okay." Kevin would have preferred a steak, but this night was about Karen and her preferences.

"Second, you cook your own entrée in a fondue pot on your table. Eating here is not just having a meal; it's a unique dining experience."

This was starting to sound more like work and less like a romantic evening out. "I guess that's all right."

"You'll be fine. Men are always skeptical. Trust me, women love it. Lastly, we will not be offering our normal menu on Valentine's. We have planned something very special, instead. Let me explain."

Kevin had no idea what their regular menu was, so he waited silently.

"We will be serving only the Extravaganza Spectacular." The animation in the hostess's voice told him that this was a meal he wouldn't want to miss. "The Spectacular is a delicious four-course meal. The first course is cheese fondue. This is followed by salad. The entrée for the evening includes a bit of everything—lobster, shrimp, filet mignon, teriyaki steak, and chicken, along with a variety of vegetables. You'll absolutely love it! The finishing touch is our fabulous chocolate fondue. It's the perfect ending for a wonderful meal."

The hostess's voice grew quiet, and Kevin waited a moment to be sure she was finished with her spiel.

"That sounds great," Kevin replied.

"The cost is $105 per couple. The price does not include beverages, tax, or gratuity."

"That will be fine." It was a bit pricier than Kevin had planned, but he had no problem affording it. It better be as good as Josh claimed.

"We can seat you at 6:30," she replied. "You should plan to be here a minimum of two hours."

⌘ ⌘ ⌘

After cleaning up the kitchen and tucking the younger boys into bed, Karen went to the garage and carried the two kitchen chairs into the house. As it was too cold to work in the garage this time of year, she had cleared enough space in the oversized laundry room to begin the process of removing the old stain.

She poured nail polish remover on a cotton ball and dabbed it on one chair leg. The cotton ball stuck to the finish. Okay, so the finish was not polyurethane-based. She jotted "Buy furniture refinisher" on her to-do list and added the other items she'd need to purchase for the project. She should have time to shop on Friday and planned to begin the project on Saturday. Excitement surged through her as she anticipated the work. It had been far too long since her last project.

She said good night to Trevor and headed upstairs to her bedroom. She had called the three teenage girls she used regularly as babysitters but had struck out on finding one available for Valentine's Day. They all had dates, as she should have expected. She would ask around at work tomorrow. Someone might know of a sitter who was available.

Karen flipped on her computer and waited for it to warm up. The computer had been her salvation when things had been at the worst. Internet chat rooms had provided her with anonymity and allowed her to pour out her pain and her guilt without fear of reprisal or condemnation. Her faceless chat room companions offered sympathy and shared their own pain and guilt. The Internet had also rekindled her hopes of meeting someone new. Karen had met Mike Sloan on a chat room for single parents.

She saw that she had an e-mail from him. Warily, she opened it, unsure of what to expect, and read:

> Karen, I've had a change of plans. I won't be able to make our lunch on Friday.

She rolled her eyes. *Like I was really going to have lunch with you.*

> Since the weatherman is calling for snow later in the week, my boss is sending me to F'burg in the morning. Lately, I've been coming through every couple weeks, so I'll take a rain check on lunch. See ya soon.

Karen was surprised that she was slightly disappointed. It would have been nice to see him. Mike had helped her through the darkest period of her life. Of course, he'd done so through deception and lies.

"Well, what difference does it make? He isn't coming anyway."

A sudden *ding* alerted Karen that she had an instant message. She was delighted to see that it was from Kim.

Kim: I thought you might be on-line. How are you?
Karen: Excited about a new project. Remember those kitchen chairs I was going to refinish?
Kim: The one's you got at the flea market in South Hill?
Karen: Yes. I'm going to get started on them.
Kim: Did you get a table yet?
Karen: No. I haven't been looking. But, I plan to soon.
Kim: What else is happening?

So Karen told Kim about the nightmare, Chad's upcoming visit, and her plans for Valentine's Day.

Kim was Karen's best friend. She had been the one to spark Karen's interest in furniture restoration. She had initiated Karen by having her paint unfinished furniture for Trevor's nursery. Their first project was a bookcase for his room. Trevor was too young to read, so lower shelves were used to hold Trevor's trucks and stuffed animals, while the upper two shelves displayed photos and the ceramic piggy bank Karen's mother had made when he was born. Karen, with Kim's help, had painted it a lovely moss green to match the leaves in the jungle-themed curtains and bedding. Karen's next project had been a chest of drawers painted it in the same green. After that, with help from Kim, she had moved on to restoration projects. She had a dream, shared only with Kim, of someday earning a living by restoring furniture.

Kevin called at 10 p.m. and filled her in on his day. He had sold two cars. He had expected one of the sales, as the buyer had been in three times in the past two weeks and, obviously, knew he could get the best deal on the final day of the month. The other was a total surprise, a very nice surprise. He had exceeded his self-imposed quota for the month. They talked for a few more minutes, without Karen mentioning her nightmare.

Karen breathed a quick prayer that she would not be troubled by the nightmare again tonight. Being particularly tired from her early morning, she was asleep almost as soon as her head hit the pillow.

37

7

The anticipated snow did not materialize on Thursday, although the area received an inch of snow on Friday evening. Not enough to cause any problems with driving, and certainly not enough to deter Chad from his mission of visiting his sister on Saturday. The day was cold, but the skies were clear.

Chad arrived at 10 a.m. as promised. He was hauling something in the bed of his pickup truck. "That's your surprise." He pointed proudly at the lump hidden under a green tarp.

Pulling off the tarp, he revealed a white kitchen table large enough to seat six comfortably. Karen walked around the bed of the truck assessing the table's condition and the work needed to turn it into a prized possession. "I found it when I was helping a friend clean out a repo," Chad was explaining.

Karen set aside her evaluation and focused on her brother's words.

"The bank wanted the house emptied. We could dispose of the belongings anyway we wanted, including keeping them for ourselves or selling them. I thought of you as soon as I saw this."

"Thanks a lot." Karen hugged her brother. Excitement welled up in her. "I can't wait to strip off that awful paint and reveal the true nature of the wood."

Chad laughed. "I knew you would see the potential in it. Mom said you need a table for your kitchen. I figured you could work your magic and create a thing of beauty."

"I hope so. It's certainly fits the bill."

It took Chad, Karen, Trevor, and Austin to carry the table into the house. They moved the card table to make room for it in the breakfast nook. It seemed to be sturdy and in good shape. Karen liked the mission style of the table. The straight edges and legs would make stripping the paint off a fairly quick process.

Karen did not, however, like looking at the chipped, marred surface, even temporarily. She dug a tablecloth out of the linen closet and covered the table. "Much better," she declared. She grabbed the chairs from the laundry room and placed them on either side of the table. "I think these will go well with the table. I'm going to start work on them today." Chad beamed, pleased with himself over the find.

Karen thanked him profusely. "I think this has earned you a home-cooked meal. Can you stay for dinner?"

"I'd love to. Right now, I'd like a cup of coffee." Karen dumped the remains of yesterday's coffee, filled the carafe with cold water, and set about brewing a fresh pot.

"Trevor, give me a few minutes to drink my coffee and chat with your mom, then we'll go." Chad sat down in one of the chairs.

"When did you start cleaning out repossessed houses?" Karen asked as she waited for the coffee.

He smiled. "There's not a big demand for decks this time of year. Work has been pretty slow throughout the winter, so I let my friends know that I was available to do some other jobs on the side. Craig Johnson asked me to help him clean out some repossessed houses. That didn't pay much, but it kept me busy, and he let me have first pick on the items I wanted to keep. You'd be amazed at the things people leave behind."

The coffee was ready. Karen poured them each a cup and sat down at the table with her brother. The twinkle in his eyes alerted her that he had some news he was bursting to tell. *Is Chad in love?* She pondered that thought and sipped her coffee as she waited for him to spill the beans. He took his time, staring into the hot, brown liquid before speaking. "I may be moving up here."

"Here? Fredericksburg?" That was the last thing Karen expected her little brother to say. "How did this come about?"

"Another friend, Josh Stevens, asked me if I could finish his basement for him. I don't think you know Josh." Karen shook her head no, puzzled as to what all this had to do with Chad's moving plans.

"Josh is new in the area. I met him at church. Anyway, his basement was completely unfinished. I put in a bedroom, full bath, and a media room for him. It turned out even better than I hoped. His father was impressed—very impressed—particularly with the media room. Mr. Stevens lives in this area and owns a couple old houses in Fredericksburg, down near the river. He wants me to restore them to their former grandeur, so he can resell them. Each house could take several months, maybe up to a year, to complete. If he hires me, I'll have enough work to last a couple of years. So it would only make sense to move here."

"Wow." Karen was speechless for only a moment before jumping up and hugging Chad's neck. "That is *wonderful* news." It would be terrific to have Chad close by. The siblings had always been tight and missed each other tremendously since Karen's move.

"It's not a done deal, yet. I'm going to drop by the houses while I'm out with Trevor. I want to make sure I'm not biting off more than I can chew. Now, it's time for Trevor and I to get out of here. We'll be back in plenty of time for dinner."

⌘ ⌘ ⌘

Karen couldn't wait to tell Kim about Chad's surprises. The table was just what she had hoped to find. Now, if she could only scavenge a couple more chairs and apply lots of elbow grease, she would be set. The table was an answer to prayer, but having Chad nearby was more than she'd ever have dared to pray for. With seemingly boundless energy flowing from a grateful heart, Karen was ready to tackle the job at hand.

While running errands on Friday, Karen had purchased the wood stripper, fine steel wool, and tung oil she needed to begin the process of stripping the stain from the chairs and preparing them to be re-stained. She had not made a final decision on the finish, so she put off purchasing wood stain until later.

The prospect of refinishing the table was so inviting that Karen would have started on it instead of the chairs, except that she hadn't purchase paint remover. Also, paint removal required a greater time commitment than stain removal. She would work on the chairs for the next several days and begin work on the table next Friday, when she was off and the boys were in school.

Kyle and Austin went out to play in the snow before the sun melted it, giving Karen time to begin work on the chairs. She removed the upholstered seats, then spread newspaper on the laundry room floor. She soaked a steel wool pad with stripper and gently rubbed it over the wood. It took a bit of effort, but the finish began to lift and the bare wood to appear. She had stripped most of one chair when she heard the back door open.

Time to stop. The nice thing about furniture stripping was that she could quit whenever she needed to and pick up the project where she left off.

"Mom, I'm hungry."

"I'll be right there, Kyle."

⌘ ⌘ ⌘

Chad and Trevor returned while Karen was preparing dinner. The pair had been busy. They had managed to bowl two games, eat lunch, meet with Mr. Stevens and his architect, and catch a matinee. Chad sat at the bar and kept Karen company as she diced carrots and potatoes to go with the pot roast.

"I'd offer to help, but…" Chad's voice trailed off as he gave a little chuckle.

"But we'd like to eat tonight. Thanks, but no thanks."

Chad's lack of culinary skills was legendary in the Butler family. Karen slid the vegetables into the pot.

"Are you okay, sis?" Chad's question caught Karen by surprise.

"Sure, I'm fine. Don't I seem okay?"

"I talked to Kim yesterday. She told me you've been having nightmares about Jeff. I'm concerned, that's all."

"I had a couple this week." She grabbed the celery and onions from the refrigerator. "They have interfered with my sleep, so I'm more tired than normal. But I don't think it's anything to be overly concerned about."

"Maybe, maybe not. Did you ever talk to anyone, a counselor, about Jeff's death?"

"No. I'm fine."

41

Chad didn't look convinced.

"If the nightmares get worse, I'll talk to someone. I promise."

Chad let it go for the moment. "Remember Jeff's dreams and how he used to insist on telling them to you every morning?"

"How could I ever forget? He remembered every excruciating detail. I'd be trying to snatch five more minutes of sleep, and he'd be describing wild car chases or fishing expeditions or whatever it was that he dreamed that night. I learned to sleep with my eyes open, so he'd think I was listening."

Chad grinned. "Then he'd come into work and tell them to me and the other guys. He derived a lot of pleasure and mileage out of his dreams." Chad had worked with Jeff and Mr. Harper for a couple years before going into business for himself building decks and screened porches.

Karen nodded. "He'd get so frustrated with me because I rarely recalled having had dreams, much less remembering them in any detail. He tried to teach me techniques to help me remember my dreams." Karen sobered. "I've always been able to remember nightmares, though. I went over the details as soon as I woke up. I wonder if they might have some underlying meaning…." She shook her head and changed the subject. "How did the meeting with Mr. Stevens go?"

"Wonderfully. The architect will design the changes, making sure they are consistent with the homes' original designs. I'll do the carpentry, electrical work, and painting. Jeremy, er, Mr. Stevens, will hire a plumber and landscaper to take of those details. I can hardly wait to get started." Too excited to sit still, Chad paced around the room as he spoke.

"So, is it a done deal?"

"Absolutely. I am definitely taking this job."

"What's your time frame for moving here?" Karen slid a pan of rolls in the oven and scooped out some broth from the roast to make gravy.

"We hope to start in April or May. The architect will need the time to finalize his designs and pull permits. That will give me a chance to finish up a couple jobs I have going and get moved."

Karen hadn't seen Chad this excited in a long, long time.

⌘ ⌘ ⌘

At dinner, Trevor seemed more peaceful than Karen had seen him in recent weeks. He was actually pleasantly talkative, filling the family in on his success in bowling and describing the movie he and Chad had seen. Karen breathed a silent prayer of thanks for Chad's visit. It had been a blessing in more ways than one. Chad left soon after dinner.

Karen put away the leftover pot roast and cleaned up the kitchen. The boys were occupied watching a video. Not able to wait any longer, Karen called Kim to tell her about the table. Kim was as excited as Karen and promised to be on the lookout for a good deal on some more used chairs.

"I'm sure I can find some chairs. The problem is finding chairs that match the ones you already have."

"They don't have to match. As a matter of fact, I think it would be nice to have an eclectic mix. Three sets of two matching chairs would be perfect."

"I think you should go with a mahogany finish," Kim suggested.

"Great idea. I think I agree. By the way, I hear you've been talking to Chad."

"I called him. I thought he should know about the nightmares."

Karen sighed. "I'm glad you told him. I was struggling to find a way to bring it up without alarming him. You know how Chad worries about me. You'd think he was the older sibling. By the way, Chad will be moving up here in the spring."

"He's probably trying to keep an eye on you," Kim teased.

8

When Greg's radio alarm when off at 5 Monday morning, he was surprised to hear the DJ announcing a list of local school closings, "Caroline County schools are closed. Also closed are King George, Stafford, and Spotsylvania schools. Germanna Community College will open two hours late." The DJ continued on to private school closings.

"At least it won't affect me; the city never closes school unless we have a blizzard," Greg said to himself.

"We have a new closing to announce. Fredericksburg city schools are closed today."

"Oh, brother." Greg yawned and opened his eyes. "At least I have plenty of time to make arrangements for the girls, but it's too early to call anyone yet."

Greg rolled out of bed and peeked out the window before heading to the shower. Snow blanketed everything, but it had stopped falling. He estimated they had received about 3 inches. In the distance, he could hear the snowplows already at work clearing the roads.

I'll have a few cancellations, but most patients will make it in, he thought. Robin's husband would most likely drive her to work, and Karen never came in on snow days. Jenna would be in—she loved to drive in the snow—but he wasn't sure about Katie. Either way, they should manage just fine.

Although he didn't open the office until 10 on Mondays and Wednesdays, Greg arose at five o'clock each morning. He found that maintaining his routine made it easier to get up on Tuesdays and Thursdays, when he opened the office early. Greg appreciated the slower pace to his late-opening days. It afforded him the opportunity to have breakfast with the girls and to spend a considerable amount of time in prayer and devotions before heading to work.

One of the great things about his schedule was that he only missed breakfast with the girls twice a week. He also missed dinner with them twice a week—Gretchen picked them up from school on his late days, fed them, and saw that their homework was completed before Greg came to get them.

Normally, Gretchen was happy to have the girls stay at her house on snow days. She loved spending time with her precious granddaughters. Unfortunately, Gretchen and Tom were visiting friends in Chapel Hill; they had planned to head back around noon and to be home in time to get the girls from school. Greg had not thought to make alternate arrangements, as the city only had one or two snow days a year—unlike the surrounding counties that averaged 9 or more per year.

I wonder if Karen would let them stay at her house. The thought occurred to him as he was shaving. Greg had allowed Karen to schedule her work around her children's school schedule so she could get her children off to school and pick them up from the after-school program without paying any extra fees. Greg had further agreed that if her children's schools were closed due to inclement weather, he would expect Karen to take the day off.

Greg did not know how early he could call her. He assumed she normally rose by 6, but she may have heard the school closings and gone back to sleep. He decided that he would wait until 7 to call, to be on the safe side.

⌘ ⌘ ⌘

The phone's ringing woke Karen from a sound sleep. She had awakened at 5:45 when her alarm had gone off, only to roll over and go immediately back to sleep after she heard the DJ announcing the area school closing. It took her until the fifth ring to wake up enough to answer it.

"Hello," she said through a giant yawn.

"Karen, it's Greg Marshall." Karen was so startled to hear her employer's voice that she thought perhaps she had dreamed the snow day and overslept.

"I hope I didn't wake you. I need a favor, and I didn't know anyone else to call. Were you asleep? I could call back later."

"No, no. It's okay. I'm awake now. How can I help you?"

Greg explained his dilemma with the twins, and Karen readily agreed that the girls could spend the day at her house. She supplied Greg with the directions, and he informed her that he would drop Bethany and Brittany off around 9:30.

Karen was thinking how nice it would be to lounge in bed awhile longer when she heard Kyle waking his brothers. "It snowed! Hurrah! No school! It snowed!" The one day that they could sleep in and, of course, the boys got up without any difficulty.

⌘⌘⌘

At ten o'clock, Kevin had awakened to the snow piled up outside his bedroom window and quickly concluded that Karen would be home with the boys. As it was his day off and he had no plans, he decided that today be an excellent opportunity to spend time with Karen's sons. He phoned Karen.

"Do you want another kid for the day?" It had been quite a few years since he'd actually played in the snow, and the idea made him feel like a kid again.

"Well, I don't know. I'm not sure I can handle any more children. What kid are we talking about?" she asked warily.

"Me." He was delighted to have caught her totally off guard.

"You? Did I hear that correctly? You I would love to see. What did you have in mind?"

"Sledding, snowball fights. You know, the usual snowy day fun."

"So, you are asking if you can come over and play?"

"That's the idea. I want to play with you and the boys."

Karen was ecstatic and invited him to lunch, after warning him that there were two extra children at her house for the day.

"Does this mean that I'm forgiven for yesterday?" Kevin asked a bit sheepishly.

Immediately, he regretted bringing up the subject. If Karen were still sore at him, it would have been best to not remind her that he had turned down her invitation to eat dinner and watch the Super Bowl with her family. He had tried to be vague when he turned her down: "Sorry. But, I've already made plans."

"Aw, c'mon. I made a big pot of chili, and I bought some buffalo wings. I even made homemade bread. It will be great."

"Wish I could. It sounds nice, but I've got plans." He hoped that Karen took his words at face value and didn't try to analyze them. There was no way he could enjoy the game with Karen and her kids. There would be too much talking and too many distractions. He wanted to watch the game with people who shared his love for football. While the Harpers liked football, they weren't passionate about it unless the Redskins were playing. And it had been a long time since the Redskins had made it to the big game.

"Some of the guys are coming over to watch it on the big screen in high def. We planned this months ago." He couldn't cancel on the guys at the last minute. Besides, Karen's 30-inch TV could not do justice to the biggest game of the year.

Karen had sounded miffed but had eventually relented. Today was a different story. She was giggling like a schoolgirl. All was forgiven.

When Kevin pulled into Karen's driveway, a large snowman in the front yard provided evidence that the children had already been outside. He found them all in the kitchen warming up with hot chocolate loaded with miniature marshmallows. Karen handed Kevin a steaming mug.

"Be careful; it's hot," she advised.

He raised one eyebrow and nodded in the direction of the children, who were gulping theirs down rapidly. "I added cold milk to theirs. It's barely lukewarm," she whispered conspiratorially.

A quick count told Kevin that someone was missing. It was Trevor, of course. Karen informed him that Trevor was spending the day with friends.

Too bad, Kevin mused to himself. *Trevor is the one I need to win over.*

Karen introduced Kevin to Bethany and Brittany. Although they were very similar in appearance, the twins were not identical. The one with the big brown freckle on the tip of her nose was Brittany, Kevin

47

duly noted. He quickly learned that she was the shy one of the pair.

"How about some lunch?" Karen suggested.

Everyone agreed, as the exertion of building the snowman had made the children quite hungry. In short order, Karen and Kevin whipped up grilled cheese sandwiches for everyone. Karen added a handful of potato chips and two chocolate chip cookies to each plate to complete the lunches.

Soon they were all bundled back into their hats, scarves, mittens, jackets, and boots. It was quite an undertaking getting six people ready to face the wintry bliss. The afternoon passed quickly as forts were built and snowball fights ensued. In the first round, it was boys versus girls. The girls were outmatched and quickly surrendered. In the second round, it was Kevin and the twins versus the Harpers. The Harpers took round two. Two rounds were enough for Karen, who begged off with the claim that she had to work on dinner. She had taken a roast out of the freezer when Kevin had called, and she needed to get it in the oven.

Dinner preparations were well underway when the gang trooped in.

"Shake the snow off your boots and clothes before you come in," Karen hollered.

Soon discarded hats, scarves, mittens, jackets, and boots filled the laundry room. Karen hung up the jackets and wiped off the boots. Everything else went into the dryer. Karen made a second pot of hot chocolate and passed out more cookies.

"I've had a great afternoon, Karen, but I have to be going," Kevin announced a short while later.

"You're not staying for dinner? I made a roast. It will be ready soon."

"Sorry, I didn't know I was invited. It's poker night. You know we play every Monday night at Josh's house. We're ordering pizza." He could see that Karen was disappointed, and that was the last thing he wanted. "Hey, I had a great time today, with you and the kids—all of them," he added quickly. "But I'm really 'kidded out' for now. We have to take this a little bit at a time. I'm ready for some guy time."

⌘ ⌘ ⌘

"We closed early tonight," Greg explained to Karen when he arrived moments later. "We had so many cancellations that we worked everyone in early or rescheduled them."

Karen introduced him to Kevin, who was getting ready to head out the door. The men shook hands and exchanged pleasantries, but Greg noted Kevin's frown as he made his exit.

Bethany and Brittany bounded into Greg's arms, both of them talking at once.

"We made a snowman," Bethany said excitedly.

"Did you see it outside?" Brittany asked.

He nodded as the girls filled him in on their day.

"We built forts and had snowball fights."

"Our team lost."

"We're having roast for dinner."

Greg couldn't get a word in edgewise, but that last comment got his attention. He caught the surprise on Karen's face before she schooled her expression.

"We have plenty. I'd love for you to stay," she offered, "if you don't have plans."

"No, we don't have plans, but I don't want to impose." *Is this a good idea?* he wondered.

"Please, stay. It's really no imposition at all. I made plenty because I assumed that Kevin and the girls would be eating here." Karen wondered what Kevin would think when she told him—*if* she told him.

"We'd be honored." Greg still wasn't sure it was a good idea, but it was certainly preferable to scrounging up dinner at home. When he had told Gretchen not to come over today, he hadn't considered that he would be on his own for dinner. Of course, he could pick up something on the way home, but why let a perfectly good roast go to waste?

9

Life was back to normal on Tuesday. The roads were cleared and schools reopened. At noon, Robin and Karen found that they had the break room to themselves.

"How did it go yesterday?" Karen questioned Robin as she waited for her lunch to heat in the microwave.

"It was kind of quiet," Robin answered as she unwrapped the turkey sandwich she had brought. "We had quite a few cancellations. Katie didn't make it in, but we really didn't need her. But the important question is, how was your day? I understand you had a houseful."

"It was surprisingly wonderful," Karen replied, taking her dish from the microwave and sitting down beside Robin. "Bethany and Brittany are little angels. I think they had a calming effect on the boys."

"I found, when my two were children, that they didn't bicker as much if other children were around. And I have to agree with you concerning the girls. They are precious."

"Kevin came over and 'played' with the kids. I think he truly enjoyed himself."

"Kevin's the man you're dating?" It was more of a question than a statement.

"Yes, for about three months now. I really like him. I think he may be Mr. Right."

Robin lifted an eyebrow. "I didn't realize it was getting serious."

"It isn't all that serious yet." Karen was uncertain how much she should say. But Robin was a good listener, and she didn't have any one else she could talk to face-to-face on a regular basis. "I'm just looking down the road and hoping. He's everything I'm looking for. He's kind, attentive, and responsible. He's got a great job, which he loves…maybe a bit too much. And he seems to get along great with my boys, at least the younger ones."

"What about Trevor? How does he feel?"

Karen took another bite of leftover roast before answering, carefully considering how much she wanted to reveal. "Trevor is antagonistic towards Kevin, but he would feel that way about anyone I was dating. He feels that if I dating someone, I'm being disloyal to Jeff. He took off yesterday when he heard that Kevin was coming over. He spent the entire day at his friend Tim's, only coming home for dinner."

Robin reflected on that silently as she slowly chewed her last bite of sandwich.

"Trevor didn't seem to mind Greg and the girls having dinner with us," Karen mused. "Maybe he doesn't see Greg as a threat to take his father's place."

⌘⌘⌘

So, Greg had dinner with Karen last night, Robin thought. *Maybe that's a hopeful sign.* She had long held the opinion that Greg needed to start dating. Those girls needed a mother, and Greg could use some looking after as well. Of course, it was probably nothing more than a simple meal shared by two friends, and their five children. Five children! That was too much to wish on anyone.

Robin had wanted to talk to Gretchen for some time about "fixing" Greg up. There were a number of single women at their church. Surely one of them would be right for Greg. She was hesitant to broach the subject with her best friend, however. The situation was sensitive, as Robin didn't want Gretchen to feel that they were replacing her daughter. She'd give it some thought and prayer.

⌘⌘⌘

Karen couldn't believe the way Kevin was acting. She had casually mentioned that Greg and the girls had stayed for dinner, and Kevin went off the deep end. He sounded like a jealous schoolboy. Jealous of Greg Marshall, of all people! Why, Greg was her boss. Besides that, Greg was too old for Karen. He was too old, wasn't he? Now that she thought about it, Karen wasn't certain what Greg's age was. His children were about the same age as hers—in fact she had one significantly older than his—but she and Jeff had started their family early. Greg had spent years in school becoming an orthodontist before having children, hadn't he? Maybe being the boss made him seem older. Anyway, she was getting herself off track. Good grief, it had only been dinner at home with the family. A body would think she'd gone out for a date with Greg from the way Kevin was ranting on and on.

I should never have told him, she fumed silently, tuning Kevin out. *Here I am trying to be honest and above-board with him, and he makes a federal case out of it.*

"Kevin, lighten up," she finally said, frustrated. "He stayed for dinner, that's all. The dinner you should have stayed for. The dinner I fixed for you. And there were five other people at the table. You are being ridiculous." A little part of her was secretly pleased that Kevin cared enough about her to be jealous, but mostly she was annoyed. He had no right to be acting this way.

"I guess you're right." It seemed she had finally penetrated his thick skull. "Just dinner, huh?"

"Just dinner."

"I'm sorry I blew up at you. I guess I just don't like the idea of another man having dinner with my girl."

His girl. Karen's heart did a flip. *He called me his girl.* In an instant, that comment made up for his childish behavior. All was forgiven.

Karen decided she wouldn't mention that Greg had sat in the kitchen and kept her company while she put the finishing touches on dinner. Nor would she mention that he had set the table and helped her with cleaning up after dinner before taking his girls home. Best also not to mention the note she had found on her desk this morning. A note from Greg thanking her for taking care of the girls and for making dinner and offering to take she and the boys out in return. No, she definitely wouldn't mention any of that. Some things were best kept to one's self.

⌘ ⌘ ⌘

Karen felt as if her head had barely touched her pillow when the nightmare occurred. She awoke sobbing and shivering. After calming herself, she flicked on the lamp and picked up the small notebook she kept on the nightstand. Taking Chad's advice, Karen had begun documenting the nightmares. She recorded the date, time, and anything unusual or stressful that had happened during the day. Chad thought that stress might be contributing to the nightmares. The only thing stressful today had been Kevin's attitude when Karen told about Greg staying for dinner. She wrote that down. If she decided to see a counselor, the information she was recording might be helpful.

It was only 2 in the morning. Karen was always apprehensive of going back to sleep after a nightmare, and tonight was no exception. She decided that working on stripping the chairs might provide her with a needed distraction. Going downstairs, she brewed a cup of apple-spice tea and set about her work.

Working for a bit each night after the boys were in bed, she had finished removing the finish from the first chair and was nearly done with the second. Her natural inclination was to move ahead with sanding and staining the first chair before turning her attention to the other one, but she had promised herself not to do so. She felt that stripping both chairs before moving on to the sanding step would teach her patience. It would also build her appreciation for the final outcome.

As she worked, she thought back to Kevin and Greg's differing responses to her project. Even though Kevin sat at the "new" table to eat his lunch, he didn't seem to notice the addition to the kitchen. Then he had walked past the stripped chair in the laundry room on his way outside without noticing it either. To say that Karen was disappointed in his observational skills was an understatement. She'd hoped he would compliment her progress on the project; after all, she had excitedly told him about the table just a few days earlier and updated him on her progress during their nightly phone conversations.

Greg, who was previously unaware of Karen's project or her passion for it, had noticed the chairs as he passed the laundry room while carrying dishes from the kitchen to the dining room table. He not only asked her about the project but showed a genuine interest in hearing all about her hobby. He had even asked to see some of the other pieces she had done. Karen had proudly showed him the coffee table and end tables in her living room. Greg had been properly impressed and expressed his opinion that God had blessed her with a special talent.

Karen prayed as she worked on the chair, asking God to take away the awful nightmares. Soon Karen felt the tension melt away and exhaustion set in. She was able to sleep peacefully for the remainder of the night.

10

Valentine's Day was all that Karen had dreamed it would be. Kevin called her just as she was rising from her bed and wished her a wonderful day. He even ended with "Love ya" rather than his trademark "Talk to ya later." Karen's heart soared with his words. She sang in the shower before heading downstairs to start the coffee and have her daily devotion. Two weeks into her new routine, she could no longer envision starting the day without taking a few minutes for prayer and Bible reading. She had picked up a woman's 5-minute devotional and was working her way through it; it was ideal for her and, as she read it each morning, she was reminded of truths of God's love and provision that she had forgotten.

Every aspect of the family's morning routine had improved since Karen had begun forfeiting a little sleep and taking care each night to pack the family's lunches. Before heading upstairs for the night—to chat with Kevin—she made sandwiches. Each sandwich and a piece of fruit went into a brown lunch sack and then into the fridge. In the morning, each boy grabbed his sack and added a bag of chips and a dessert of his choosing. Austin made a point of helping Kyle. With these few steps, Karen had downgraded the morning rush from total havoc to organized chaos. She was pleased that the new routine required that she sacrifice only 15 minutes of sleep.

A less-frazzled Karen was freed up to concentrate on breakfast. While bagels and cold cereal were still the breakfast of choice, Karen made an effort to cook at least twice a week. This morning she wanted to do something special. She settled on Belgian waffles with strawberry topping. And while the boys were eating, she tossed a Valentine and a box of "message" hearts into each lunch sack.

She arrived at the office to find that Robin had decorated for the occasion. The walls were covered with red lace hearts. Bundles of helium-inflated balloons were arranged in each corner, and the candy dish beside the reception window contained chocolate hearts. Each patient would receive a balloon and a heart. Karen smiled at the thought of the patients whose day Robin would brighten as she offered balloons and candy to the young and the old. So far, her day could not have been any better.

Lunchtime was special, too. Dr. Marshall ordered subs from a nearby deli for everyone, and the staff of five all ate together in the break room. While they were eating, the bell on the front door rang. They considered ignoring it, but Robin said that would be rude and went to tell whomever it was that they were closed. When she re-entered the room, her face was hidden behind a vase filled with the most beautiful red roses Karen had ever seen.

"Oh Robin, did Chris send you roses?" Jenna exclaimed. Jenna was the hopeless romantic of the office. "They are sooo beautiful."

"They are beautiful, but they're not from Chris—he's too practical to pay a florist for roses on Valentine's Day—and they're not for me. Let me look at the card and see who they are for," Robin teasingly tormented the anxious women.

"I'll look." Katie snatched the envelope from the vase and retrieved the card.

"Umm, it looks like they are for…" Katie pretended to be unable to make out the card. "Take a look, Greg. Can you read it?"

Katie passed the card over to Greg, who seemed to be having difficulty reading today.

"This is ridiculous!" Jenna moaned, taking the card from Greg. "They are clearly for Karen!"

Karen squealed with delight and snatched the card. She knew, of course, that they were from Kevin, but she couldn't wait to read what he wrote.

"I'm looking forward to a special evening with you. Happy Valentine's Day, Kevin."

Before lunch was over, another florist delivered flowers for Jenna and Katie—Jenna's from her longtime boyfriend; Katie's from her husband of three years. Robin's husband, Chris, delivered his roses personally soon after lunch; he had picked red tea roses from his own plants and artfully arranged them in a lovely vase. Robin was thrilled.

"I didn't know you could grow roses in the winter," Karen had commented.

"Chris grows them indoors in pots. He has quite the green thumb." Robin was deservedly quite proud of Chris's gardening abilities.

⌘⌘⌘

While the women in his office were all a-flutter with the promise of a romantic evening spent with the one they loved, Greg faced the prospect of a lonely dinner at home. *Of course, I won't be alone,* he chided himself, *I'll be with my two favorite girls.* He missed Cindy as deeply as ever, but more and more he felt the loneliness of not having a partner to share his life with and considered the idea that maybe it was time to move on.

⌘⌘⌘

Karen was almost giddy with anticipation before Kevin finally arrived at 6 to pick her up. Karen had had no luck in finding a sitter for the evening until Robin suggested that she and Chris would be delighted to stay with the boys. Karen naturally had protested, but Robin had been adamant.

"We don't go out for Valentine's Day anymore," Robin told her at lunch last Thursday. "We long ago got tired of the crowds and prefer a more intimate dinner at home. We'll have a nice dinner out on Monday, and we'll make something special for the boys on Tuesday."

Karen had not wanted to impose on her friend, but Robin was so insistent that Karen finally yielded.

"It will be a blessing to us to help you out," Robin said repeatedly.

Chris and Robin had shown up at Karen's just after 5, carrying two bags of groceries.

"Don't say a word," Robin spoke up before Karen could say anything. "We want to do this. It will be great practice for when we take care of our own grandchildren."

As Karen and Kevin left, the smell of homemade pizza was beginning to waft through the house. Karen knew the boys would have a fun evening. She wondered where Kevin was taking her. But he was offering no hints.

Karen fingered the wrist corsage Kevin had brought her as she dreamed about all that this night could bring. Deep into her revelry, she didn't realize they had arrived at the restaurant until the car stopped and Kevin cut the engine. She looked up, startled.

"Where were you just now?" Kevin asked.

"Just counting my blessings. It's been such a wonderful day already."

"And the evening's just getting started," Kevin added as he opened the door and climbed from the car.

Karen waited for Kevin to walk to her side and open the door for her. He didn't always do that, but she knew he would on a special occasion like tonight.

For the first time, Karen directed her eyes toward the restaurant and saw that they were at Fondue Extravaganza. She'd heard of the fondue chain but had never been to one. Jeff had not been the romantic sort, and they could never have afforded it anyway.

They were greeted enthusiastically by the hostess, who handed Karen two red roses and escorted them to their table. They were seated in a cozy, corner booth. A fondue pot sat on a burner in the center of the table. The hostess told them that Michael would be their server and gave them a souvenir copy of the special Valentine's Day Extravaganza Spectacular menu for the evening.

Michael quickly greeted them. Then he led them through the decisions they needed to make concerning their meal.

The meal began with cheese fondue; they choose a Swiss cheese. Michael prepared it at the table before them. The aroma was enticing. As soon as he declared the cheese ready for consumption, Karen dipped a piece of cauliflower into the creamy concoction. She stabbed a chunk of pumpernickel bread even as she munched on the cauliflower. Kevin took a more cautious approach, preferring to wait until Karen had declared judgment.

"Mmm…mmm." Karen next tried a slice of Granny Smith apple.

"So, what's the verdict?" Kevin eyed the bowl of raw veggies warily.

"Best stuff I've ever eaten. Hence the yummy noises."

"I wondered what those sounds were." Kevin decided to start with bread. He chose a piece of rye. "Not bad."

"Try the apples. I could make a meal of this." And, apparently, Karen could, as she didn't stop eating until she had scraped every last bit of cheese from the pot. Kevin ate a few bites before deciding to save his appetite for the entrée.

The cheese was followed by the salad course. Both Kevin and Karen had chosen the Caesar and agreed it was delicious. Karen declared she was feeling comfortably full by the time the main course was ready.

"Good. More meat for me." The fondue concept was beginning to grow on Kevin.

Michael whisked away their salad plates and explained that, for the entrée course, they would cook their own meat and vegetables at the table. He suggested that they cook in *coq au vin*. When the liquid was hot enough, he explained to them the proper cooking times and left them to enjoy themselves. Karen didn't know what she liked the best—the succulent lobster or the tender filet mignon. Kevin declared the entire selection of meats to be delicious, but Karen noticed that he avoided all of the vegetables except one.

"Kevin, you define 'meat and potato man.'"

"I eat what I like. I gotta tell you, though, a man could starve waiting for his food to cook. I get one bite every two minutes. No wonder the meal takes two hours—one hour and 50 minutes to cook the food and ten minutes to eat it."

"Don't spoil a perfectly wonderful day by being a grouch."

"I wouldn't be grouchy if I weren't starving to death."

"By the way, the roses were lovely. Thank you." Karen quit eating just as Kevin was getting warmed up.

"Can I use your fondue forks? I can cook twice as much at one time that way." He reached over and picked up her forks without waiting for her response. "And you're welcome. I'm glad you liked the roses."

"I loved them! It's the first time I've had flowers delivered to me."

"Your husband never sent you flowers?"

"Jeff? That's funny. Jeff's idea of a romantic gift was a box of chocolates. He would give them to me and then eat most of them himself."

When Kevin had consumed the last morsel of meat, Michael returned to clear away the main course dishes and describe to them the delicious options for ending their evening. They chose a decadent mixture of white and dark chocolate fondue for their final course. The fondue was accompanied by a selection of fruits, cake, and marshmallows.

"Now, this is my idea of a romantic dessert." Kevin dipped a strawberry in the chocolate and fed it to Karen.

"Incredible," Karen declared as she spooned chocolate over a bite of cheesecake.

Kevin popped a chocolate-covered brownie in his mouth and reached for a banana. "That's the best, the very best."

By the time all the chocolate had been consumed, even Kevin said he was stuffed. Karen was enthralled with the restaurant, the food, and the atmosphere.

"Are you up for a bit of dancing?" Kevin asked Karen, as he opened the car door for her. "I hear they have a good band tonight at the Holiday Inn."

Karen had to wait for him to walk around to the driver's side and climb in the car before answering.

"Sure, that's sounds wonderful." Karen hoped she didn't disappoint Kevin with her lack of ability; Jeff hadn't liked dancing, so Karen had never danced. But, as dancing always sounded so romantic, she was looking forward to giving it a try.

Before Karen had a chance to get nervous about dancing, Kevin had parked the car and was opening the car door for her. Kevin took her hand and led her into the club and onto the dancing floor. Swaying to the music in Kevin's arms felt so right to Karen. She could have stayed there forever.

After a couple of dances, Karen saw a man approaching. He tapped Kevin on the shoulder.

"Mind if I cut in?" Kevin was scowling as he turned to face the interloper who dared to compete with him for Karen's attention. But the scowl quickly turned into a big grin.

"Donnie. Good to see you, my man." The two men shook hands and pounded each other on the back.

"This is Karen, the lady I told you about. Karen, I'd like you to meet Donnie. He is a customer who has turned into a friend." Karen felt Donnie's eyes appraising her as he extended his hand.

"It's nice to meet you, Karen. I've been waiting a long time for Kevin to bring a lady in here for a dance. He spends far too much time at the dealership."

Karen nodded her agreement, even as she felt Donnie reach for her hand.

"Now, how about that dance?"

The next hour passed quickly as Kevin and Karen visited with Donnie and took a few more turns around the dance floor.

"I hate to break this up, Donnie, but I promised Karen we would make an early night of it. It seems some people have to get up before the crack of dawn and go to work."

Donnie chuckled and wished them a good night.

⌘⌘⌘

When Karen returned to the living room after saying good night to Robin and Chris, she found Kevin sitting on the couch looking a great deal like the cat who swallowed the canary.

"What are you up to?"

He thrust his hand forward. Karen saw that it held a small white box. "Happy Valentine's Day." Kevin managed to look both quite pleased with himself and extremely anxious at the same time.

"Oh, my. For me?" *How stupid can I be? Of course, it's for me.*

⌘⌘⌘

"Oh, Kevin." Her breathless whisper as she peered into the open box told Kevin everything he needed to know.

61

"I hoped you would like them."

"Like them? I love them. They are exquisite." Karen was sounding like she was on the verge of crying. "I've never been given anything so lovely."

"Didn't Jeff give you jewelry, either?"

"Hardly ever. And never anything as nice as these earring."

Kevin was beginning to wonder what kind of man Jeff had been. To have a wife as special as Karen and never send her flowers, take her dancing, or buy her the jewelry was unthinkable. Heck, it was almost criminal. Jeff could not have been worthy of a woman as wonderful as Karen. But Jeff was only a memory now. Kevin looked forward to many opportunities to take Karen dancing and to shower her with jewelry.

"I've got to try them on right now."

Karen removed the earrings she was wearing and inserted the emeralds Kevin had just given her. She went to the mirror in the entrance hall to see how they looked.

"They look even better on than they did in the box." Joy radiated from Karen's face.

Kevin walked to the foyer and studied her in the bright light on the entryway. "They match your eyes perfectly."

"Yes, they do. How clever of you to remember my eye color so accurately!"

"I love your eyes."

Karen's pleasure more than made up for all the time Kevin had spent selecting the earrings. He had looked at more pairs of earrings than he cared to remember. He had first been attracted to a pair of ruby teardrops, then pearl studs, but when he saw the sparkling emerald ones the same shade as Karen's lovely green eyes, his decision had been made.

She smiled at Kevin, and he lowered his mouth to meet hers.

⌘ ⌘ ⌘

His first kiss was gentle. The next one was more passionate. *Too passionate,* Karen thought. She was determined to not let physical attraction and passion cloud her judgment regarding their relationship.

When the kiss ended, Karen edged away, giving Kevin space to breathe.

Kevin took the hint. He led her back to the couch. "I think it's time for us to take our relationship to the next level." He reached over and stroked her cheek.

"What exactly do you mean by the next level?" Karen's heart raced in her chest. *Could he be talking about getting engaged? It's soon. But not that soon, if we really love each other.*

"I'm talking about intimacy. Trusting each other completely. Opening up and being honest with each other."

"I do trust you. I have been honest with you."

"Have you?" Kevin's voice wasn't accusing, yet Karen felt threatened by his words.

"Of course, I would never lie to you."

"I'm not saying that you would. I'm talking about being honest with your feelings and about your past. I need you to open up to me. To share more of your past. I need to know that you're over Jeff and truly ready to move on."

"Oh," she said in a small, quiet voice.

Kevin's words shouldn't have been surprising. After all, Karen had been telling herself this for weeks, yet she couldn't bring herself to talk about the past. There was too much hurt, too much pain, and too much guilt.

"I'll try," she said meekly.

"That's all I'm asking. And I'll make an effort to get to know your sons better. If this relationship is going to work, I have to do a better job of bonding with them."

Karen was thrilled. Hadn't she prayed only yesterday that God would put it in Kevin's heart to spend time with her boys? If Kevin was going to be the father to her boys that she hoped he would be, then he needed to start becoming part of their lives.

Just as Karen was handing Kevin his gift, he dropped the bombshell she'd been dreading. "There's more, Karen. We need to become more intimate physically. We need to find out if we are…compatible."

Karen didn't reply but shoved the gift into his hands. He ripped off the paper, revealing a Texas Hold 'Em poker set and the DVD *Maverick*.

"Hey, this is great. I love this movie."

"You don't have it already, do you?"

"No. I don't have many movies. My ex took all of our movies when she moved out, and I haven't replaced them."

"I know how much you enjoy playing poker with your friends. So I thought you might enjoy these."

"I do. They're great. Thank you."

"So, Karen, I've been thinking that you and I should go away together for a couple of days. Maybe around Easter. Didn't you say that the boys will be spending their break with their grandparents?"

"Go away together?" Karen was caught off guard by Kevin's sudden switch back to the subject of intimacy. "Maybe. I guess, uh, that it might be a good idea."

"Will the boys be at their grandparents? Will you be home alone?"

"Yes, to both questions. They'll be staying with Jeff's parents. I'm not welcome, er, I mean, comfortable, there. Besides, I have to work."

"Everyone is entitled to a vacation."

"Of course. Greg closes the office for two week in the summer. I have to take my vacation then. If I take off at Easter, I won't get paid."

"The dealership is closed on Easter Sunday. I thought we could both take off Monday and Tuesday. I'm sure you could manage two days off without pay."

"Well, maybe. I could ask Greg." Karen couldn't think clearly and it seemed she was agreeing despite her best intentions.

"We can leave Saturday night and come back on Tuesday. My uncle has a place on the Northern Neck. I can use it anytime I want."

Kevin seemed to have given this some thought. Karen needed some time to think about it. She was certain Kevin would expect them to share a bed. Hadn't he said they needed to be physically intimate and find out if they were compatible? *I don't know if I'm ready for that.* Karen had been raised to believe that physical intimacy was for marriage only. She didn't want to compromise her beliefs, but she didn't want to disappoint Kevin, either.

Kevin left, with Karen promising to give his idea some thought. *Maybe Greg won't let me off of work, and I will have to say no. Why don't I have the courage to tell Kevin the truth?*

64

11

"Jeff. Grab the life preserver. Reach for it, Jeff. Come on, you can do it. Just reach a little further." Jeff was struggling to keep his head above water. Karen had tossed the life preserver to him three times, but each throw fell short of his reach. Jeff was unable or unwilling to make the effort to swim to the ring.

Karen made a couple more attempts to no avail. Deciding that it was no use to continue her efforts, Karen gave up and walked back to their children huddled together on the shore.

"Help, Daddy," Trevor yelled to her.

"It's no use. I can't reach him," Karen answered sadly.

Karen gathered the two youngest boys to her and watched helplessly as Jeff tired and began to surrender to the water. Trevor, being the oldest, refused to stand by and watch his father drown. He ran to the water and swam with all his might toward his father. But he was too late. Jeff had sunk beneath the surface and, though he dove again and again, Trevor could not find him.

Trevor emerged from the water exhausted, tears streaming down his face. "You let Daddy die," he screamed at Karen. "You could have saved him, but you let him die."

"No," Karen screamed back at him, "I tried to help him, but I couldn't save him It's not my fault, it's not my fault...."

⌘⌘⌘

"Mom, wake up." Trevor shook Karen awake. "It's just a nightmare, Mom. It's just a nightmare." Trevor put his arms around her and stroked her hair. For a few moments, Karen felt bonded to her oldest child in a way she had not been since Jeff's death.

For all of his preschool years, Trevor had Karen all to himself while Jeff worked; the two had formed a connection stronger than those she had with the younger boys. Since Jeff's death, however, he had kept her at a distance. Karen knew he was hurt and angry about his father's death. Rather than face his hurt and anger, Trevor kept it bottled up inside, refusing to talk to her about it or to see a counselor. She occasionally caught glimpses of the old Trevor, especially when Chad visited or at times, like tonight, when Karen seemed vulnerable. Karen quickly recovered, but she stole a few extra moments in her son's embrace.

"I know. It just seemed so real."

Trevor, seeing that she was fine, headed back to his own bed. Karen reached for the notebook on the nightstand and duly recorded the nightmare. She noted the stress caused by Kevin's desire for a more intimate relationship. Seeing that it was after five, she rose from the bed and headed downstairs to the kitchen. A cup of tea, reading a couple of Psalms, and expending some energy refinishing the chairs had become the antidote of choice whenever a nightmare occurred.

While waiting for the teakettle to whistle, Karen worked on smoothing the now stain-free surfaces of the chairs with the sandpaper.

Sanding required little conscious thought and allowed her to reflect on the events of previous night. Some of Kevin's surprises had been pleasing and welcomed; others had been, well, shocking. Kevin had never brought up the subject of physical intimacy before, but Karen recognized that she should have expected it. Kevin, after all, had been married before, too. He had known the pleasures of a physical relationship with a woman and certainly would want to enjoy that type of relationship again.

Kevin had said Karen was his first steady girlfriend since the divorce. Karen had, quite naturally, drawn the conclusion that Kevin had been celibate since his wife deserted him. *Maybe that's not what he was implying.* Karen had assumed that she and Kevin would marry before sleeping together. *What do I really know of Kevin's values? What about my own? Am I being a hypocrite?*

After the mistakes of her past, Karen had vowed never to engage in sex outside of marriage again. Now she was having the feeling that her willpower would be severely tested in this area.

⌘ ⌘ ⌘

Karen knew she could not repay Robin for taking care of the boys the night before, but she wanted to do more than say "Thank you." On her way to work, Karen stopped at Starbucks and purchased Robin a bag of her favorite blend of coffee, which she gave to her as soon as she arrived at the office. "Thank you so much for watching the boys last night. I hope they behaved themselves for you." She placed the bag of coffee beside Robin's computer. "Just a small token of my appreciation."

"You know you didn't have to do that. We enjoyed ourselves. Your boys behaved quite well." Robin picked up the bag. "Guatemala Antigua. My favorite. You remembered?" A couple weeks earlier, Karen and Robin had been discussing their current "comfort foods" and Robin had mentioned that the coffee was a new favorite. "I love the hint of cocoa," she had said. Karen had mentally stored away the information.

"It's the least I could do. Thanks again."

Karen headed for her desk after promising Robin to fill her in on the details of the evening during lunch.

⌘ ⌘ ⌘

The day moved along quickly and before Karen knew it, it was lunchtime. She had brought a couple slices of leftover pizza—the homemade pizza Robin and Chris had made for the boys. By the time her pizza was hot, Robin had joined her in the lunchroom.

"I had forgotten how good homemade pizza is." Robin had her head in the refrigerator trying to find her lunch. "Chris and I used to make pizza all the time when our children were small, but until last night, it had been years since we had done so."

"It's really delicious. I haven't had pizza in a while."

"Me neither. Chris is trying to lower his cholesterol, so we have been eating a low carb diet."

Karen swallowed another bite. "I hope you didn't blow your diet on account of my boys."

"Not at all. We ate before we came over." Robin added dressing to the salad she had brought. "The pizza smelled so good that I ate some anyway. Chris had more willpower than me. He scraped the toppings off a couple of pieces and ate them, but no crust. I was proud of him."

Robin took time to eat a bite of salad. "Now, tell me about your evening. Spare no details."

Karen gushed forth with a description of their meal at Fondue Extravaganza and dancing together afterwards. She was hesitant to bring up the conversation Kevin had initiated, but she needed to talk to someone and Robin was a trusted friend.

"After you left, Kevin gave me my gift." Karen tugged at the emerald earring dangling from her right lobe.

"They're beautiful."

"Aren't they? I love them. Although, I have to admit, when Kevin pulled out the white jeweler's box, I did think, just for a second, that it might be a ring....I know," Karen quickly added, "it was silly to think that. It's too soon. But I guess I keep hoping that he's the one.... Well, the emeralds were so lovely, they took my breath away."

Robin agreed that they were. "It sounds like you had a wonderful night. I'm happy for you."

"We did. Except....it's not important," Karen said nervously.

"Except, what?"

Karen knew Robin wasn't going to let the comment slip. "He wants me to go away with him," she murmured. "You know, spend a few nights together."

"What did you say?"

"I told him I would have to think about it. I'm not sure that it's a good idea."

Robin frowned. "No. It's not. I think you know that."

"I tossed and turned for hours, thinking about it last night. Then I had another nightmare. The same one, where Jeff dies, although it wasn't exactly the same."

"I thought you looked a bit tired this morning." Robin patted her hand in a maternal gesture. "Maybe you should talk to someone about the nightmares. You may have some unresolved issues from Jeff's death that you need to deal with before you are ready to commit your life to

Kevin, or whoever God has for you."

"I'll think about it." Karen knew that Robin was giving her good advice, but she wasn't sure she would act on it.

"You should also think about coming to church. Your boys need to be in church and so do you."

Every few weeks, Robin brought up the subject of church. Karen usually ignored her comments, but lately, she had been thinking that Robin was right. Although the Harper family had avoided church for the last two years, Karen and Jeff had faithfully attended during most of their marriage. Karen had continued going even after Jeff had quit a few years before his death.

"You're right. I'll try to make it this Sunday."

Robin didn't say anything. She just smiled and continued eating her lunch.

⌘⌘⌘

Greg had walked by the lunchroom as Karen was reciting her account of her Valentine's date. He had noticed her earrings when he had encountered Karen at the coffee station earlier. Robin had shown him the watch Chris gave her, and Jenna was sporting a new necklace. Katie and Jenna had chatted all morning, between patients and with patients, about romantic dinners, chocolates, and jewelry. It seemed that everyone, except Greg, had thoroughly enjoyed the day. He hated to admit it, but he was jealous.

How petty of me, he thought, *to be jealous of the women who work for me because they all have someone to share their lives with.* But the chiding didn't change his envy or desire for someone to share his life.

Greg had spent a quiet evening at home with Bethany and Brittany. Gretchen and Tom were having a special evening out, but before she left for the evening, Gretchen had prepared Greg's favorite meal—chicken parmesan—and baked an apple pie for the three members of the Marshall family to enjoy. Gretchen and Tom gave the girls red wicker baskets filled with chocolate hearts and other treats. After dinner, Greg and the girls had played Bingo and watched

Dunston Checks In, currently the girls' favorite movie. Greg gave them each a card that told them how proud he was to be their father. He also gave them coupons to each have a one-on-one "Date with Dad." Gretchen would keep one girl while Greg took the other out for a special dinner and an activity of her choice. The girls gave Greg handmade cards proclaiming him to be the "World's Best Daddy."

But when Greg climbed into the king-sized bed, the familiar loneliness crept in. He missed Cindy so much. Yet, he knew that God was telling him it was time to let go of Cindy and move on. He knew he would always love her. Letting go would not mean forgetting her or the love they had shared. No, she would always be a part of him. But he needed to make room in his heart for a new love.

"Dear Heavenly Father, I know your Word says it's not good for man to be alone. I'm asking You now to give me another helpmate, someone who loves You and will love me and the girls. I need someone to share my life. Help me to be open to your direction in this area. I praise You, for You always hear and always answer. In the precious name of Your Son, I ask this. Amen."

As he listened to his staff share their experiences from the night before, Greg's heart longed for someone to share a romantic dinner with or to shower with jewelry. The only women he knew were the ones in his employ and the ones who attended his church. All the women at work were claimed. But there must be some available women at church. Greg had overheard Gretchen and Robin whispering together last Sunday after services. They were discussing which single women at church would be suitable matches for Greg. If they wanted to play matchmaker, perhaps he should let them.

Greg smiled. He'd let them know he was definitely interested in their interference—or rather, help.

12

After showering and putting her spaghetti-stained blouse in the sink to soak, all Karen wanted to do was talk to Kim. It had been one of the most frustrating days she had ever experienced, and she needed to vent to her best friend. She dialed Kim's number and got a busy signal. *How could Kim be on the phone when I need to talk to her? Hasn't she ever heard of call waiting?*

While she paced around the kitchen anxiously, Karen started a pot of coffee—decaf. She was hyped up enough; she definitely didn't need caffeine. She tried Kim's number twice more while the coffee brewed. Still busy. She poured a cup of coffee and dialed Kim's number a fourth time. *Good grief, Kim, get off the phone.* As she took her first tentative sip of the steaming liquid, the phone rang. It was Kim.

"I'm so glad you called back! Boy, do I need to talk to you!"

"What's going on?" Kim sounded worried. "Are you okay?"

"Yes, sort of. I've had a terrible day. I needed to talk to someone who would understand."

"That's all? No one is seriously injured or in the hospital?" The worry in Kim's voice had been replaced by annoyance.

"No." Karen was beginning to feel a bit abashed. Patience had never been one of her strengths.

"I tried to ignore the call waiting signal, but when you called back every two minutes, I thought it must be something urgent."

"Did I interrupt anything important?"

"I was just planning my father's 65th birthday party with Mom. The party is still a few weeks away, so we have plenty of time. But let's get back to you. You had a bad day and need to talk. That means you are having problems with either Trevor or Kevin. Which one is it?"

"Both. I made such a mess of things. It's all my fault."

"Start at the beginning."

⌘ ⌘ ⌘

Kim curled up in her most comfortable chair. She had a feeling this was going to take awhile.

"If only I hadn't agreed to have lunch with Mike." Karen settled down on the sofa, with the phone in one hand and her coffee in the other.

"Mike? Who's Mike?" Kim was confused momentarily, and then it hit her. "You don't mean that guy you were dating last summer! Tell me, you are not talking about *that* Mike."

"One and the same."

"I thought you weren't ever going to see him again. You said he was out of your life for good. What were you thinking?"

"I wasn't thinking; that's the problem. He called this morning and said he was in town on business. He wanted to buy me lunch and catch up, see how I was doing. I knew it was him from the caller ID. I should never have answered the phone. But I did. Of course, I told him I wasn't going to meet him, but he persisted and I gave in. What harm could it do? It was only lunch in a public restaurant."

Kim could hardly believe her ears. How could Karen let that jerk back into her life, after the way he had misled her and hurt her?

⌘ ⌘ ⌘

Mike had come to Karen's rescue in the months following Jeff's death, when she looked at the future and saw only hopelessness and despair. After the boys went to bed, the house was too lonely, too quiet. She would lie in bed for hours, unable to sleep and plagued by nightmares when she did manage to sleep. On one of those sleepless nights, several months after Jeff's death, she had logged onto the Internet and found a chat room for parents without partners. This sounded like a place where she might find someone who could empathize with her grief and loneliness. It was there one night that Karen met Mike.

Mike told her he too had experienced a great loss, and they

commiserated in their shared pain. Mike's wife—his first and only love, the mother of his children— had died after being hit by a drunk driver on her way home from a PTA meeting a year earlier. He still hadn't gotten over it; he didn't think he ever would. Mike was left to raise their two children, a boy and a girl, on his own. They expounded on the difficulties of being both mom and dad to the children and the loneliness that was strongest at night as they climbed into their respective beds alone. The fact that everything Mike told her would later prove to be lies didn't diminish the comfort those conversations had given Karen in the darkest period of her life.

Karen and Mike became more than friends; they became each other's lifeline. If they clung to one another, they might survive the terrible emptiness and come out whole on the other side. Mike suggested that they meet. Karen could take a personal day from work; Kyle was in daycare, and the other boys were in school. She could meet him somewhere, spend several hours together, and be back to Chester in time to get the boys from afterschool care before the 6 p.m. deadline.

"How about King's Dominion?" Mike had suggested. The theme park was midway between their two homes, and it seemed an ideal place to spend their first afternoon together.

"Great. I have an annual pass." Ironically, Karen's annual pass had been purchased on her last visit there with Jeff, only days before he died.

They met at the Eiffel Tower. Mike was everything he had described himself as—handsome, athletic, fun-loving. It was the best day Karen had spent since, well, since she had come here with Jeff. Before leaving the park, they rode to the top of the Eiffel Tower. Looking out at the park and surrounding landscape, Mike had taken her into his arms and kissed her. The kiss had left her breathless and wanting more.

Two weeks later, Karen took another personal day. She met Mike for lunch in Ashland. After lunch, Mike suggested they get a hotel room. By then, Karen knew she was in love; she told herself that it wasn't wrong as long as they loved each other. Plus, they were both single, consenting adults who knew what they were doing. Ashland became their meeting place. About once a month, Karen would call in sick or take a personal day and make the 40-minute trip to meet Mike for "lunch."

By the first anniversary of Jeff's death, Karen knew she had to get out of Chester. It was a small town, one of those small towns where everyone knows everyone. No anonymity there. No chance for a new start. She knew that people gossiped about her—and that some of them, particularly Jeff's family, thought she bore some responsibility for Jeff's death. She would never get beyond the rumors.

Karen decided to move away from Chester as soon as school let out. Fredericksburg seemed to be the logical choice. It was only 80 miles away. She could easily drive down to visit her parents and let the boys see Jeff's family. She didn't know anyone there—except Mike—so she could start a new life with a clean slate. She and Mike were in love, and it was time they got to know each other's children. If they were going to blend these families—and Karen was positive they were—they needed to spend time together.

It was in another chat room—one targeting 30-something singles—that she had met Kevin about a month after she made the move. At the time, she still believed that she and Mike had a future together and let Kevin know she was only interested in being friends with him. It was several weeks later, when Mike told her that he was being transferred and revealed that his wife was very much alive, that she began to shift her hopes of a romantic future to Kevin. Now she had risked her relationship with Kevin by having lunch with Mike.

⌘ ⌘ ⌘

"What harm did it do?" Kim asked. In that moment, she knew Karen's plan for a simple, innocent lunch had totally backfired.

"At first, it was therapeutic to see Mike," Karen explained. "I realized that I was totally over him. He apologized for deceiving me, and I nearly fell for it. Then he gave me that silly grin and said he'd like to start seeing me again. I wasn't even tempted and told him so. He said, 'Well, you can't blame a guy for asking.' The next minute, I heard Kevin say, 'What's going on here?' I nearly choked on my food."

"You should know by now that your sins will find you out. I bet

Kevin was furious." Kim didn't bother to remind Karen that she'd told her friend this many times in the past. It seemed to be a lesson Karen had difficulty learning.

"I'd never seen him like that. His body was completely rigid, and his eyes were black with anger. He looked at me as if I had betrayed him. He didn't say a word for the longest time. Finally, he said. 'I can't believe that my girl is having lunch with this slime ball.'" Karen spoke each syllable slowly and deliberately.

Kim got the picture of Kevin's anger. She shivered.

"I told him it wasn't what he was thinking. And he yelled back, 'How do you know what I'm thinking?' Every head in the restaurant turned to look at us. I tried to tell him that Mike was an old friend and that we were only having lunch." Karen's quivering voice told Kim how painful the scene had been for her friend.

"I've never seen Kevin angry before, and it was frightening. He was fighting hard to maintain his composure, but he kept his right hand clenched in a fist. I thought he was going to punch Mike right in the middle of the restaurant. Mike just sat there with a stupid smirk. He actually looked amused. Then he said, 'It's been a long time, Kevin. How have you been?' I couldn't believe that they knew each other. I kept looking from one man to the other, trying to figure out what was going on."

When Karen paused, Kim took advantage to ask, "How do they know each other?" But she had a sinking feeling she could guess the answer.

"I asked that question myself. Kevin turned to me and said, 'I sold Mike a pickup a few years back, and he picked up more than the truck. Soon after, I caught him in bed with Christine.' I thought I was going to be sick. The room started spinning. I got up from the table and ran toward the restroom. Unfortunately, I ran smack into a waiter carrying a tray full of food."

"You didn't!" Kim gasped.

"Knocked him flat. Food went everywhere. I wound up in a sitting position on the floor with a pile of spaghetti on my head. My blouse was covered in sauce. I burst into tears. I've never been more embarrassed."

Kim tried her best to be sympathetic but found herself laughing so hard tears were welling up in her eyes. "I can just picture you. I wish I could have seen it."

"Some friend, you are." Karen tried to sound cross, but the laughter was contagious…and well needed.

When Kim was able to talk again, she ventured to ask what happened next.

"I shook off the spaghetti and made a mad dash for the restroom. I stayed in there for the longest time, picking noodles from my hair and wiping the sauce off my blouse as best I could. I was considering staying in there forever. I don't know how long I was in there, but after a while, Kevin opened the door and poked his head inside."

"Inside the ladies' room! You're kidding!"

"Sorry, but I'm not. He had my purse and coat over his arm and my cell phone in his hand. He said that Trevor's school had called, and I needed to get to the school right away to pick Trevor up. I was so scared. I thought something bad must have happened to Trevor. I grabbed my things and ran out of the restaurant. I didn't even say goodbye to Kevin or Mike."

Kim had so many questions that she didn't know which one to ask first. "Is Trevor all right? Have you talked to Kevin? Did you two make up? Tell me what happened before I burst."

"I don't know why, but I didn't think to call the school back and ask them what had happened. I just raced over there as fast as I could. I kept praying that Trevor wasn't hurt."

"Was he?" Kim knew that if anything bad had happened to Trevor, Karen would have told her already. Still, she needed to hear Karen say he was okay.

"No, he was fine. At least physically. When I finally got to the school, Trevor was sitting in a chair in the office looking angry. The secretary told me he had been suspended for three days. I was so frustrated by this time that I took it all out on poor Trevor. I screamed at him. I told him he'd worried me half to death. How could he do something that would get him suspended? I told him I was angry and disappointed in him. He didn't say a word. He walked out of the office and went to sit in the car."

"Suspended? What did he do?"

"I didn't even think to ask, until after I yelled at him. It turns out he had taken his pocketknife to school. The one that Jeff gave him for Christmas—the last Christmas. You remember how proud he was of it. He carried it with him everywhere. I guess he's been taking it to school with him. It seems that the state has a zero tolerance policy on kids bringing weapons to school. The principal had no choice but to suspend him. And he kept the knife. I have to go back with him next week to get the knife back."

"Whew. You have had a rough day. How's Trevor now?"

"Angry. Upset. Not speaking to me."

"Have you talked to Kevin?"

"No. When I got home, Trevor went to his room, and I called you. I don't know what I'm going to do, but somehow I have to make things right with both of them."

Kim suggested that Karen first start by making things right with God and asking him to help her repair her relationships with the two men in her life.

"I will," Karen said. "Just pray for me."

13

It had been one of the longest weeks of her life. And now she had to take a couple hours off from work on a Thursday morning to speak with the principal. Since Trevor got in trouble at school last Friday and Karen yelled at him, he hadn't spoken a solitary word to her. He obeyed any order she gave him, but he refused to acknowledge her. When he looked at her, he glared so hard Karen thought he might burn a hole in her. If all that wasn't enough, she'd had three nightmares in the past seven days.

Karen sat in an orange vinyl chair in the high school office waiting her turn to see the principal. It brought back her own high school days. While she'd never been an unruly student, Karen often had trouble guarding her mouth. On more than one occasion, she had mouthed off to Mrs. Carter, the gymnastic coach and Karen's ninth grade PE teacher. Karen hated PE, particularly gymnastics. When Mrs. Carter chided Karen about her fear of the balance beam, Karen had told her to take the balance beam, and…oh well, better to not go there. Karen had served two days' detention for that comment. She didn't bother to dredge through her memory bank for the other comments. Eventually, Karen had learned to calculate the cost of speaking her mind and determined that the satisfaction of telling off Mrs. Carter wasn't worth spending of couple of extra hours at school. At least, she had never been suspended. But she couldn't be too angry with Trevor. He hadn't purposefully violated the school rule for which he'd been suspended.

Karen still felt terrible about the way she had railed into Trevor, without even finding out what he had done or hearing his side of the story. Trevor knew he couldn't bring weapons to school, but it was doubtful he considered his pocketknife to be a weapon. The knife, the last gift from his father, was Trevor's lifeline, a link to his father. He had probably carried it to school every day all year but had only gotten caught last Friday. Best not to mention that to the principal.

"How much longer do you think it will be?" Karen asked to no one in particular. Trevor, who was sitting across the room from her doodling, gave her one of his patented *I-really-don't-know-and-I REALLY-don't-care* looks. The office secretary ignored her and continued shuffling papers on her desk.

Trevor had not minded missing three days of school; lately, he seemed to hate school—and life. It seemed the only time he was happy was as he was going out the door to Tim's house or when he was spending time with Chad. Karen hadn't been sure she could trust Trevor to stay at home by himself, given his present state of sullenness, and she couldn't take the time off from work. It was only a month before tax day, and Greg's accountant needed some additional information before he could file the taxes for the dental practice. Additionally, their finances were tight, and Karen couldn't afford to take any time off without pay right now, particularly since it seemed likely that she would be taking two days off at Easter. She'd finally determined that her only course of action was to take Trevor to work with her. Sunday afternoon, when Karen informed Trevor of her decision, he had gone to his room and slammed the door, refusing to come out for dinner. But when it was time to leave Monday morning, he was standing by the door with his backpack.

Karen had set Trevor up at an unused desk and had gotten his assignments for the three days off the school's website. Trevor had completed them all by the time she was done for the day on Monday. *Great,* Karen had fumed inwardly. *Now what am I going to do with him Tuesday and Wednesday?* Fortunately, Greg had come to her rescue. He suggested that Trevor shadow him and help out a bit. Trevor actually seemed to enjoy the attention from Greg. She could hear him asking the orthodontist questions and volunteering to do tasks. He even ate his lunch with Greg in Greg's office.

He needs a male role model. Dear God, please send him one, Karen prayed silently as she waited for the principal. After their Valentine's Day "talk", Karen had thought that Kevin was going to step up where the boys were concerned, but the only change had been that he was making plans for their weekend away together. Karen still wasn't

79

comfortable with the idea, but Kevin had been so persistent that she had reluctantly agreed. Whenever he called, she tried to feign enthusiasm.

Chad will be moving here in a few months, she reminded herself. Chad would spend as much time as he could with Trevor, but his new business would demand most of his time. *I can't expect Chad to put Trevor ahead of his work, but it will be a big help having him around.* Karen was so deep into her thoughts that she didn't notice the door to the principal's office open or the principal himself indicating to the secretary that he was ready for the next person.

"Mrs. Harper, Mr. Adam will see you now." The sudden announcement startled Karen. She jumped from her seat, knocking her purse to the floor and spilling the contents. Trevor was already in Mr. Adam's office by the time Karen collected her things. She was a bit flustered as she entered the office and took a seat in a brown vinyl chair across the desk from Mr. Adam. *What a way to get started!*

"Please make yourself comfortable, Mrs. Harper." Mr. Adam seemed friendly enough, yet he was the principal. "I'm Jeff Adam, the ninth-grade assistant principal."

So he's not THE principal. That knowledge helped Karen feel a bit more at ease.

"As you were told on Friday when you picked Trevor up, we have a zero tolerance policy towards anyone bringing a weapon on campus. Pocketknives fall into that category. We had no choice but to suspend Trevor. If he brings the knife, or any other weapon, to school again, we will have no choice but to expel him from our school."

Karen nodded, signaling that she understood.

"Trevor, do you understand what I'm telling you?"

"Yes, sir. When do I get my knife back?"

"I'll give the knife to your mother when she is ready to leave. You do understand that you cannot have this knife or any other knife or any type of weapon at school ever again, or you will be expelled. Is that correct?"

"Yes, sir. I just want to have my knife back."

"I need you to sign this form acknowledging that we had this conversation and that you understand everything I told you."

Trevor signed the form, and Mr. Adam added it to Trevor's file on his desk.

"Trevor, this is your knife, correct? Good. You may go to class now. Mrs. Jacobs will write you a pass. I'll give the knife to your mother to take home." With a nod, Mr. Adam dismissed Trevor.

Trevor left the room without so much as a good-bye to his mother. A frown flickered across Mr. Adam's face.

"While you're here, Mrs. Harper, we have some concerns about Trevor that I would like to discuss with you."

Oh, no. Here it comes. And I was just thinking that this visit to the principal's office hadn't been all that bad.

"Several of Trevor's teachers have reported to us that Trevor seems withdrawn. He hasn't made many friends, and he doesn't voluntarily participate in class discussions or activities. He's always been quiet, but in the past few weeks has appeared to become even more withdrawn. Is there anything going on at home that would be impacting Trevor?" Mr. Adam got out of his seat, walked around to the front of the desk, and leaned back on the edge.

There were so many things going on that Karen didn't know where to begin.

"I suppose you know that I'm a single mother. My husband, Jeff, died about two years ago. In fact, it will be two years on April 2."

Mr. Adam scratched the back of his neck. "Well, that could certainly account for his recent behavior. He's probably missing his father and thinking about him more as the anniversary approaches. That is helpful. Anything else?"

Karen focused on her lap and twisted her hands. "I have to support the family, so I work more than I did before. And I'm dating someone. It's getting serious, and Trevor doesn't seem like it. I'm not sure if he has a problem with me dating or if he doesn't like the man I'm seeing. We haven't communicated well since his father's death." Karen kept her head lowered but looked up cautiously. "I think that he blames me for everything."

"What do you mean, everything?"

"He doesn't have a father, we moved away from his friends, he has to help out with his brothers. Things like that." Karen glanced up wistfully. "I'm doing the best I can, but it's very difficult."

"Tragedies like yours can either bring families closer together or drive them apart. It sound like this one is driving you and Trevor apart. What about your other children? How are they handling things?"

"They are quite a bit younger. They don't have as many memories of their father, and I think they want me to remarry so they'll have a dad."

"Trevor is what, about fourteen now? So he was twelve when his father died?" With his arms crossed over his chest and standing over her, Mr. Adam reminded Karen of her own principal. She felt like the schoolgirl she had been, awaiting her punishment.

Karen nodded but did not speak.

"That's a tough age. Did he see a grief counselor?"

"No. His school tried to get him to go, but he refused. He didn't want to talk about that night. I don't think he has ever talked about what happened."

Mr. Adam paused. "Would you feel comfortable sharing with me what happened?

Karen shook her head from side to side. Her voice was barely above a whisper. "I'm sorry. It's still too painful. It was so sudden and unexpected. Trevor was there and witnessed it. Can you imagine how horrible it would be for a kid to see his father die?"

Mr. Adam waited quietly for Karen to continue.

"That's why the pocketknife is so important to Trevor. His father gave it to him for Christmas a few months before his death. He carries it with him everywhere. I think it gives him some comfort, like he always has a little bit of his father with him wherever he goes."

Mr. Adam took a deep breath and slowly exhaled. "I get the picture. However, bringing the knife to school is a violation of state law. There's nothing I can do about that."

"I know. He'll be okay."

"Well, I'm not so sure about that. He really needs to talk to someone. We could arrange for him to see a grief counselor here at school. Or maybe you have a pastor he could talk to?"

"He won't talk to a grief counselor. I'm positive about that. But he might talk to a pastor. We recently began attending a church here. I'll check into it."

"He needs it. Insist that he go to counseling. What he experienced is way too much for him to handle on his own or ignore. Please promise me you will make him get some help."

Karen knew the principal was right. "I promise."

"You might want to find a man you trust for him to spend some time with, kind of a 'big brother' Trevor can confide in."

Karen nodded. She had just asked God for the same thing.

"And I don't mean the guy you are dating," Mr. Adam went on. "Since Trevor doesn't get along well with him, it will only make things worse."

"My brother will be moving to Fredericksburg soon. They get along well. I'm sure he'll be a help with Trevor."

Mr. Adam returned Trevor's knife and saw Karen out the door. "I have one other suggestion."

Karen turned back toward Mr. Adam.

"See if you can find some other object that Trevor can have with him at all times. Maybe a picture or, I don't know, his father's cap, a favorite belt buckle. Something like that."

The visit to the principal's office left Karen spent. When she pulled out of the high school parking lot, she didn't head to Tidewater Orthodontics but turned toward home.

She called Robin on her cell phone as she drove. "Hi, it's Karen. I'll be in after lunch. I need to take care of some things."

Robin was her usual cheerful self. "I'll let Greg know. The accountant called already. I left a message on your desk. He said he needed to verify some payroll information."

"Thanks. I'll take care of it as soon as I get in."

What Karen needed right now was a cup of tea and a good cry. Life seemed to be closing in on her in all directions.

It was tax time, so work was more stressful than normal. She and Trevor were getting more distant; the silent treatment Trevor had given her since the suspension was becoming unbearable. Kevin had gotten her to agree to spend a few days with him at Easter and was expecting her to enter into a physical relationship with him. The constant fear of nightmares and the interruption in her sleep that they caused had left her exhausted and fragile.

As Karen cuddled up in the recliner in the den sipping tea, she wondered how she could bridge the gap between Trevor and herself. She wished she hadn't let so much time pass before making an attempt. "I should have apologized in the car, or at least as soon as we got home." She hadn't done so because she'd been embarrassed by her behavior in the school office and couldn't come up with the appropriate words to justify her actions. The fact that she was drenched in spaghetti sauce did nothing to improve her sour mood. Karen had fully intended to apologize to Trevor before going to bed Friday night. But then Kevin had shown up and her good intentions toward Trevor were forgotten until the next day. By then Trevor had built a wall between them that would take enormous effort for Karen to break through. If only Kevin hadn't come over…but, truthfully, she was thankful he had, as she had been at a loss as to how to mend that broken relationship also.

The doorbell had rung that Friday night just as Karen was heading upstairs for the night. After a stressful day, she wasn't thrilled to have a visitor.

"Ten o'clock at night. I can't imagine who that would be." She took the precaution of grabbing her cell phone before she went to answer the door.

The bell rang again, then once more in quick succession.

"Hold your horses. I'm coming," Karen called out. *They better not wake the boys.*

She looked through the peephole. "Kevin!"

She quickly unhooked the chain and released the bolt lock. Kevin turned the handle and opened the door immediately, but he did not come in.

"Come in. It's freezing out there." Karen was shocked that Kevin would come by so late; she had hoped that he would call her after he was done at work and they would talk things over on the phone.

"We need to talk."

Kevin looked upset. Karen hoped this wasn't one of those *I-never-want-to-see-you-again* talks." He was still standing on the porch.

"Yes, of course. Let's go in the living room. Would you like something hot to drink—maybe some coffee, or I could make some tea?" Karen's rapidly spoken words were running together, the way they always did when she was nervous.

Kevin shook his head. This wasn't a pleasant social call.

"This may get loud. I don't want to disturb the boys. Let's talk in my car." Kevin turned and walked toward the pickup, without waiting for Karen's reply.

Karen shut the door enough to open the coat closet and grab her winter coat. She slipped her arms to the sleeve, closed the front door, and hurried after Kevin. She could hear the hum of his truck's engine. Kevin sat in the front seat of the Avalanche, looking every bit as distraught as when he confronted Mike at the restaurant earlier in the day.

"You slept with Mike Sloan." It wasn't a question. Kevin made the accusation even before Karen was fully in the car.

Karen shut the car door. There was no sense in trying to deny it. "It was months ago, before I met you. Today was the first time I'd seen him since August."

"So you admit you slept with him." Kevin wasn't going to make this easy for her.

"Yes. Yes, I slept with him. It was a huge mistake, and it was over months ago. It has nothing to do with you." Karen was frustrated but tried not to let it show in her voice. *This really is none of your business.* Karen tried to see Kevin's face in the dark car. The street lamp provided some light, but Kevin's face was in the shadows.

"Why did it have to be Mike Sloan?" Kevin's voice sounded more hurt than angry. "If it had been anybody other than that slime ball, it wouldn't be so bad."

"I don't know what else to say." Karen knew she had made a big mistake in getting involved with Mike, but she had truly believed his lies right up until the end. She didn't feel she owed Kevin an explanation. Still, she didn't want to lose him.

"I'm not going to go into all the gory details. But I will tell you this much. I met Mike on the Internet. He said he was a widower. My husband had died, and we seemed to have so much in common. I needed someone who understood what I was going through. Mike seemed to be that someone. As soon as I found out he was married, I ended it."

Well, that last statement wasn't exactly the truth. Mike had ended it before he moved away.

"How long did it go on?"

"Several months, actually close to a year." Karen hated to admit that she had been duped for so long.

Kevin put his head on the steering wheel. He was quiet for a long time. "You ended it when?"

"Last July."

"A year before that would have been about the time he dumped Christine."

That's what this is really about. Mike stole Christine and broke his heart, and he didn't really even want Christine.

"How did Christine get involved with Mike?" Karen thought Kevin might need to talk about his pain.

"Christine worked for a construction company, in the office as a receptionist. Mike would come in to repair the copier. It seemed the copier was broken more than it was operational, so he was there a lot. I guess Christine was attracted to him and flirted with him. He asked her to lunch, and things took off from there." Kevin's voice cracked as he struggled to get the words out.

"So he didn't meet her through you after he bought the pickup from you?"

"No. They had been having an affair for about four months when he bought the pickup. Christine actually sent him in. Said he was a friend from work and that I should give him a discount. I really bent over backwards to get the jerk a great deal. If I'd known he was sleeping with my wife..." Kevin didn't finish the thought.

Karen exhaled loudly. Her heart ached for Kevin.

"They were...in our bed. I wasn't feeling well one day and came home early and...and there they were. Christine didn't apologize or anything. I told her to get out. She didn't argue. I think she wanted to go. Funny thing is, Christine thought Mike loved her and that he was going to marry her. When she moved out, he set her up in an apartment. She had no idea he was married. I found that out and let her know. I thought she might come back to me." Kevin's voice broke, and Karen could tell he was crying.

"I was sure she had been blinded by him, that when she knew the truth, she would realize she still loved me...that she had made a terrible mistake." Kevin had been staring straight ahead, but now he turned and looked at Karen. "You know what she said?"

Karen shook her head.

"She said that Mike wasn't the first. She said she was bored with me, that I worked too much, and that there had been others. She said Mike had helped her to get out of a bad marriage and that she would always be grateful to him." Kevin put his head back on the steering wheel.

Whew. This was a lot deeper than Karen had realized. Karen knew she had to say something. "And then I told you that Mike helped me through a difficult time. I can see now why you are so hurt." Karen reached out her hand and caressed Kevin's head. "I'm so sorry Mike and Christine hurt you, but I would never hurt you. Please, you've got to believe me. I'm not Christine. I didn't cheat on you. I would never cheat on you. Please, Kevin, please believe me." Karen scooted over close to Kevin and laid her head on his shoulder, her arms wrapped around him.

Kevin took her in his arms. They huddled together for a long time, comforting and drawing strength from one another. Kevin bent his head and kissed her tentatively, as if her kiss could tell him if she told the truth. He kissed her again, harder, deeper. Then he held her so tightly Karen thought he might squeeze the breath from her. He seemed to still be struggling with whether to believe her.

Then the heart of the matter hit Karen like a lightning bolt. *I slept with Mike, but I won't sleep with him. That's what's really bothering him.* She knew the only way Kevin would be satisfied that she was telling the truth was if she agreed to be intimate with him. It was in this moment that she had been persuaded to agree to Kevin's plan to spend a weekend together. She whispered in his ear, "I can't wait until Easter when we can go away. I can't wait until you take me in your arms and make love to me." Then she felt Kevin relax. She knew she was still his girl.

She had the nightmare again that night and twice more since. The data recorded in the notebook provided convincing evidence that the nightmares were linked to the stress in her life. Whether it was the stress of her diminished relationship with Trevor or the stress Kevin was putting on her for intimacy was unclear. But what was crystal clear was that the nightmares had to stop or she would lose her mind.

Karen drew herself back into the present. She needed to eat some lunch and get to work. It had been less than a week since she made her promises to Kevin and already she was regretting them. Easter was still three weeks away. A lot could happen in three weeks.

14

Karen was rinsing the shampoo from her hair when the phone rang. She climbed from the tub and made a mad dash into the adjoining bedroom to answer it. She grabbed the phone on the fourth ring, just before the answering machine picked up.

"Hello." She hoped her voice sounded normal.

"Karen. Is that you?"

"Yes. Who is this?" The voice sounded familiar but she couldn't place it.

"Good morning. It's Greg Marshall."

"Uh, yeah, good morning." The only other time Greg had ever called her was to ask her to watch the girls the day it had snowed. Karen was pretty sure it hadn't snowed. At least there had been nothing on the radio about school cancellations.

"Are you all right? You sound out of breath."

Great. He noticed. "I'm fine." *Well, not fine, but I can't say I'm standing here naked, dripping water on the carpet.* "I was in the shower."

"You were in the shower? Don't you have an answering machine?" Greg was yelling, but for the life of her, Karen couldn't figure out why. "That's what answering machines are for. Promise me you'll never get out of the shower to answer the phone again. Is that clear? Promise me."

"Sure, okay, I promise." *What's up with Greg?* He was making a federal case over her answering the phone. *If you didn't want me to answer, why did you call?* Was this some sort of test? Surely Greg didn't call just to find out if she would jump out of the shower to answer the phone.

"All right then." Greg sounded a bit sheepish. He cleared his throat. "I called because I wanted to check with you about your plans

89

for today."

This is the strangest conversation I have ever had with Greg Marshall.

"Did I correctly overhear you telling Robin you would be in the office today?"

"Yes. Is that a problem?" *Greg, help me out here.*

"No, no problem at all. I usually go in on Fridays and make dental appliances. I thought we could coordinate and be there at the same time. I would worry about you if you were in the office by yourself."

This was news to Karen—that Greg would worry about her and that Greg went in on Fridays. She had never given any thought to when Greg made retainers and such. "I was planning to be in at my normal time and stay until noon, to make up the time I missed yesterday."

"Great. I'll see you at 8:30 then. Good-bye." Greg hung up the phone before Karen even had a chance to say good-bye in return.

Karen headed back to the bathroom to finish her shower, pondering what had gotten into Greg. He usually seemed so normal and calm. However, he might have had a point. In the case of this particular call, it had been foolish to risk breaking her neck to answer it.

⌘ ⌘ ⌘

Karen pulled into the parking lot just as Greg was unlocking the doors. She could see that he was holding a tray of some sort in his left hand, balancing it on his knee, as he turned the key with his right hand. Karen hurried up the sidewalk to lend a hand.

"Here, Greg, let me help you with that." She reached out and took the tray. It held two cups of coffee and a couple of bacon, egg, and cheese bagels. "Smells delicious. Is this breakfast?"

"For both of us. Sort of a peace offering." Greg had opened the door. He flicked on the lights and took the tray as Karen entered.

"Peace offering?" If Karen was puzzled before, she was even more so now.

"I owe you an apology. I went a bit ballistic on you over the shower thing." Greg, normally very confident and self-assured, looked a bit uncomfortable.

"It's okay. Don't worry about it." Karen genuinely meant it. No peace offering was needed, but it was appreciated nonetheless. Things had been a bit rushed this morning, with the interruption to her shower, and she had only taken time for a quick cup of coffee and a piece of toast.

Greg offered no further explanation but instead handed Karen a cup of coffee. "I didn't know what you take in it, so I brought a bit of everything." Karen saw that indeed he had. In the tray were sugar and artificial sweeteners—pink, yellow, and blue packets—plus packets of powdered creamer and small containers of half-n-half, hazelnut, and French vanilla creamers. Karen knew their own lunchroom was fully stocked with all of those condiments and more, but there was no reason to make mention of that.

Karen and Greg ate the bagels quickly, then headed to their respective offices to get some work done. It took awhile for Karen to gather the information the accountant needed. It was nearly 11 by the time she had finished relaying the data to the accountant. She hadn't seen Greg during all this time, although she did hear him occasionally as he worked on the necessary appliances for his patients.

Fifteen minutes later, he stuck his head in her office. "I'm going out. I'll be back in a few minutes." If he hadn't made that announcement, Karen would probably have never noticed his absence.

"Time for lunch," Greg's voice bellowed through the halls on his return.

"Lunch, how nice. I'm famished." Karen thought she smelled Chinese.

"I didn't know what you like, so I got my favorites. Hope you like at least one of these." Greg was pulling cartons from a large paper sack. It looked like he was planning to feed more than just the two of them.

"This is beef and broccoli." He set the container in front of Karen. "One of those is General Tso's Chicken, and the other is triple delicacy." He nodded in the general direction of two containers already sitting on the desk. He pulled out two smaller containers. "I got fried rice and white. There're also a couple of egg rolls. They threw in two sodas to boot."

"It looks and smells wonderful. I love Chinese food. You got all my favorites."

Greg's smiled. "I'll ask the blessing before we eat."

Karen bowed her head. A twinge of excitement coursed through her when she felt Greg reach over and take her hand. She remembered that the family had held hands when he asked the blessing at her house. She supposed it was a normal thing to do. So why did she have this strange feeling of butterflies in her stomach?

"Heavenly Father," Greg began. Karen brought her thoughts back in line. "We thank You for this bounty of which we are about to partake. Bless it, Father, and us to Thy service. Amen."

For the first time Karen felt a bit ill at ease; she supposed it was being here alone with Greg. That must be it. During a normal workday, Greg was so intent on his work that he had little time to engage in conversations of a personal nature with his staff.

"How was your visit to the principal's office?"

Greg must have overheard her telling Robin about her fear of facing the Mr. Adams. Karen noted the hint of teasing in his voice.

Karen swallowed the bite of egg roll she was chewing before replying. "Terrifying. Just like when I was a kid."

"Spent a lot of time there, did you?"

"Not a lot, but definitely more than enough." Greg's easy banter helped Karen relax and be herself. She felt like she was seeing Greg's true self for the first time. He seemed less like her boss and more like her friend today.

"The principal says Trevor isn't adjusting very well to high school. He says he needs a male role model. Someone Trevor likes and trusts." Karen shrugged. "I think it will help when my brother moves up here. Chad is the only adult Trevor seems to get along with these days."

"He and I seemed to get along just fine."

Karen had to agree; she had caught an occasional glimpse of the old Trevor during his two days shadowing Greg.

Greg had finished a plate of beef and broccoli and an egg roll. He reached for the General Tso's chicken. "Does he like to hike?"

"He's never been, as far as I can recall. He loves fishing and hunting." Karen speared a shrimp. "His father used to take him hunting, but he always fished with my dad." As she chewed the shrimp, she wondered where Greg was headed.

"I like to fish, too. But it's the wrong time of year for fishing." Greg served himself some fried rice and triple delicacy. "I'm free all day next Saturday. The girls are invited to spend the Friday night with a friend and go ice-skating in D.C. Do you think he would want to go hiking with me? I like to drive up to the Blue Ridge Mountains and hike the trails. There's a fairly easy one that leads to a beautiful waterfall."

"It's worth asking him, although he's still not talking to me. Would you be willing to call him and ask him yourself?"

Greg nodded his assent.

"He'd probably agree to anything to get out of the house and away from me for the day." Karen had finished eating, but Greg was eying the last of the General Tso's. "You might as well finish it," she prodded.

"So, Trevor hasn't spoken to you in what—a week?—now. I know that must be hard on you."

"You wouldn't believe how hard. I have apologized again and again. I know I was wrong to yell first and ask questions later, but it's time he got over it."

Greg decided to change the subject. "I saw you in church Sunday. I don't think I've seen you there before. Was it your first visit?"

"We came one other time. Robin invited us a few weeks ago. We had planned to come back the next week, but Austin had a cold. Then Kyle and Trevor caught colds. Last week, after all the stress with Trevor, I knew I needed to be in church. We used to go all the time, but lately we got out of the habit."

"What did you think of the sermon?"

She sighed. "It was just what I needed to hear. I have enjoyed both of Pastor Vinson's sermons. Actually, *enjoyed* is not the right word. Both Sundays, I felt like he was talking directly to me. Like he knew what I was going through and wrote his sermon with me in mind."

"I feel that way myself frequently. That's the work of the Holy Spirit. He speaks to us through the pastor's sermons and helps us to apply God's Word to our present situation."

Karen had never thought of that before, but Greg's words certainly made sense.

When Karen didn't respond, Greg asked, "Will I see you there again this Sunday?"

"If it doesn't snow and the boys are well, we'll be there." Karen began clearing the trash from the table. It was nearly twelve thirty. The time with Greg had flown by.

"I guess we should be getting out of here," Greg noted.

As they packed up the food, Karen was surprised that there wasn't as much left as she'd expected. What did remain went in the refrigerator to be eaten on Monday.

⌘⌘⌘

Karen left the office and headed for the hardware store near her home. The chairs were coming along well and would be ready for stain soon. She'd purchase the supplies she needed for staining them and also get some paint remover. She was hoping to get started on the table this weekend. She'd decided to stain the table a rich mahogany. While she preferred darker stains, particularly cherry for more formal furniture, she thought a lighter shade worked best in the kitchen. She had in mind the shade she'd used on her first staining project--a gun rack she had given Jeff for Christmas one year. Jeff had been very impressed and pleased. Karen estimated that she had plenty of time to purchase the necessary supplies and apply the stain to the chairs before she had to pick up the boys. She'd let them dry for a few days before applying the polyurethane sealer.

⌘⌘⌘

Greg whistled in the car as he drove home from the office. He'd enjoyed having Karen in the office today. Normally, he was by himself on Fridays. While the solitude proved best for being productive, it was too lonely at times. Lunch had been a pleasant diversion, as well.

"I really should make a point of eating lunch with my staff once or twice a week." God had been showing Greg how much he had isolated himself since Cindy's death. He occupied himself with work and the girls to the point that he had no real social interactions outside of

Cindy's parents and the occasional lunch with Chris and Robin. He was making a concerted effort of late to engage in some social activities with adults. Take tonight, for example.

Tonight, Greg would have his first date with Sandy. He had given Gretchen and Robin his blessing to play matchmaker only a few weeks ago, and they had been hard at work. Their first "match" was Lynn, a young elementary school teacher who had attended their church only since the beginning of the current school year. *Young* was the operative word. Although she was sweet and wonderful with children, Greg could not get past the age difference—she was only 32 while Greg would turn 47 in May. They had gone out twice before Greg called it quits.

Sandy, on the other hand, was a woman more of his own age. If he had to guess, Greg would have said she was in her late 30s. Greg had been acquainted with Sandy for several years. He recalled that she had been Brittany and Bethany's Sunday school teacher when they were in the Primary class. She also sang in the choir. Other than that, he had known very little about her. Gretchen had invited Sandy to lunch last Sunday. Greg and the girls, of course, were regulars around the Sullivan's table.

Greg had come to expect, since the matchmaking began, that Gretchen's guests would include at least one eligible woman. The women were always prescreened by Gretchen and Robin. Greg could rest assured that each woman shared his faith in the Lord Jesus Christ, loved children, and did not come with a lot of "baggage." Of those invited so far, only Lynn and Sandy had captured Greg's interest. He thought that Sandy offered real potential. He had learned that she was a registered nurse working at Mary Washington Hospital, she had never married, and she loved the outdoors.

Tonight, he would take Sandy to dinner at Old Town Eatery. He hoped she would enjoy the quaint restaurant located in downtown Fredericksburg. The Old Town area had been a thriving business center since its establishment in 1671. Like many cities around the nation, it had suffered greatly when the local mall was built about 30 years ago. The department stores and theater had moved to the mall, leaving many storefronts empty. Those shops that remained saw their patrons dwindle more each year. To combat this decline a restoration effort was undertaken in the '80s.

Old Town was now the gem of the city; tourists flocked to the historical sites and antique shops. Local residents came downtown for the boutiques and family-owned restaurants. Old Town Eatery had been Greg and Cindy's favorite date spot. Greg hadn't been back since Cindy's death. The memories of being there with Cindy would have been too painful, plus it wasn't the type of restaurant where one went without a date. Greg hoped that by bringing Sandy there, he would be taking a big step towards moving forward with his life. If the food was as good as he remembered and if Sandy was as agreeable a dinner companion as he expected her to be, this first date could prove to be a thoroughly enjoyable experience.

15

It had been a week since Kevin caught Karen and Mike together. Although he and Karen had made up, and she'd agreed to go to the Northern Neck with him, doubts about her story still lingered.

"I know she's hiding something. I can feel it. She's so guarded whenever she talks about her past, which isn't often," Kevin confided in Josh as they ate their lunch in Kevin's office at the dealership.

"Hiding something? Like what?" Josh was a good friend, but he wasn't the sharpest tack in the box.

"For starters, she never talks about Jeff. They were married a long time. You'd think she'd have some stories to tell about Jeff and her or Jeff and the kids." Kevin ate a bite of sandwich.

Josh seemed content to sit quietly and hear Kevin out.

"She refuses to talk about how he died. And the oldest kid—Trevor's his name—seems at odds with her all the time. She mentioned once that Trevor blames all their problems on her. If my dad had died when I was a teenager, I think I'd have been protective of my mom."

"Have you checked her out?" Josh had that look he got when he thought he had a really good idea. "We could 'Google' her on the Internet and see if we can find out anything."

"Anything like what?" Kevin was curious.

"Like, maybe she did something terrible. Maybe she murdered Jeff. Something like that, something she wouldn't want you to know."

Kevin rolled his eyes. Sometimes Josh's imagination got the better of him. He knew Karen wasn't a murderer. But come to think of it, maybe "Googling" Karen wasn't such a bad idea.

He reached over to his desk and jiggled the mouse to get the computer out of screen saver mode. Clicking on the Internet, he typed "Karen Harper, Chester, VA" in the search box. A moment later, the results appeared on the screen. There were only two: Jeff's obituary and an archive from the *Chester Herald*.

He first accessed the archive. It was a listing of graduates for John Tyler Community College. The article was several years old; Karen Harper was listed among the graduates as having earned an AAS degree. The article was published 15 years ago. That sounded about right. At least she had told the truth about her education.

Next, Kevin clicked on Jeff's obituary:

> Jeffrey "Jeff" Michael Harper, 35, died on April 2 at his home in Chester. Mr. Harper, a lifelong resident of Chester, was a graduate of Chester High School, where he led the football team to a conference champion and was named first team All-Conference during his senior year. He was employed in the family business, Harper Construction.
>
> He is survived by his wife, Karen Butler Harper, and three sons, Trevor, Austin, and Kyle Harper, all of the home. He is also survived by his parents, Carl and Marsha Harper of Chester, and a brother, Tommy Harper. Mr. Harper was preceded in death by his twin sister, Jessica.

Kevin scanned the rest of it. Jeff had been involved in a number of community organizations. That might explain why Karen said there were too many memories in Chester. Everyone probably knew him and had a story they wanted to share with her. He read the final paragraph out loud to Josh:

> "Services for Mr. Harper will be held at Oak Hill Church, where he was a member and served as a deacon. In lieu of flowers, the family requests that donations be made to the American Cancer Association or to Hospice."

Kevin felt like a heel. Karen's husband, and his twin sister, had died of cancer. It was probably a protracted illness. He must have wanted to come home to die. Hospice only got involved in situations like that. How terrible it must have been for Karen to watch her husband suffer and die a slow, agonizing death. Poor Trevor must have blamed Karen for Jeff's suffering, not realizing that Karen was doing everything she could.

16

Karen woke early, feeling completely rested and alert after the best night's sleep she'd had in weeks. She had determined last night that she and the boys would be in church this morning, excepting snow or illness. Before going to bed, she had prayed, asking God to let nothing interfere with her plans. She jumped from the bed and peeked out the window onto the front lawn. No snow. So far, so good. She headed downstairs to brew a pot of coffee

"Seven-thirty. I can let the boys sleep awhile longer." As she filled the pot with fresh, cold water, she mentally calculated what time she needed to call the boys.

Church starts at 11:00. It takes about 20 minutes to get there, get in the door and find a seat, and about an hour and a half for the boys to eat breakfast, shower, and dress. I better get them up at nine. Good, that gives me plenty of time for a leisurely cup of coffee and devotions, before I shower and start breakfast.

Karen now looked forward to quiet time in God's Word before beginning her day. It gave her a measure of peace and serenity to carry her through her normally hectic days. Once the boys were up, she wouldn't have a moment to herself until they were in bed for the night.

⌘⌘⌘

After settling the younger two boys in children's church, Karen made her way to the sanctuary. She spied Trevor sitting with a group of teens. She assumed they were students he knew from school. Looking around the auditorium for Robin, she caught Greg's eye. He motioned for her to come over to where he was seated with an older couple. She recognized the man and woman as Greg's in-laws.

"Karen, I believe you know Cindy's parents, Tom and Gretchen

Sullivan."

"Yes. It's very nice to see you again." Karen shook Tom's outstretched hand. When she turned to Gretchen, the older woman embraced her warmly.

She turned back to Greg. " I usually sit with Robin and Chris, but I don't see them this morning."

"They are in New York City for the weekend," he informed her. "They're celebrating their wedding anniversary."

"Their 30th," Gretchen piped in. "Robin has wanted to go to New York for years. Chris said if they were going, they were going to do the city right. They are staying at the Ritz-Carlton. He got them tickets to a couple Broadway plays—*Phantom of the Opera* is one of them. He even made dinner reservations at Sardi's. Can you believe it?" Gretchen looked at Tom expectantly as she asked that question.

"Don't look at me like that! We are well past the 30-year mark, even the 40. You'll have to wait until 50 if you want me to spring for a trip like that."

Gretchen shook her head in mock disgust. "I guess I should feel grateful to get you to the beach once a year."

"I like going to the beach. Putting on a penguin suit and going to a Broadway show is a whole other thing."

Karen was amused watching the couple spar. Her heartstrings tugged at her chest. *Would Jeff and I ever have been able to work out our differences and stick it out 30 or 40 years?* She'd been thinking about Jeff more frequently. What was that all about?

"Sit here with us. There's plenty of room." Greg shifted closer to Gretchen and made room for Karen in the pew.

"What about...aren't you dating someone?"

"Sandy? She's in the choir. Sit."

Karen felt rather ill at ease, sitting next to her boss in church. *Kevin won't like this.*

"How's Trevor today? A bit sore, I suspect."

Karen relaxed visibly. "If he is, he hasn't admitted it. Of course, that's not the sort of thing he would admit. He didn't say much, but from the little he said, I could tell he enjoyed himself." Karen whispered a quick prayer of thanks that Trevor had finally spoken to her after two weeks of the silent treatment.

"Mountain hiking can be tough for the uninitiated. Trevor kept up pretty well. Of course, keeping up with me isn't too hard. I'm an out-of-shape old man."

"You look like you are in pretty good shape to me." Karen's face reddened. *I didn't mean to say that out loud.*

Greg just laughed and shook his head. "Clothes cover a multitude of sins."

"Thanks again for spending the day with Trevor yesterday."

"I was glad to do it. I enjoyed myself, and I think Trevor did too."

"Well, I appreciated it. Trevor and I needed some time apart. He seemed less hostile this morning than he has since his suspension."

Their conversation ended as the worship leader made his way to the podium to start the service.

I wonder what Sandy thinks, seeing me sitting here with Greg. Suddenly, Karen was nervous again.

The worship leader opened the service in prayer then directed the congregation to join in singing "Shout to the Lord."

The singing was over, and the offering had been collected. After a brief time of fellowship, Pastor Mark Vinson walked to the podium and flipped open his Bible

"Turn with me in your Bibles to the book of Romans. We will be reading from Chapters 5 and 6." He waited patiently as the congregation found the reference. When the turning of pages quieted, he cleared his throat. "We'll begin with verse 20 of chapter 5. I'm reading today from the New King James Version."

> "Where sin abounded, grace abounded much more, so that as sin reigned in death, even so grace might reign through righteousness to eternal life through Jesus Christ our Lord. What shall we say then? Shall we continue in sin that grace may abound? Certainly not! How shall we who died to sin live any longer in it?

"Let us pray. Heavenly Father, we ask You to bless the reading of your Word. Open our hearts to hear Your message for us today. Allow Your Holy Spirit to work in hearts today to bring conviction and repentance. In the precious name of Your Son, Jesus, we ask these things. Amen.

"When we come to God, He forgives us. Often, the more we are forgiven of, the more grateful we are. Consider Mary Magdalene. Jesus cast seven demons from her. Was she grateful? Absolutely. We are told that she was one of several women who traveled with Jesus and His disciples and used their own money to help to support them. She was present at the cross and was one of the first to see Christ after the resurrection. But she didn't continue to live a sin-filled life in order to receive more of God's grace. She turned from sin and lived for Christ.

"There are people in this congregation today who have accepted God's gift of forgiveness, yet are contemplating allowing sin into their lives. I don't know who you are, but God does. There may be a student here who is planning to download a term paper off the Internet this afternoon and turn in it as her own work tomorrow at school. There may be a businessman who is considering cheating on his taxes or participating in a shady business deal. Some among us may be considering engaging in sexual sin—fornication or adultery. You are thinking that you can commit this sin and then run back to God and confess it, and God will forgive it.

"If you come back to God with a truly repentant heart, He will forgive you. But why get into that situation in the first place? You know what you are contemplating is sin. Flee from it. If you belong to God, you are no longer in bondage to sin. As we read further in Chapter 6 of Romans, Paul tells us in verse 14, 'For sin shall not have dominion over you, for you are not under law but under grace.' He goes on in verse 18 to say, 'And having been set free from sin, you became slaves of righteousness.'

"God has set you free from the bondage of sin. Don't let Satan trick into going back into bondage. Remember that you are free in Christ—free to live for Him and free to avoid the snare of sin. If the Holy Spirit spoke to you today, I urge you to come to the altar and ask God to help you resist the temptation you are facing."

Pastor Vinson closed the service in prayer, inviting those who were facing particular temptations to raise their hands, while all eyes were closed, so he could pray specifically for them. Karen thought she could feel the pastor's eyes on her. Did he know about her plans with

Kevin? How could he? Yet, his message seemed tailored for her.

Karen covered her eyes with her hands, so Pastor Vinson would not notice her peeking around through her fingers. She could see hands raised all over the sanctuary. Maybe he hadn't been addressing her alone? Karen felt the Holy Spirit convicting her, prompting her to raise her hand, but she could not do it. Raising her hand would be an acknowledgment that her plans were wrong and she would never be able to go through with them.

Lord, I heard what the pastor was saying to me. But Kevin and I are both single. It wouldn't be adultery. And I'm sure he's the man for me. Since we're going to get married, at least I hope we are, it's not really sin. Is it? Karen tried to pray, but she felt as if her words were not getting through to God. As soon as the service was dismissed, Karen said a terse good-bye to Greg and made a beeline out of the sanctuary.

⌘ ⌘ ⌘

Greg was puzzled by Karen's hasty exit but also a bit relieved. He had been debating with himself over whether to ask her to lunch. On the one hand, he still owed her for her hospitality the day the girls were out of school for snow. On the other hand, he had already asked Sandy to lunch. Taking both ladies, plus Karen's offspring, to lunch could prove awkward and expensive. Karen's departure saved him from making a decision.

Sandy had made her way from the choir loft and greeted Greg and the Sullivans. Since their dinner date to Old Town, Greg had taken Sandy to a movie one night and to a play at the local college another night. Today would be their first outing with the girls.

"Who was your friend?" Her voice held no trace of jealousy, just curiosity.

"Karen Harper. She's my business manager. I was hoping to introduce the two of you, but she was in a hurry." Greg was pleased that Sandy wasn't threatened by his inviting Karen to sit with him during the church service. Sandy's gentle spirit was only one of the many things Greg liked about Sandy.

17

Jeff had taken Karen and the kids out on the boat. They had cruised the lake all afternoon, and Trevor had skied until his legs felt like jelly. Jeff had decided to take a turn on the skies. Trevor was old enough to drive the boat, and Karen would act as the spotter.

Jeff was doing great and seemed to be enjoying himself. Karen thought she hadn't seen Jeff this happy in a very long time.

Jeff's not wearing a life vest. He always wears a life vest when he skies. I wonder why he's not wearing one. The thoughts ran through Karen's head as she watched him. *If he fell, he might drown.*

Suddenly, Jeff was in the water. He was holding the rope, but the rope was dragging in the water. Someone had untied the rope from the boat. With a gasp of horror, Karen realized that she had untied the rope. *Why did I do that?*

Trevor hadn't noticed his father fall. He was taking the boat away from Jeff. Karen knew she should scream at Trevor to rescue his father, but instead she watched silently as Jeff struggled and then succumbed to the water. When his head disappeared below the glistening surface, something snapped inside her.

"Trevor, Trevor, turned the boat around," she screamed.

Trevor slowed the boat and turned it around as quickly as he could. "Where's Dad?" he yelled. "I don't see him anywhere."

It was too late. Trevor saw that the rope was missing. "You untied the rope, didn't you? You killed Daddy. You killed Daddy."

"I didn't mean to," Karen sobbed.

The reality of what she had done hit her. Her boys did not have a father, and it was all her fault.

⌘⌘⌘

The nightmares were coming with greater frequency. This was the fourth night in a row that Karen had awakened with her heart pounding, her body drenched in sweat. Every night since Sunday, when she had avoided the Holy Spirit's gentle tug on her heart, she had dreamed of Jeff's death. Of course, the dream never depicted Jeff's actual death. That was what perplexed Karen the most.

She was also puzzled that while the dream took on different forms, the end result was always the same: Jeff always drowned. Karen noted that her efforts to save him had declined as the dreams continued. Tonight's dream, however, was the first one in which she had actually caused his death. *Is there some significance to the dreams?* Surely, her subconscious was trying to communicate with her through the nightmares.

Lord, you know I didn't kill Jeff. I may bear some of the blame, but I had no way of knowing what the outcome would be. Please take the dreams away. I'm sorry Jeff is dead. I'm sorry my boys do not have a father. But it's not my fault. Jeff is the one who turned his back on you. He's the one who ruined our marriage by drinking and cheating. Please help me, God. I really need your help.

Karen desperately needed to talk to someone; she knew that now. The obvious choice was Pastor Vinson. She had been trying to gather her courage to make an appointment with him for weeks—Robin had suggested counseling soon after the dreams started, and the principal had made her promise to get counseling for Trevor and herself. Yet, she continually put it off. She felt uncomfortable talking to the pastor when she was planning an illicit weekend with Kevin. And, after last Sunday's sermon, she was even more ill at ease. She'd just have to wait until after the trip, only about a week away. After that, she'd confess her sins to God, all of them, and make everything right. Then she would start counseling. Karen recognized that her decision flew in the face of the pastor's teaching, but he'd said that God's grace abounds. She was certain God would understand her predicament and forgive her.

Since Karen had agreed to the trip, her nightmares had increased, as had the tension with Trevor. They were on speaking terms again, but just barely. Tuesday morning, Karen learned that he was taking a field trip to the Holocaust Museum in Washington, D.C., only because

Trevor had to have her signature on his permission slip. When he came down for breakfast, he thrust the permission slip at her.

"Sign this," he said tersely.

"What is it?" Karen asked, even as her eyes scanned the single sheet outlining the pertinent information. Trevor poured himself a bowl of cereal and began eating, making it abundantly clear that he saw no reason to respond to her question.

"It should be very informative," Karen said, trying to illicit a response from Trevor.

Trevor continued eating.

Karen signed the form and laid it on the table beside him. "Will you need any money for the trip?"

"Dunno," Trevor managed.

Karen had fared little better on Wednesday evening, as she questioned him about the trip. "How was the trip?" she had asked.

"Okay," came Trevor's one-word response.

"Did you enjoy the museum?"

He rolled his eyes at her. "Holocaust Museum," he said, his irritation evident. "It's about the Holocaust."

"Oh, right. Well, then, what impressed you the most?" Karen was determined to engage him in a real conversation.

Her efforts were rewarded. "The shoe room," he said quietly.

She arched her eyebrows, hoping he would clue her in to what he meant by the shoe room and was mildly shocked when he complied. "There are thousands of pairs of shoes that were collected from the Jews before they were…executed. It's overwhelming to think that each pair of shoes represented someone who died."

Karen crossed the room and gave him a gentle squeeze. Trevor said nothing more for the rest of the night.

As the nightmares and the tensions with Trevor increased, so did Karen's desire to have reach out of God. She had been praying every morning before she went to work and every night before she went to bed. She thought the prayers would ward off the bad dreams, but so far, they had been of no help on that front. She prayed about her relationships with Trevor and Kevin. She pleaded with God to let Kevin be the man she needed him to be.

Robin looked surprised when she mentioned her prayers about Kevin at lunch. "That's not the way God works."

"You mean I'm not supposed to pray for Kevin."

"No, I didn't mean that. I simply meant that you shouldn't ask God to turn Kevin into the man you want him to be. It sounds like you are trying to talk God into believing that Kevin is the right man for you."

Karen looked puzzled.

"I'll be right back," Robin said and left the lunchroom. When she returned, she was carrying her Bible. She flipped it open and pointed to a passage in Jeremiah 29. "Let me read verses 11-13:

> "'For I know the plans I have for you,' declares the Lord, 'plans to prosper you and not to harm you, plans to give you hope and a future. Then you will call upon me and come and pray to me, and I will listen to you. You will seek me and find me when you seek me with all your heart.'

"God has a wonderful plan for your life. He will bring His plans to fruition if you will allow Him. Seek Him with all your heart, and He will lead and guide you in the path he has for you. God's plan may or may not include Kevin. You need to let God make that decision. You should ask God to give you the life He desires you to have."

"That makes sense. But what prayers should I pray for Kevin?"

"You can pray that his heart will be sensitive to God and that he will allow God to transform him into the man God wants him to be. But, bear in mind, God cannot change Kevin unless Kevin wants Him to. Kevin must come to God himself. You have never said anything about Kevin's relationship with God. Is Kevin a believer?"

A knot formed in the pit of Karen's stomach. She had been deliberately avoiding this subject so far. "I don't know. We've never discussed church or religion."

"I think you know that I'm not talking about what church he attends or what denomination he claims." Robin spoke gently but firmly. "I'm talking about whether he has a relationship with Jesus Christ. Has he accepted Christ's free gift of forgiveness for his sins? Has Kevin made Jesus his Lord and Savior?"

Karen hesitated. "I don't know for sure, but I don't think so."

⌘ ⌘ ⌘

Robin felt impressed by the Holy Spirit that she needed to find a time to ask Karen about her own relationship with the Lord. But now was not the time. They had covered enough ground for one day.

⌘ ⌘ ⌘

The Lord provided the opportunity the next day at lunch for Robin to probe Karen about her own salvation.

"Karen, tell me about your relationship with Christ."

"Jeff and I accepted Christ at the same time, when Trevor was just a baby. We asked Jesus to forgive our sins. He changed us completely. Before we were saved, our focus was totally on having fun in life. We partied and drank every weekend. And we fought a lot. The neighbors called the police on us more than once. When Christ entered our hearts, He set us free of that lifestyle. People noticed the change. They would ask us about the change. We had many opportunities to share how God had turned our lives around."

Robin was relieved to learn Jeff and Karen had truly given their lives over to God. "Were you part of a church? Did you grow in the Lord?"

"Oh, yes. We joined a church that taught the truth of God's Word. We were in church every time the doors opened. We studied the Bible and prayed together night. It was a wonderful time in our marriage."

"It certainly sounds that way. I take it something happened to change that. Can you tell me what happened?"

"Jeff's twin sister, Jessica, got sick. Jess had accepted the Lord about a month after we did. She was the sweetest, kindest person in the world. She loved the Lord and served Him with all her heart."

"Then she got sick?"

"She went to the doctor for a routine checkup and the doctor discovered a suspicious looking mole. It was in a spot Jess couldn't see—high up on the back of her thigh, just below her tan line." Karen twisted her body and pointed out the spot on her own thigh. "The doctor took a biopsy. It was skin cancer. Jess was diagnosed when she was 29." Karen's voice quivered as she relived the horror of the day they learned of her diagnosis.

Robin patted her hand. "Skin cancer is bad, but today it's very treatable. I've read that it's nearly 100 percent curable if it's caught in time."

"Yes, that's what the doctor told us. We were very optimistic that Jess would have a fairly minor surgery and that would be that. Unfortunately, the cancer was melanoma and by the time the doctor found out, it had spread to her lymph nodes." Karen spoke very softly.

"Jess was sent to the UVA Cancer Center. The doctors there tried chemotherapy, but the cancer continued to spread. Eventually, it metastasized to her left lung. She fought a good fight, but it wasn't enough. She died about 18 months after the melanoma was discovered—just after she and Jeff turned 31. Watching Jess suffer so and then die changed Jeff. He got angry with God. He kept saying that if God were who He claims to be, He would have healed Jess and not allowed her to suffer. After the funeral, Jeff didn't go back to church. He started hanging out with his old friends that he had known before we were saved. He began drinking to dull the pain. Things went downhill from there."

"What was going on with you during this time?"

Robin didn't say "spiritually," but Karen understood what she meant.

"I continued to go to church and to take the boys. I grew more dependent on the Lord than ever before. Then Jeff died, and it was too painful to go to church. I stopped going and gradually stopped praying and reading the Bible."

"What is your relationship with the Lord now?"

"I'm working on it," was all Karen would reveal.

"That's a start. Keep working on it. God will be found if you seek him." When Robin heard Greg unlocking the front door to let a patient in, she knew lunchtime was over. "I'd better get to my desk. Thank you for sharing all that with me. I hope to hear more soon." Robin headed to the reception area.

⌘ ⌘ ⌘

As Karen settled in at her desk for an afternoon of reconciling the checkbook and readying invoices for the mail, she couldn't get Robin's words out of her mind.

She took a moment to talk to the Lord before attacking her work.

Dear Heavenly Father, please help me to be the person You want me to be. I know I've made bad choices. I haven't even shared my faith with Kevin. Help me to tell him about You and help him to be the man You want him to be. You know I'm hoping he's the one You have to share my life. But if that is not your will, please make it clear to me. I want Your best for me, even if Your best is not Kevin.

18

"What will it be?" The waiter's sudden question startled Karen so that she dropped the menu she had been holding but not reading. Her mind had been on how she could rearrange her living room furniture to accommodate the table she had purchased from the antique store around the corner. She bent over and retrieved the menu from the floor.

She ordered the first thing that came into her mind. "I'll have a ham sandwich on rye bread with lettuce and tomato. Mustard, no mayo."

"You want chips with that?"

"Sure. And a dill pickle."

"Something to drink?"

"Hot tea. Herbal."

"I'll be right back with your tea." The waiter took the menu and left.

Karen was having lunch by herself at the Downtown Deli on Princess Anne Street. Since it was Friday, she didn't have to work, and as the boys were in school, she had the day to herself. She used most Fridays to catch up on housework, shop for groceries without a bunch of kids in tow, and work uninterrupted on her refinishing project. The chairs were stained and varnished, and the table had been stripped of its paint. The hours of removing the old finishes and sanding had been therapeutic, reducing her stress level. Under the layer of white paint, she had found a layer of light blue paint, and under that a layer of forest green. She was now down to the wood grain. Karen was pleased to discover that the wood was in good shape. She still had many hours sanding ahead of her; they were hours she looked forward to. She often found herself praying or singing as she worked.

Today, however, she had wanted to get out of the house. The

nightmares were taking a toll on her. She decided she deserved a day off. There was no better way to spend a lazy free day than meandering through the unique shops of Old Town. It was particularly beautiful at present, as the cherry trees were in full blossom.

Karen had wandered into the Antique Emporium looking for more chairs to go with the table. She found two that complemented the mission-style of the table. The chairs didn't perfectly match the other two, but Karen thought the eclectic mix would go well together. She was waiting in line to pay for the chairs when she discovered a beat-up sofa table. Actually, it was brought to her attention when she heard two female shoppers commenting on how badly damaged it was.

"I like the style of that table. What a shame it is in such bad shape," one lady commented.

"Yes, it was probably nice once," her companion replied. "But now it's ruined. No one would want it, even at that price."

Karen looked at it and saw potential. *Actually,* she said to herself, *I would want it.* Priced at $30, it was a real bargain. She purchased the table, along with the two chairs. The shop owner agreed to hold the items for her until she was finished with her shopping.

"If you pull up in front of the store," he told her, "when you're ready, I'll load them for you."

Her stomach had begun growling about then and she'd decided it was time for lunch. So she'd walked around the corner to the deli and sat at the first empty table she encountered.

The waiter interrupted her thoughts. "Here's your tea, ma'am." He set the cup and saucer in front of her.

She stirred in a packet of sugar, still musing. *I'll have to move the couch away from the wall, so I can place the table behind the couch. I wonder if the couch would look best facing out the front window or turned toward the foyer.* Several layouts seemed to have promise.

Her sandwich arrived, pulling her once again from her revelries. The sandwich looked delicious and tasted even better than it looked. *Kevin would like this. He loves ham on rye.* Kevin was never far from her thoughts, particularly as their planned getaway loomed on the horizon. Karen was still planning to go, although she increasingly felt it was the wrong decision. She mentally assessed where she stood on the subject at present.

I think God is trying to make it clear to me that I am not to go away with Kevin. Sleeping with Kevin would be a clear violation of God's command to be pure and holy. I know God forgives sin when we repent, but if I deliberately sin and then repent...well, I'm not sure I want to chance that. The more I think about a weekend away with Kevin, the less I want to go. If I tell Kevin I don't want to go, that will probably be the end of our relationship. On the other hand, if that's true, do I really want to be in this relationship? Does Kevin even love me? He's never actually said so. I'm not sure I want to be "test-driven" so Kevin can decide if we are compatible.

By the time Karen had paid for her food and exited the restaurant, she was certain she didn't want to make the trip with Kevin to the Northern Neck. At least not now and certainly not for the purposes Kevin had stated.

She unlocked the door of her minivan and climbed behind the wheel. She put the key in the ignition but did not start the engine. Laying her head on the steering wheel, she fully gave her relationship with Kevin over to God.

"Heavenly Father, help me to make wise decisions concerning my life and my relationship with Kevin. I'm convinced that going away with Kevin is not what You would want me to do. I'm feeling trapped. I made a promise that I no longer want to honor. Please give me a way out of my promise without hurting Kevin. Help me to know if Kevin is the man You have for me. You know how desperately I long for a man to share my life and to be a father to my sons. I'm still hoping that Kevin will be that man, but I'm willing to give him up, if he is not part of Your plan for my life. I want Your best. Help me to trust You and to know Your will for my life. Thank You. Amen."

⌘⌘⌘

Sandy had a rare Friday off, and Greg wanted to take her to lunch. He had called her Thursday night after the girls were in bed to ask her out and make plans.

"I only have two retainers to make in the morning. I can be

finished by ten o'clock. I thought we might drive over to Maryland and have a nice seafood lunch."

"That sounds great. I love seafood, especially blue crabs."

"Crabs it is. I'll pick you up about 10:30. That will put us in Maryland by lunchtime. If we're going to pick crabs, I want to allow *plenty* of time. You can't rush crab picking."

The next day Greg picked Sandy up right on time at her townhouse.

"Do we have time to drive along the river?" Sandy asked the questions before she was fully ensconced in Greg's Lexus. "I hear the cherry blossoms are magnificent this year."

"There's always time to please a lovely lady." Greg was once again astonished at how comfortable he was with Sandy. Maybe because they were friends before they started dating. She had been casual friends with Cindy and had prayed for Greg as he grieved over her death. Greg was relieved that she didn't ask questions about his past—probably because she already knew the significant details.

Greg drove slowly down Riverside Drive, then cut back to Caroline and made a pass through Old Town. The beauty of the cherry trees had not been overstated. The fluffy pink blossoms were glorious. "This is my favorite time of year to walk along the riverbank or stroll around downtown," Sandy had commented. Greg had heard Cindy make similar comments many years as spring arrived.

"It's a shame we don't have time for a walk today, but we need to head on over to Maryland."

"That lady looks familiar." Sandy pointed to a woman on the sidewalk. " I think I've seen her at church. Do you know her?"

A man was securing a table to the luggage rack of her minivan.

"Yes. That's Karen. She's the woman I wanted you to meet on Sunday." Greg honked the horn, but Karen didn't respond. "We better not stop. I hear crabs calling my name, and I'm starved."

"I've noticed that you're usually starving. How do you manage to stay so trim when food is constantly on your mind?"

Greg chuckled. "I get that question a lot. Good genes, I guess."

They were crossing the Nice Bridge into Maryland when Greg had a sudden inspiration—two actually. Crab season was about to open, and the annual Cherry Blossom Festival in the nation's capital was in full swing. He acted on the second one first.

"The Cherry Blossom Festival is going on right now. It would be nice to drive up to D.C." He looked expectantly at Sandy.

"I have to work a 12-hour shift tomorrow, but I'm free on Sunday."

"Let's go after church. We'll grab a quick lunch and head up right after."

"Sounds wonderful. Will you bring Bethany and Brittany?"

"I'd like to, although I'm not certain that they will find the cherry blossoms as interesting as we do. What do you think?"

"Please bring them. I enjoy spending time with them. Maybe we would have time to visit the Smithsonian or a monument."

"Great idea. They love the Museum of Natural History."

With that settled, Greg turned his thoughts to crabbing. "I know your family lives in Baltimore now. Did you grow up in Maryland?"

"Yes, in a small town near the coast. My parents moved to Baltimore when I was in college."

"Did you ever go crabbing?"

"Do you mean, did I ever catch my own crabs?"

"Yes."

"No. My brothers did, however. I love to eat them, but someone else can catch them."

Greg pulled into Billy's Crab Shack. "Time to get us some of those crabs someone else caught."

As they ate, Greg shared with Sandy his memories of crabbing in the Potomac River off the dock at his uncle's house. "My father and uncle would gather all of the cousins and take us down to the dock to give my mom and aunt a break. We'd spend the entire afternoon on the dock catching crabs. We would tie one end of a string to a stick and tie a chicken neck on the other end. Then we would toss it in the river and wait. It didn't take long. Pretty soon, you would see crabs swimming as fast as they could to get the chicken necks. When one bit into the chicken, we would haul it up. Someone else would snag it with a net. Occasionally one got loose and ran around the deck. We sometimes let them loose on purpose because chasing them was so much fun."

Sandy giggled as she envisioned a bunch of kids chasing crabs on the deck.

"I haven't been crabbing in years. I think it's time I took it up again."

"Will you take the girls?"

"My prima donnas? They wouldn't touch a crab if their life depended on it. They don't like to get the smell on their hands. They will eat crab, however, if I pick the meat out for them."

"How sweet of you. I admire your devotion to your daughters."

"Yeah, right. They're spoiled rotten."

"No, they aren't. They are the most precious girls ever."

"You wouldn't say that if you had to spend hours picking crab meat for them."

"So if the girls and I refuse to go crabbing with you, who would you take?"

" I think Trevor might like it."

"Hmm." Another trait of Greg's to be admired. He had told Sandy about his hiking trip with Trevor last Saturday. It spoke volumes about Greg's character that he would give up a free day to spend it with a fatherless boy.

19

April 2
The anniversary of Jeff's death

"I'm not going to church. Don't even ask." Trevor had made his announcement as soon as Karen came down the stairs. He was upset. Karen had known he would be. But she was surprised to see him up so early. It was only 6:30.

Trevor must have seen the shock on her face, so he offered a rare explanation for his early rising. "I couldn't sleep. I've been thinking about Dad all night."

Karen sat down beside Trevor on the faded brown floral couch in the den. Intent on ignoring her, Trevor pretended to be engrossed in a video game.

"I know it's hard for you. I miss him too." She reached her arm around his shoulder, but he shrugged her away.

"Do you miss him? It sure doesn't seem like it."

"Of course, I miss him. Why would you say something like that?"

"You started dating again right away. Most people wait at least a year before they start dating."

Karen stood and walked a few paces away. She silently prayed that God would give her a reply to ease her son's pain. But no words came.

"You can't answer me, can you? Because you know I'm right." Trevor spoke with a vengeance Karen had never heard from him. "I know all about your boyfriends." He hissed the angry words. "The one you dated last summer and the one you wanted to leave Dad for. If you hadn't told Dad you wanted a divorce, he would still be alive. It's your fault Dad's dead. I hate you." After spewing the final acrid words, Trevor ran from the room and up the stairs. His bedroom door slammed shut.

Karen was stunned by Trevor's anger and shocked by his harsh words. She thought she had protected him from the accusations and shame. *I should have realized that I couldn't shield him from the gossip. No wonder he's been so distant and angry.*

It was true that Karen had met someone else before Jeff's death. She wouldn't try to deny that. What Trevor didn't understand was that Jeff had abandoned her long before she met Danny. Jeff hadn't moved out of the house, but he had abandoned Karen nonetheless. He made no investment in their marriage, emotionally or physically, during their final three years together. The last time they'd made love, Kyle had been conceived. Karen could understand that Jeff was angry about his sister's death; what she had never understood was why Jeff took his anger out on her.

Karen crouched on the floor, hugging her knees to her chest, and let the tears flow. It had been a long time since she had cried over all that she had lost. With Jessica's death, she had lost her loving relationship with Jeff, the closeness they enjoyed as a family, and the peaceful home they had created together. With Jeff's death, she had lost her partner and the father of her children, her close bond with her oldest child, and the love and support of Jeff's parents. She had even lost her personal relationship with God. She determined in her heart to regain what she could, beginning with her relationships with God and Trevor.

Her tears spent, she sat on the couch, her head resting on her hands, feeling the tension as she rubbed her forehead and temples. *Dear God, I need Your help. I can't do this on my own. I need Your guidance in all my relationships. I don't want to do things my way anymore, Lord. I give up. I surrender. Please help me.*

⌘⌘⌘

The rest of the morning dragged by. The family stayed home from church, as Karen wasn't up to facing anyone and there was no way she was leaving Trevor home alone, given how upset he was. *He's so much like his father. Always holding in his pain and despair, never talking about it until he's so full of anger that it all spills out like venom.*

Karen decided to let the younger boys sleep until they woke up on their own. As the morning slipped towards noon, she concluded they might sleep the day away and made the decision to entice them downstairs with delicious aromas.

Brunch was in order. While a pound of bacon sizzled in the frying pan, she washed lettuce and sliced tomatoes. She heated apple cider in a pot on the stove and added mulling spices. *If the bacon doesn't wake them, the cinnamon and cloves should do the trick.* It didn't take long for Austin and Kyle to traipse down the stairs. As they filed into the kitchen, Karen toasted bread and made them each a triple-decker turkey club sandwich. She fixed a sandwich for Trevor and sent Austin to deliver it to him in his room. To her great relief, he opened the door and accepted the food.

In the afternoon, Karen called the boys into the den. "Let's watch old family videos," she told them without preamble. If they were surprised to see their father in the videos, they didn't express it. This was the first time since the tragedy that they had seen the footage.

Kyle did not catch on right away that the characters on the screen were the members of the Harper family. "That boy looks like me."

"It is you." Karen hadn't been aware that Trevor was in the room until she heard him answer Kyle. "There's Austin, and that's me."

"Where's Mommy?" Austin asked.

"I was filming. You can't see me, but I'm there." Karen answered as she took a seat on the couch beside Austin.

"Who is that man?" This came from Kyle, seated in the beige recliner.

"That's our daddy." Trevor picked Kyle up as he answered. He sat in the recliner and settled Kyle on his lap.

"That can't be our daddy," Kyle argued. "We don't have a daddy."

"Of course, we have a daddy. Everyone has a daddy." Trevor was doing such a great job of answering Kyle's questions that Karen kept quiet.

"Where is he? I've never seen him."

"Yes, you have. You just don't remember. He went to Heaven when you were little." Trevor shot a glance at Karen, warning her to not argue with his assertion that his father was in Heaven. Karen hoped

119

that Trevor was correct. Pastor Lewis had said Jeff was in Heaven at the funeral, and Trevor clung to that hope. There was no way Karen was going to dispute it.

Trevor continued to narrate whenever he thought Kyle needed an explanation. Austin never spoke a word, although Karen noticed that he wiped tears from his cheeks occasionally. She did also.

After the videos had all been watched, Austin and Kyle disappeared into the basement to play while they waited for the pizza Karen had ordered for their dinner. Trevor remained seated in the recliner, starring at the dark television set.

"I don't hate you." Trevor's sudden pronouncement caught Karen off guard. He turned to look at her and repeated his words. "I don't hate you. I'm sorry I said that."

It only took a moment for Karen to cross the room and gather her son in her arms. Suddenly, it seemed as if the dam Trevor had erected around his heart burst. The tears he had held back for so long came in great choking sobs. Karen recognized it as the beginning of the healing process. Trevor had a long way to go before he could fully release the emotional baggage he had clung to for the past two years, but at least he had made a start. Karen whispered a silent prayer of thanks.

By the time Karen climbed the stairs for bed, she was drained emotionally. The day that had gotten off to such a bad start had ended with her having a better understanding of Trevor's pain and hurt. His tirade had hurt her to be sure, yet his tears had been soothing. A door of communication had been opened for the two of them. As she crawled into bed, she spent a few moments praising God again for the breakthrough with Trevor. Now if she only knew what to do about Kevin.

20

Karen arrived at work at 8:20 to find the staff standing in the reception area admiring the ring on the fourth finger of Jenna's left hand. It was a marquise diamond solitaire engagement ring.

"Wow. That is so beautiful." Karen was truly happy for Jenna, yet she felt a twinge of jealousy. Was is because she had found someone who loved her and wanted to spend the rest of his life with her, or was it because the ring was the loveliest she had ever seen? Her own engagement ring seemed tawdry in comparison. The diamonds were tiny chips with a total weight of about one-third of a carat. However, she clearly remembered being thrilled with it when Jeff had gotten down on one knee and slipped it on her finger. As poor as they had been starting out, Karen figured she was lucky to have received an engagement ring at all.

"How big is the diamond?" Of course Katie would ask, Karen thought.

"It's a half-carat." Jenna's cheerful reply gave no indication that she thought Katie's question out of line.

Katie held out her left hand and admired her own one-carat ring. An uncomfortable silence ensued until Robin jumped in and saved the day. "That big? We were so poor when Chris proposed that he bought me a ring with a diamond chip so small you had to use a magnifying glass to see it. We were married ten years before he got me a ring as nice as yours."

"I think a celebration is in order." All heads turned toward Greg as he made that announcement. "We're going out for lunch. I'm treating. Jenna, you get to choose the place. The only restriction is that we have to be able to eat and be back in time for our afternoon patients."

A couple hours later, Greg popped his head into Karen's office between patients. "Have you been to the bank yet today?"

"No. I'm planning to go after lunch."

"Excellent. While you're out, would you mind picking up a cake and a couple bottles of sparkling cider? I'd like to have a small celebration for Jenna before we leave this afternoon."

"Sure. I'd be happy to." Karen was thrilled for Jenna and glad to be able to help with the celebration. "Is there any particular type of cake you had in mind?"

"No. Go to Paul's Bakery and pick out whatever looks good to you. Everything they make is delicious."

⌘⌘⌘

Karen managed to sneak in the back door and put the cake and cider into the refrigerator without Jenna spotting her. She heard the phone ringing out front as she was returning to her office. When it rang for the fourth time, she concluded that Robin was unable to answer it and got up to see to the task herself. Katie beat her to it.

"Where's Robin?" Karen asked Jenna as she cut through the examination area on her way back to her office.

"Robin left; her daughter went into labor."

The examination room chairs were filled with patients needing the attention of Greg and the assistants, so Karen spent the rest of the afternoon at Robin's desk.

Despite being one employee short, the staff seemed to be holding their own. That was until about an hour before closing.

Karen saw a blur as Katie ran past her and made a beeline for the ladies' bathroom.

Katie emerged a few minutes later, looking a bit queasy.

"Are you all right?" Karen was genuinely concerned for her co-worker's health. "Did lunch disagree with you?"

"Everything disagrees with me these days." Katie grinned.

Karen squealed and jumped up from the desk. "Congratulations." She grabbed Katie in a big bear hug.

Greg popped his head around the corner. "What in the world?"

"Katie's pregnant," Karen blurted out.

If Katie smiled any bigger, she would crack her face.

⌘ ⌘ ⌘

"Oh, my. What a day." Greg collapsed into a chair as soon as the last patient left the building. He waited until Jenna and Katie had put all the instruments in the autoclave for sterilization and changed the covers on the headrests, before signaling Karen to bring out the items she had purchased for the celebration.

The cake and cider were a big hit.

"Thank you so much, Doctor." Jenna beamed. "First, lunch at my favorite seafood restaurant and now all this. I don't know what to say."

"You don't have to say anymore. It turned out to be quite a day for celebrations. Congratulations to you and to Katie." Greg beamed so big that a stranger might have assumed him to be the proud father of the bride or the grandfather-to-be.

Karen did some quick calculations. She had overheard him say that he was turning 47 soon. That would indeed make him old enough to be the father of 23-year-old Jenna and 25-year-old Katie. Jenna had started working as his assistant as soon as she had finished her training, nearly five years ago. Katie had started soon after. She concluded that Greg had every right to feel paternal where Jenna and Katie were concerned.

"Don't forget Robin," Jenna added.

⌘ ⌘ ⌘

Karen found the phone message on her desk as she was leaving for the day. The handwriting was hard to decipher—Robin must have scribbled it as she raced out the door for her new grandchild's entrance into the world. It was from Kevin—that much was legible. The first word started with "fa" but the rest was just a wiggly line. The second word looked like "emer." That could stand for 'emergency.' "Family emergency." Well, maybe. Karen toyed with the idea of calling the Chevrolet dealership where Kevin worked. No, she would just wait. Surely, Kevin would call her soon and let her know what was happening.

21

The phone rang itself almost off the wall. After the craziness of the workday, Karen had looked forward to nothing more than a quiet evening at home and a hot bubble bath before bed. But now, after hanging up the phone for the umpteenth time, she merely looked forward to a few moments of peace before crashing into her bed.

The incessant phone calls had begun as she was unlocking the front door, her purse dangling from the arm holding the key and her other arm laden with grocery bags. Thinking it might be Kevin, she made a mad dash to pick it up before the answering machine kicked in. "Hello."

"Are you all right? You sound out of breath." The voice belonged to a woman. It took Karen a few seconds to identify the voice as Robin's.

"I'm fine. I was just coming in the door and raced to grab the phone."

"I called to give you an update on Hannah. No baby yet. The doctor says her labor is progressing normally. We should have a grandchild in the next few hours."

Karen expressed her pleasure at the news and thanked Robin for keeping her informed. Robin promised to call back after the birth occurred.

Karen pressed the button on the answering machine and listened to the messages as she began putting away the groceries. Three messages. The first was from her mother wondering when to expect her and the boys on Friday. "I have to tell you again how disappointed I am that you will not stay until Sunday afternoon. It's not like you to abandon the boys on an important holiday. They need their mother, you know."

Karen slammed the refrigerator door, toppling a glass pitcher that she had stored on top of it. She fumed as she bent to pick up the larger pieces of glass. "Thanks, Mom, for making this harder than it already is." Even as that thought crossed Karen's mind, she knew it wasn't her mother she was upset with. She was upset with herself for her reluctance to tell Kevin she didn't want to spend the weekend with him. As if on cue, she heard his voice coming from the answering machine.

"Karen, Kev. I have to go to Florida. Family emergency. I'll explain later. Bye." The message helped, but it didn't explain much. Karen grabbed the broom and swept up the broken glass.

"Hi, Karen. It's Kim. I saw your mother at the grocery store this afternoon. She told me that you'll be home for Easter. Let's get the boys together Saturday. We can have lunch, and the boys can color Easter eggs. I haven't had any luck finding chairs for your table. We could get up early Saturday and hit the yard sales. Let me know if you want to. Either way I hope to see you Saturday."

It would be great to see Kim. Though they communicated regularly through phone calls and the Internet, Karen hadn't actually seen her best friend since Thanksgiving. "Thank you, Lord, for friends like Kim." Karen breathed as she finished putting away the groceries.

Karen would never have survived those first few horrible weeks after Jeff's death without Kim's support and friendship. In the immediate aftermath, Kim had fielded phone calls from the concerned and the curious as word of the tragedy spread throughout their small community. She accompanied Karen to the funeral home and helped with everything from selecting a coffin to choosing hymns for the service. As the shock wore off and things settled down, it was Kim who contacted the Social Security Administration and started the paperwork for the benefits that Karen and the boys were entitled to. She even phoned creditors and arranged debt refinancing and, in a few cases, forgiveness.

"I don't know about going to yard sales at the crack of dawn, but lunch and coloring Easter eggs sounds like a good plan." Karen knew she could spend a few hours with Kim and still be back in Fredericksburg by six to meet Kevin—assuming the trip was still on.

Karen was putting the last of the canned goods in the cupboard when the phone rang. "Hi, Mom. I'm eating dinner at Tim's house. I'll be home later." Trevor hung up before she had a chance to even respond.

Okay, no Trevor for dinner. She hadn't had time to notice that he wasn't home yet. The tears on Sunday had relieved much of the tension between the two of them, but there were still issues to be resolved. Eventually, Karen knew she had to ask Trevor's forgiveness for her contributions to his pain and grief. And they would have to come to an understanding about her relationship with Kevin. Those conversations would have to wait until later, however. Karen had enough to deal with right now.

⌘⌘⌘

Karen was frying chicken in her largest skillet and had the boys settled at the kitchen table working on homework when Greg Marshall called. "I wanted to let you know that I lined up Emily Clark to fill in for Robin for the next two weeks. But she can't come in until Monday. I'll need a receptionist for tomorrow and Thursday."

"Do you want me to cover for her?"

"Either that, or I could call a temp agency and get someone."

"I'm pretty much caught up on my work. Why don't I just do it?"

"That's great. Thank you. Bye."

Greg hung up before Karen had a chance to ask who Emily Clark was. Greg mentioned her name casually, as if he expected Karen to know her. "Well, I guess I find out who she is on Monday." Karen set to work making cacciatore sauce. She was interrupted by two phone calls from telemarketers. She considered it a small miracle that they made it through dinner without the phone ringing. The dishes were partially loaded into the dishwasher when Austin's homeroom mother called to remind Karen that she was expected to make 30 cupcakes for Thursday's class party. *Remind me?* "Don't forget to send them in a disposable container—I don't want to have to return dishes."

"Do you want any particular flavor?"

"No chocolate. Yellow or vanilla cupcakes, with white icing. Did you get my note?"

"Of course," Karen lied. "I seem to have misplaced it, however. Can you give me the details again?"

"Remember to dye the coconut green before you sprinkle it on the cupcakes."

"Green coconut?"

"Easter grass. Then tuck colored jellybeans into the coconut. You'll need to put the coconut and jellybeans on before the icing hardens so they will stick. Remember that the top of the cup cake should remind the children of Easter eggs in a bed of Easter grass. Send them to school with Austin on Thursday morning. Thanks. Good-bye."

"Austin," Karen said as soon as she hung up the phone, "we need to have a little chat."

⌘ ⌘ ⌘

Chad was the next to call. Karen must have sounded exasperated when she answered because he inquired as to whether she was all right.

"You wouldn't believe the day I've had." She proceeded to tell him about Jenna's engagement, Katie's pregnancy, and Robin's soon-to-arrive grandchild. "Plus, you must be the tenth person to call tonight. I guess you didn't call for a full report on my day, however."

"I wanted to find out what your plans are for next week. I need to come to Fredericksburg one day to apply for a building permit. We are going to start the renovation work soon."

Karen filled in him on her plans as they stood at the moment. Since the boys would spend Monday through Thursday with Jeff's parents, Chad decided to come to Fredericksburg on Thursday.

"Great," Karen told him. "Plan to have dinner with me—I'll cook—before you head home."

"Sound like a plan. See you Thursday." Chad hung up.

⌘ ⌘ ⌘

When the phone rang at ten minutes until 9, Karen was certain that it would be Kevin. It was not.

Robin was calling with her happy announcement. "It's a girl. Nicole Marie. 7 lbs. 2 oz. Everything went well. Hannah is doing wonderfully."

Karen extended her congratulations on the new arrival before hanging up. "Can I please have a few minutes of peace and quiet?" Karen pleaded with the phone to not ring again tonight unless it was Kevin calling. She got her wish.

As she collapsed on the bed in exhaustion, the reprieve she had been praying for came in the form of Kevin's phone call. Since finding Robin's indecipherable note and then listening to his hasty message, she had wondered what was happening with Kevin. To make matter worse, the "weekend," as she had come to think of it, was only days away.

On Friday, she planned to make the hour and a half drive to Chester to deliver the boys to her parents. Despite her mother's wishes, she would stay only until midafternoon on Saturday. Kevin wanted to get in a full workday, ending at 6 p.m. His plan called for Kevin to come straight to Karen's after work; they would get on the road immediately and grab a quick bite to eat at a fast-food restaurant along the way. With any luck, they would reach his uncle's cabin in Kilmarnock by 9.

Kevin had made it very clear over the past few weeks that, once they reached the cabin, he planned to waste little time before consummating their relationship. He felt he had been quite stoic in waiting this long. He suggested that if this weekend revealed the two of them to be "compatible," that they might consider the next step—Kevin sleeping over at her house occasionally. If the relationship progressed from there, they might move in together. But at no point had Kevin said he wanted to spend the rest of his life with her. Karen had tried desperately to convince herself that marriage was his ultimate goal and that he was just taking things slow. But she was having doubts.

She reached over and picked up the ringing phone. *This better be Kevin.*

"Hi. I'm in Florida. My grandmother had a stroke this morning. It's doesn't look good." Kevin's voice was cracking so it was hard to understand him. Karen wasn't sure if it was a bad phone connection or if Kevin was crying.

"I'm so sorry." Karen said the only words that came to mind, hoping they didn't sound trite.

"Thanks. I'm not sure how long I'll be down here. It depends how she progresses over the next few days. I have to cancel our plans for the weekend. I know I won't be back until after Easter."

Karen expressed her concern. She was disappointed, of course, but she understood. *Another lie...two in one evening. I'll have to repent of them before I go to bed.*

Kevin promised to call her daily and keep her updated. He had no idea how long he would be gone. He apologized profusely for disappointing her. Karen was very understanding.

"I'll pray for your grandmother's recovery."

"Uh, sure, okay, whatever."

Karen had the distinct impression that Kevin didn't think that prayer would help the situation. The two of them needed to have a serious discussion about spiritual matters when Kevin returned. Kevin knew she had been attending church somewhat regularly, but she had never opened up to him about her growing relationship with the Lord.

"Thank You, Father." Before falling asleep, Karen spent a few minutes offering up praises to God. She was glad she had let God back into her life. "Thank You for not giving up on me. Thank You for keeping me from making another mistake."

Karen had been toying with the idea of meeting with Pastor Vinson for counseling for several weeks. Now that God had given her a way out of her promise to Kevin, she could face the pastor without the guilt of deliberate sin weighing on her conscience. She would call the church office in the morning and make an appointment. She would also call her mother to let her know that she would be staying until Sunday after all.

22

Easter weekend was everything Karen had hoped it would be and more. She slept better than she had in many weeks. Perhaps it was sleeping in her old bed in her childhood home. Or perhaps it was the feeling of relief that had enveloped her since Kevin had been forced to cancel their plans. Having opted out of early morning bargain hunting, Karen slept until after 9 Saturday morning; she couldn't remember when she had slept so late.

Karen thoroughly enjoyed spending Saturday afternoon with Kim. In many respects, Kim was the sister Karen never had. After lunch, they helped the boys color Easter eggs and hid them more times than they cared to count. Karen filled Kim in on her latest finds, and Kim shared her newest passion—quilting. Kim promised to keep an eye out for the two additional chairs Karen needed to complete her set.

Karen attended sunrise services with Chad at Oak Hill Church and visited briefly with a number of old acquaintances. She avoided the Sunday morning worship service—too many eyes, too much gossip—but sent the boys with her parents. She took advantage of the quiet time to call Kevin and get an update on his grandmother.

"It's looking pretty bleak." The strain of the weekend was evident in his voice. "The doctor has told us to contact family members who would want to see her one last…" He choked back a sob. "Unless she makes a miraculous improvement, it will probably only be another couple of days."

"Is there anything I can do?"

"There's nothing to be done but wait. I may be down here for a while."

Karen wanted to wish Kevin a Happy Easter, but it seemed so trivial. Instead she told him to be sure to rest and that he would be in her thoughts and prayers.

The best part of the weekend was working in the kitchen preparing the Easter feast with her mother. Karen glazed the ham, while her mother fried bacon for the seven-layer salad. Karen made grandmother's sweet potato casserole, and her mother whipped up a batch of biscuits. Deviled eggs and peach cream pie completed the meal. While they worked, Karen filled her mother in on the boys' latest antics and got caught up on the local gossip. Years of cooking together had taught Karen the family's favorite recipes and much, much more.

⌘⌘⌘

Wednesday at noon Karen found herself sitting alone in the break room eating her lunch. Eating alone, again. It was one of her pet peeves. She'd always hated it and probably always would. With the boys in Chester and Robin off helping Hannah with the new baby, Karen had eaten every meal of the past three days by herself. So when Greg popped into the room to pour a cup of coffee, she practically begged him to be her lunch partner.

"If it's not an intrusion," Greg said.

"An intrusion! I'm going stir crazy sitting here all by myself. Last night I set an extra place at the table and pretended I had a dinner guest."

"I know the feeling. I'm all alone this week, also. Tom and Gretchen took the girls to South Carolina to visit Cindy's sister."

"Hey, I've got an idea," she blurted. "You can come over tonight, and we can be all alone together."

Greg cocked one eyebrow at her, the way he always did when she said something that didn't quite register.

"You know what I mean." Karen swatted Greg on the arm. "What do you say? I'll cook a nice dinner, and you come over when you're done here."

"That sounds wonderful. Are you sure you want to cook? It's a good chance to not cook."

"I love to cook. It's cooking for one that I hate."

The phone rang. Greg looked at the caller ID on the lunchroom extension. "It's from South Carolina. Must be my girls. I'll take it in the office." He called back as he exited the room, "Thanks for lunch. I accept the dinner invitation."

"Well, for three minutes there I carried on a conversation with another human." Having no one else to talk to, Karen decided to talk to herself. "Let's see, I'm done eating, there's no one around, and I have 35 minutes of my lunch hour left. I think I'll take a walk and plan my dinner menu."

⌘ ⌘ ⌘

Karen stopped off for groceries on the way home and bought the ingredients for chicken marsala. She would serve it with rice and steamed broccoli. She hoped Greg liked mushrooms. Fresh mushrooms were on sale so she had purchased a pound. She planned to stuff some for an appetizer and add the rest to the chicken. For dessert, she bought a frozen blueberry pie and a carton of vanilla ice cream.

The chicken was simmering in the marsala sauce when Greg called to say he was leaving the office and heading to her house. That was her cue to pop the mushrooms into the oven and start cooking the rice and broccoli. By the time Greg arrived, Karen was ready to serve dinner.

Greg blessed the meal and declared that everything smelled delicious. Karen was amazed at how natural it felt to eat dinner with Greg. She concluded it was because this wasn't a date; it was just a casual meal shared by two friends.

"So, where's Sandy?"

"In Baltimore, visiting her parents. Kevin?"

"Still in Florida. His grandmother is not doing well."

"I'm sorry to hear that. And the boys are in Chester?"

"Yes, they're visiting my parents and Jeff's. I took them down Friday."

"I thought you were going to stay down there for a while yourself. I noticed you didn't take Monday and Tuesday off, as you had planned."

"I, uh, changed my plans. I had a nice weekend with my parents, though."

⌘ ⌘ ⌘

Greg noticed that Karen was deliberately vague but decided not to pursue it. He hoped that she didn't come back early because she couldn't afford to take the two days off. *I should have offered to buy her dinner, not the other way around.* He made a mental note to make it up to her. This was twice now that she had cooked for him.

The rest of the meal passed quickly, and the conversation was easy. They shared updates they had each received from Robin and commented on how well Emily was working out. Karen learned that Emily's family had attended Riverside Christian Fellowship since Emily was a toddler; Emily had moved away after college and had only recently returned to the area. The meal passed quickly. Greg carried the dirty dishes into the kitchen while Karen loaded the dishwasher.

Karen started a pot of decaf and popped the pie into the oven. "It has to bake for 40 minutes," she said. "But I have an idea what we could do in the meanwhile. How would you feel about moving some furniture around for me?"

Greg, who was scrapping the leftover marsala sauce into a food storage container, turned so fast to look at her that he dripped sauce onto the kitchen floor.

Karen bent to wipe up the mess, giggling over Greg's expression of horror. "I guess not."

"Well, how much furniture are we talking about?"

Karen explained that she wanted to rearrange the furniture in the living room.

"No carting large pieces of furniture up and down the stairs?" Greg still sounded skeptical.

Karen smiled sweetly. "Of course not. Just sliding the couch and chairs around the living room."

Greg agreed. He began to regret the decision when Karen looked displeased with the fifth placement of the couch. "Let's put it over by the dining room to create separation." Greg had a moment of déjà vu. "Wasn't that the first idea you had?"

"Well, sometimes the first idea is the best idea."

Once the couch location was decided, the rest of the furniture was placed quite quickly. Greg positioned the sofa table behind the couch as

133

Karen instructed. The table had certainly seen better days. It seemed oddly out of place with the rest of her furniture.

"Are you sure you want this old table in here?"

"Definitely. It's the whole reason we're rearranging the room." Karen adjusted the table a bit to the left. "It will look better when I refinish it."

"Well, it certainly couldn't look worse."

Karen set a lamp and a photo of the boys on the table. "That does it. The room looks so much better. Thank you."

Even Greg had to admit the new arrangement was an improvement.

"I think you've earned a reward. Sit on the couch, and I'll bring our pie and ice cream in here."

"Do you really think that you can make that table look like it belongs in this room?" Greg asked between bites of pie. "You have some nice pieces of furniture in here."

"Thank you," Karen beamed. "You should have seen the coffee table when I bought it. It had been stored in a barn for years. It was quite a challenge, but well worth it."

"I'll say. It's a treasure. I had forgotten you showed it and the end tables to me when I was here before. You do really nice work. What else have you done?"

"I did a gun rack for my husband. I also did a couple of bookcases and a desk."

"You were working on a table and chairs the last time I was here, weren't you?"

"Yes. The chairs are done. I'm ready to stain the table. After that is complete, I'll tackle this old sofa table. You'll be amazed how nice it will look when I get through with it."

"Karen Harper, you are a woman of many talents. I am most impressed."

"That's probably the best compliment I've ever received."

23

Chad dropped by the office on Thursday afternoon as planned. He didn't recognize the new receptionist. He waited until she was finished setting up an appointment for a client before introducing himself. She was pretty cute. He flashed her a big grin. "I'm Chad, Karen's brother. Is she available?"

Emily smiled back. "She's on the phone right now. I'll let her know you're here when she's done."

"And you are..?" Chad stuck his right hand out.

⌘⌘⌘

Emily extended her hand to meet Chad's. "Emily Clark. I'm filling in for two weeks while Robin is away."

Chad held her hand far longer than was necessary for a quick handshake. He was, in fact, cradling it in between both of his.

Emily knew she should ask for her hand back. Instead, she grinned at him like a silly teenager.

"Of course. Karen told me that her daughter just had a baby." Chad reached over and picked up Emily's left hand while continuing to hold onto the right one. He ran his thumb along her ring finger. No ring. "Are you available to have dinner with me tonight?"

Emily was surprised to find she was flattered by Chad's attention; normally she was turned off by such forward behavior. "It so happens that I am. You can pick me up at 7." She freed her hands from Chad's and wrote her address and phone number down for him. The ringing of the phone claimed her attention. "Karen's free now. You can go back to her office."

⌘⌘⌘

Karen heard Chad's whistling before he reached her office. "You're in a good mood."

"I just made a dinner date with the beautiful Emily Clark."

"You two-timing skunk." Karen did her best to sound offended. "You're supposed to be having dinner with me. I thawed out two Porterhouse steaks."

"Sorry, Sis. You know a man's gotta do what a man's gotta do." Chad saw through her charade and grinned broadly. "Steak is a great idea. Where's the best place to get a steak around here?"

"Besides my house, you mean?" Karen's attempt at exasperation fell short. In truth, she was delighted that her little brother had a date. He worked too hard; a little romance would do him good. "But what am I supposed to do with two steaks?"

"I love steak." Greg poked his head in the door, his face pleading with Karen to share her bounty with him.

"You're welcome to come to dinner," Karen said, shaking her head. The man was never far from a conversation about food. "But you're doing the grilling," she called after him as he returned to his patient.

⌘⌘⌘

The steaks had been cooked and devoured, and the dishes were cleared away. "Do you have any of that blueberry pie left?"

Karen rolled her eyes. They had just finished dinner, and Greg was already thinking about dessert.

"Of course," she said. "You didn't really think I would have polished off the rest of the pie by myself since last night, did you?"

"No, it was a rhetorical question. I wanted to make sure you didn't forget to offer me some."

Karen cut two large slices and popped them in the microwave to heat. She wrapped the rest of the pie in foil and shoved it in Greg's direction. "Take it home with you. You need it much more than I do. Do you want ice cream on your pie?"

Greg feigned a look of shock.

She laughed. "Right. Why do I even bother to ask? Two blueberry pies àla mode coming right up."

They took their dessert into the den. "That table looks different than it did last night," Greg commented as they passed the kitchen table in progress.

"I stained it after you left last night. It didn't take long."

"Is it finished?"

"No, it needs a couple coats of sealant to protect the finish."

"How did you get the pattern around the edges?"

"I used two different shades of stain."

"It's beautiful."

"Thanks. I'm hoping to find two more chairs to go with the four I have already. And I want to recover the fabric seats. I've never done that before."

"You certainly don't run from a challenge, do you?"

Karen could hear the admiration in Greg's voice. A wave of shyness overcame her, and she felt her face redden. "I guess not," she said demurely.

Greg cleared his throat. "I didn't see you in church the last couple of weeks," he mentioned between bites of pie. "But, of course, you were out of town last weekend."

"The Sunday before Easter was...the..um...second anniversary." The words seem to stick in her throat, but she forced them out. "The anniversary of Jeff's death." Karen turned to Greg; the pain she still felt was evident in her troubled expression.

Setting his plate on the coffee table, Greg slid over closer to Karen and put his arm around her shoulders. She laid her head on his shoulder. He hugged her for a few moments.

"We weren't up to seeing anyone. We spent the whole day watching family videos and poring over photo albums."

"I understand. I can't believe how much I still miss Cindy. It's been more than three years since the...accident."

"A car accident?" Karen sat up and looked at Greg expectantly. Greg released her and slid over a bit on the couch.

"No, not that kind of accident," he said in hushed tones. He kept his eyes trained on the floor as if struggling to formulate the right words. Karen sat quietly, giving him the space he needed. He cocked his head toward her. "Do you remember the day I called you when you were in the shower?"

"How could I ever forget?" Karen was puzzled. Hoping to lighten the mood, she joked, "You went ballistic on me."

Greg glanced at her sheepishly, then shrugged. He stared at his hands clasped in front of him.

The pit in Karen's stomach began to grow.

"Cindy was rushing to get the phone." Greg's voice took on a distant tone, as if he had to detach himself from the events in order to speak of them. "I had told her a hundred times, maybe a thousand, to let the answering machine pick up when she was busy, particularly if she was in the shower. But, she couldn't resist a ringing phone. 'It might be important,' she always said."

Now it was Karen's turn to offer support. She reached out and stroked Greg's hand.

"It happened about ten o'clock in the morning. The girls were at school, and I was working. She'd been dead for hours when I came home and found her."

"How awful. I am so sorry."

"The doctor said she died instantly. There was nothing that could have been done, even if I'd been here."

Not knowing what else to say, Karen simply replied, "I bet the person who called felt terrible, even though it wasn't really their fault."

"I did, and I still do."

⌘ ⌘ ⌘

Kevin called as Karen was preparing for bed. He simply said, "She's gone."

"I'm so sorry." Even as she said it, she heard Kevin's sobs. She waited silently, offering up a prayer on his behalf, until he composed himself.

"The funeral will be on Monday. I need to help my mom take care of some details with the estate. I'm not sure when I'll be home. Maybe Wednesday."

Karen asked the name of the funeral home and made a mental note to send flowers. She expressed her condolences again before hanging up.

⌘ ⌘ ⌘

Greg was wide awake. Although he'd been in bed for hours, sleep evaded him. His mind kept going back to his confession in Karen's den. His rational mind told him, of course, that Cindy's life had been in God's hands. Greg accepted Cindy's death without bitterness or anger toward God. Cindy was in Heaven, and Greg had perfect assurance that he would see her again. But, back in the furthest recesses of his mind, he sometimes wondered "what if." What if he hadn't called her at precisely that moment? Would she still be alive? In those moments, he felt as guilty as if he had killed her himself.

The evidence clearly showed Cindy had slipped getting out of the shower and hit her head on the side of the porcelain tub. No one questioned the incident any further. It was an accident, pure and simple. The coroner had placed the time of death in the late morning. Gretchen had stopped by for coffee and had left around 9:30. Cindy had mentioned that she needed to take a shower before running some errands. Ten o'clock seemed the most reasonable time of death.

Every detail of the horrible afternoon was etched clearly in Greg's mind. The frantic phone call from Mrs. Warren as he was finishing up with his last patient, about four o'clock. "The girls got off the school bus, and Cindy wasn't there to meet them. The minivan is in the garage. The front door is locked. I've rung the bell and called her on the phone. You'd better come home right away." Running out the door of the office and speeding home—he'd made the five-minute drive in under three minutes. His panicky search of the main floor before heading upstairs....smelling blood as he raced into the master bedroom. Bracing himself for the worst before opening the bathroom door.

Greg knew Cindy was dead the moment he laid eyes on her still, lifeless body. He'd never seen so much blood. He cradled her head to his chest and wept. He wasn't certain how long he remained there before Mr. Warren ventured upstairs and found him. His wife had sent him over to see if he could help. There being nothing else to do, he picked up the phone on the nightstand and dialed 911. He gave the operator the necessary information in hushed tones, so as not to disturb Greg's private mourning, then went downstairs to await the arrival of the emergency personnel. Greg continued to hold his wife until the paramedics pried his arms loose and led him downstairs.

It was hours later, after everyone had gone and the girls were in bed, that Greg had finally played the messages on the answering machine. He knew what he would find, although he hoped otherwise. Greg had called Cindy between patients that morning to confirm the dates for their vacation. He wasn't certain precisely what time he had called, but it was very likely around the time of Cindy's accident. The machine verified his guilt. He had left his message precisely at **9:58 a.m.**

Until tonight, Greg had shared that information with no one in the world. He had seen his own pain mirrored in Karen's face. They had each carried their burdens for far too long. He shared his own story to let her know he understood. He found that in the sharing he had finally released his burden. He prayed that Karen would find the courage to release hers as well.

24

Friday morning before heading to Chester to pick up the boys, Karen had her first counseling session with Pastor Vinson.

"It's nice to see you, Karen. Please call me Mark."

Karen had been attending the church, rather sporadically, for about two months. The pastor had greeted her, but he didn't know anything about her other than she worked with Greg and Robin.

Before they started the session, Pastor Vinson prayed, asking the Lord to bless their time together and to open their hearts to His direction. "Let's start with you telling me a bit about yourself and why you are here."

"Well, I'm a single mother to three sons. My husband died two years ago. I'm here because I'm having a difficult time with my oldest son, Trevor, and because I have recurring nightmares about my husband dying."

"Tell me about the nightmares, beginning with when they started."

Karen summarized the nightmares. "They started about three months ago. Jeff was drowning, and I was trying to save him. I didn't give up, even though it was hopeless. I kept throwing out the life ring, but I couldn't throw it far enough. It was always out of his reach. I yelled for help and others tried to help, but it did no good. The dream always ended with Jeff drowning."

Mark made notations on a yellow legal pad.

Karen continued. "After a couple of weeks, the dream changed."

Mark held up a finger, and Karen paused. He finished making his notes, then nodded.

Karen continued. "This time, I didn't call for help, and I quit trying to save Jeff after a few minutes. I walked away and left him floundering in the water. About a month ago, the nightmare changed again. In the current version, I cause him to drown."

Pastor Vinson looked at her questioningly. Karen answered the unspoken question, "He is skiing without a life vest; I'm spotting him. I untie the line so that he goes down, but I don't tell Trevor. Trevor keeps driving away from Jeff. By the time he realizes his father is not skiing and turns around, it is too late."

"Did your husband drown?"

"No."

"And I assume you did not kill your husband."

Karen was aghast. "Of course not."

"I knew that. I just needed to hear you say it. Was your husband saved?"

"Sort of."

"It's a yes or no question. Either you are saved or you're not."

"Yes, I guess. I mean, he was a Christian, then he got angry at God and refused to have anything to do with God."

"Is that where he stood when he died?"

"No. He had repented about a month before he died."

"So, he was saved. That's wonderful news. At least you have the assurance that he is in Heaven."

Karen said yes, but inside she had some doubts.

"You said he got angry at God. What prompted that?"

"His twin sister died," she said. "She had cancer. Jeff had believed that God was going to heal her. When He didn't, Jeff got mad at God. He reverted back to the way he acted before he was saved. He started hanging out with old drinking buddies. He got drunk every weekend. He did some drugs, mostly marijuana, I think. He slept around." The last statement had cost Karen dearly. She starred at the floor, unable to face Mark.

"I believe," Mark began, "that the dreams are a metaphor for what was happening in Jeff's life and in your relationship. From what you described, Jeff was allowing alcohol and drugs to pull in back into a sinful lifestyle. He was figuratively 'drowning' by the choices he was making. Although he struggled and you tried to help him, the pull of sin was too strong and he eventually succumbed to them. Would you say that his lifestyle contributed to his death?"

Karen wasn't certain she understood what Mark was asking. "If you mean, did alcohol kill him, the answer is yes. I believe he would be alive today except for alcohol."

"Alcohol is a powerful master and has claimed many lives. I'm puzzled about your role, however. The dreams you describe seem to indicate that you did everything you could to save him from himself, at least in the beginning. And you enlisted the help of others."

"Yes, that's right. I talked to our pastor about it and got advice from him. I asked his friends from church to call him and pray for him. They would invite him to church or to go fishing or hunting, but he wouldn't talk to them or return their calls. I did everything I could."

Mark leaned forward and lowered his head until he was looking her straight in the eye. "But after a while, you got weary. You felt like you were carrying this burden all alone, and it was simply too much for you."

Karen nodded enthusiastically. He understood exactly what she had gone through.

"You still wanted to rescue him, but you didn't know what else to do, so you separated yourself from him. You walked away from the problems and went on with your own life."

A tear ran down her cheek. "I couldn't take the hurt anymore. Everyone knew he was sleeping with his old girlfriend. I heard people whispering about me when I was out. I decided I had to live my own life. I got a part-time job, so I would have my own money. I started thinking about getting divorced. I still went to church and kept my church friends. They supported me and prayed for me. But none of them really understood what I was going through. I couldn't tell them Jeff was cheating on me. I had no one I could turn to."

"You always have the Lord to lean on."

Karen sniffled and whispered, "I know, but it was so hard."

"The third version of the dream is brutal," Mark commented. "It indicts you as having some guilt in his death. Did you do something that pushed Jeff over the edge, so to speak?"

"I asked for a divorce."

"The pain got to be too much, and you were ready to walk away."

"Yes."

"How did Jeff react?"

"That was when he went to our pastor and rededicated his life to the Lord. He stopped drinking and started going back to church. He was the old Jeff again."

"So, you two got through the darkest days of your marriage, survived the turmoil and got things back on track, then Jeff died. The nightmares probably are indicative of the fact that you regret losing Jeff just when things were getting better. Subconsciously, you may be blaming yourself for Jeff's death when, in fact, your request for a divorce is what forced him to face his sins and repent. Jeff is in Heaven today because you forced him to examine his life." Mark let his words sink in before he continued. "It's time for you to make peace with the past and move forward. It's time to let Jeff go, Karen."

Karen knew that the pastor was correct. She also knew that if she told him the full story, he would likely assess the situation a bit differently. She would save that for another session.

Pastor Vinson led Karen in a prayer asking God to help her trust that Jeff was in His presence and to move on with her life.

⌘⌘⌘

Sandy and Greg were led to a table next to the windows, affording them a great view of a small town far below them in the valley. Sandy had returned from Boston Thursday evening, giving them a couple days together before the girls came home on Sunday. They had spent the morning meandering down Skyline Drive and had stopped at the Big Meadows Lodge for lunch.

"I think we stopped at every scenic overview that we came to," Sandy observed, "yet the best view of all is from inside a restaurant. I would never have expected that."

Sandy's appreciation of one of Greg's favorite spots warmed his heart. "The fresh mountain air has given me a tremendous appetite. I'm starving."

Sandy chuckled. "When are you not starving? It's amazing you stay so thin. Every time I'm with you, you eat like a horse."

The waiter arrived to take their drink orders. They both ordered decaf coffee and ice water. "We'd also like an order of sweet potato sticks."

Sandy frowned. "Sweet potatoes is one of the few vegetables I don't eat."

"I don't like sweet potatoes either, but I love these. At least try one."

The server quickly returned with their drinks and appetizer. They ordered a couple of sandwiches, then turned their attention to the fried sweet potatoes.

"Do you eat these with ketchup?" Sandy peered suspiciously at the starchy vegetables.

"No, just salt and butter." A large dollop of butter was quickly melting on top of the pile of hot fries. Greg picked up several fries, dipped them in the softened butter, and plopped them into his mouth. "Mmmm, these are soo good. Try one. What's the worst that can happen?"

"The worst possibility—let's see. I could turn out to be allergic to sweet potatoes and have severe reaction."

"Do you know anyone who is allergic to sweet potatoes?" Greg downed another handful of potatoes.

"Not a soul."

"Besides, you're a nurse. You could treat yourself."

Sandy picked up a fry and sniffed it. Greg shook his head in mock disgust. More fries went into his mouth. Greg devoured more than half of the pile while she tried to make up her mind.

Finally she took a nibble from one end. "Not too bad."

"Make sure it's salted, then dip it in the butter."

Sandy followed Greg's instructions, taking a more respectable bite this time. "Pretty good." As she reached for a handful, she noticed Greg giving her the evil eye.

"Now that you got me to try them, you are going to have to share," she teased.

Greg decided to take the high road and let Sandy have the last of the fries. He watched amused as she rubbed them on the plate, soaking up the last remnants of melted butter.

The sandwiches arrived and for several minutes the couple concentrated on their meal.

"Do you think you are up to a hike after lunch?" Greg asked in between mouthfuls.

"I love hiking."

"I thought we could hike down to Dark Hollow Falls. It's a fairly easy hike. The only problem is that it's all uphill on the way back."

"Let's go. I'm up for the challenge."

The falls were spectacular. "This is a sight I never grow tired of seeing," Greg told Sandy as they stood side-by-side watching the water tumbling down the mountainside. "I was here about a month ago with Trevor. It was his first time seeing a waterfall in person. I loved sharing that experience with him."

Halfway up the mountain, Sandy stumbled and Greg reached out a hand to steady her. After that he continued to hold her hand to prevent further stumbles. It occurred to him that this was the first time they had held hands. Something about that realization troubled Greg, but he couldn't quite figure out what.

25

Karen headed for Chester soon after lunch in order to avoid rush hour traffic through Richmond. She would be glad to see the boys. It had been a long week without them, although the peace and quiet had allowed her to make great progress on refinishing the dining room set. The table and chairs were turning out so nice that Karen had decided the set would go in the dining room and her older table would be moved into the kitchen. She prayed that the boys' week had been enjoyable.

She made it to the Butler homestead in plenty of time to help her mother with dinner preparations. Chad and their dad had taken the boys fishing, so the two women had the house to themselves. Karen was thankful for the opportunity to chat privately with her mother, as so much had transpired in the past twenty-four hours.

"Did Chad say how his date went last night?" Karen asked as she peeled potatoes at the sink. Mrs. Butler turned toward Karen, the knife in her hand poised in mid-air. Her quizzical expression told Karen that Chad had said nothing about his date. "I thought Chad had dinner with you last night."

"He was supposed to. He ditched me for Emily. Greg came over for dinner again."

"Greg. I thought you were still dating Kevin? Who's Emily?"

Karen laughed. "I guess I'd better start at the beginning." She explained to her mother how the evening had unfolded.

⌘ ⌘ ⌘

Mrs. Butler wasn't surprised that Chad had asked out the temporary receptionist only moments after meeting her. "Chad never has any trouble getting girls to go out with him. It's making a commitment to one girl that has always been his problem. It's time that boy settled down." She was surprised, however, by the way Karen's eyes lit up as she recounted her two dinners with Greg in the past two days. She wisely chose to keep that information to herself.

Changing the subject, Mrs. Butler inquired as to Kevin's grandmother's condition. "She died last night. Kevin was pretty shaken up. I talked to him earlier this afternoon. He seemed to be handling it okay. I wish I could assure him that she is in Heaven, but he hasn't said anything about her spiritual condition, and I was leery of asking."

"We need to pray that the funeral challenges Kevin to examine his own mortality and eternal future. I hope the minister uses this opportunity to share the gospel."

Karen had to agree with her mother.

⌘ ⌘ ⌘

The rest of the evening passed uneventfully. The day's fishing trip had been a success. Mr. Butler and Chad cleaned fish for tomorrow night's supper. The boys were tanned from their two-day trip to Virginia Beach with Jeff's parents. Austin and Kyle wanted to stay in Chester for another week of vacation. Even Trevor seemed to have enjoyed himself.

Karen finally cornered Chad after everyone else went to bed and insisted on hearing the details of his date.

"She's wonderful. We laughed and talked until after midnight. I didn't get back to Chester until 2:30 this morning."

"Are you going to ask her out again?"

"Absolutely. We're going out next Tuesday."

Karen was surprised that Chad would be back in Fredericksburg so soon and asked him about it.

"Mr. Stevens wants me to come up for a few days at the beginning of the week to finalize some details with the architect. I thought I'd crash on your couch for a couple of nights. I need to look for an apartment soon. I'll be moving to Fredericksburg the first of the month."

⌘ ⌘ ⌘

Saturday morning, Karen dropped by Kim's house for coffee.

"I have a surprise for you," Kim announced as she came out the front door and met Karen on the steps. "I found some chairs at the flea market. I think they'll go with your table."

Karen was delighted to see that the chairs were in great shape. They were similar to the first two chairs she had purchased, having vertically slatted backs and upholstered seats. Although the pattern of the slats wasn't identical to the others, it was similar. Once they were stained, they would look like they were meant to go together. "They're perfect! I'm not crazy about the fabric, though."

"You can always recover them."

"Of course. I was planning on recovering the other four, anyway. But I've never done it."

"You can do it. It's easy."

"Easy for you, maybe, but I don't sew."

"There's no sewing involved. You simply staple the fabric to the back." Kim explained the process, and Karen thought that maybe she could do it. It was worth a try. Kim volunteered to drive up one Friday in a few weeks and help Karen shop for fabric. Karen told Kim about her plan to move the set into the formal dining room.

"Great idea. We'll need to buy a more formal fabric for the dining room."

Kim's husband tied the two chairs to the roof of the van. Karen gave her friend a tight squeeze. Kim's impending visit gave her another thing to look forward to. Karen planned to spend the rest of the day with her parents and head back home after dinner.

As she pulled into her parents' driveway, Karen was surprised to see a Lincoln Town car parked alongside Chad's car. She recognized it immediately as belonging to Carl Harper. "What is he doing here?" Karen briefly considered backing out of the driveway and driving away to escape a confrontation with Jeff's parents. "Coward. You can't avoid them forever." She bowed her head and asked God for guidance before exiting her vehicle and slowly walking toward the house.

The door opened as she mounted the front steps. "Tell Karen I'm sorry to have missed her," Carl Harper was saying to Mrs. Butler, although Karen sincerely doubted that he meant those words.

"Actually, you haven't missed her." Mrs. Butler nodded in Karen's direction.

Carl turned and his expression revealed that he hadn't meant the words he'd just spoken. He flushed and stammered, "Ah, uh, well, hello, Karen."

"Hello, Carl." Karen kept her voice even and emotionless. "Is there something I can do for you?"

"No, nothing. I, uh, was just dropping off Kyle's blanket. He left it. Marsha figured he would want it. I was just leaving."

"I can see that. I won't keep you. Thanks for bringing the blanket over. Tell Marsha I said hello." Karen tried to be polite with Carl and Marsha whenever she was forced to converse with them for the sake of the boys. They deserved to have their grandparents in their lives, even if it put her in an uncomfortable position occasionally. Fortunately, Karen's mother generously acted as a go-between and arranged for the boys to visit the Harpers whenever they were in Chester.

Carl said a polite good-bye and left quickly. Karen made sure that none of the boys were in earshot before expressing her aggravation to her mother. "Why did he have to come here? He could have called, and Chad would have gone over there to get Kyle's blanket."

"Karen, you are going to have to forgive them. They thought they were doing what was best for the boys."

"Mother, how can you take their side against me?"

"Karen, darling, I'm not taking their side. I'm asking you to consider what they had been through and to be a bit understanding."

"Understanding. Mom, they tried to take my children away from me! They said I was an unfit mother. How can I forgive them for that?"

"I know it's hard, sweetie. Really, I do. God never said that forgiving those who hurt us would be easy, but He said that we must forgive others as He forgives us. You will end up hurting yourself if you don't forgive. If you hold onto this hurt, it will make you bitter. That's a high price to pay. You need to pray and ask God to help you to forgive. It won't be easy, but it will be worth it."

"I'll try, Mother. I will try."

26

On Thursday, Karen woke early with dread enveloping her. Thankfully, the nightmares had ceased since her session with Pastor Vinson almost a week ago. But the uneasiness she felt about Kevin's homecoming this afternoon made a full night's sleep impossible. While he was in Florida, Karen had done much soul searching and had reached a decision concerning their relationship that she knew Kevin wouldn't like. She didn't want to lose him, but she wasn't going to compromise her values to hold on to him, either.

As had become her habit recently, she made her way down the stairs and into the laundry room. The spacious room provided ample space for her to work on her restoration projects. At present, she was sanding the sofa table she had purchased downtown at the Antique Emporium. She had removed the old stain and was working to smooth all the surfaces before staining the table cherry to match her living room furniture. She found that the mindless activity of sanding allowed her to think through the problems confronting her.

She began by asking God for wisdom. That seemed to be her most frequent prayer lately. More than anything else she desired wisdom to make the right decisions.

⌘⌘⌘

Karen's cell phone rang as she was unlocking her car after work. She was expecting Kevin's call, so it was no surprise to hear his voice when she answered.

"I just got my luggage and am in the parking lot trying to remember where I parked my truck."

Karen knew Kevin's plane had been due in at Reagan National Airport an hour earlier. Kevin called Monday night after she had put the younger boys to bed. He sounded weary. His grandmother's funeral services and burial had been held that morning. The family had entertained relatives and family friends all afternoon and into the evening. He had informed her of his intention to fly home on Thursday afternoon and had asked her to meet him for dinner.

"Was your flight late?"

"A bit, not too bad. The luggage took forever to come out."

"You're going to hit rush hour in full force."

"I know, but there's nothing I can do about it." Kevin sounded weary. "I'll give you a call when I get close to town. How about meeting me at the restaurant?"

Karen agreed, knowing how tired Kevin would be after his flight. The normal one-hour drive could take two to three times that long at this time of day. She would get the boys squared away as quickly as possible and be ready whenever Kevin called. Chad was still staying with them, so Karen didn't need to find a babysitter.

⌘ ⌘ ⌘

Kevin entered the restaurant to find Karen waiting for him. She was a sight for sore eyes.

He scooped her up in his arms. "I have missed you so much."

Karen noted that Kevin looked haggard. The stress of the past two weeks had taken its toll. While they ate, he filled her in on all the details of the funeral and the work of cleaning out his grandmother's house. His mother would be putting the house on the market soon, so the family had to sort through all of his grandmother's belongings and make decisions about what to keep and what would be sold or donated to charity. Each child and grandchild had selected some personal keepsakes.

Kevin reached into the pocket in the lining of his jacket and withdrew a long, slender jeweler's box. He placed the box on the table and slid it toward Karen.

"I'd like you to have this. It belonged to Grandmother."

Karen thought it odd that he would give her a family heirloom, but she didn't want to seem unappreciative. She opened the box and let out a loud gasp. Inside the box was a strand of pearls.

"Kevin, they're beautiful. Are you sure you want me to have these?"

Kevin only smiled, clearly pleased he had impressed her with his gift.

He waited until the dessert had been served to bring up the thing that was most urgent in his mind. "So when can I redeem my rain check?"

Karen nearly choked on a bite of key lime pie. She coughed to clear her throat and took a sip of water before replying. "Rain check?"

"Yes. Rain check. I told you I would take a rain check for our trip that had to be canceled. When do I get to steal you away for a long, romantic weekend?" He waggled his eyebrows suggestively, he hoped, to insure that she understood his intentions.

Karen had known this was coming and had tried to prepare a proper response, but all her carefully practiced words flew from her head. Instead, she found herself hemming and hawing. "I really don't know. I can't ask my mother to keep the boys again this soon. They just came home a few days ago. Besides, they have school. I think a trip will have to wait until school is out."

"That's a long time. I can't wait that long."

"I can't help that. I don't know what you expect me to do."

Kevin had really hoped that their first venture into physical intimacy would be special, that they would have a few days together to get comfortable with each other. But waiting another couple of months was out of the question. He had already waited six months. He didn't know any man who would wait that long. Maybe they should explore some other options.

He considered suggesting that he spend the night at her house, but he knew she'd never go for that. Even if they could fool the younger boys, Trevor would catch on right away. Karen was having enough problems with Trevor without adding this complication.

The silence had grown uncomfortable. Kevin took a bite of cheesecake while he pondered his options. *Friday mornings! That would work.*

"What about Friday mornings?" Kevin tried not to sound overly optimistic.

"What about Friday mornings?" Karen repeated his words back obviously very puzzled. She wasn't following Kevin's reasoning.

"How about I come over on Friday mornings? You're off, and the boys are at school. We would have the house to ourselves."

⌘ ⌘ ⌘

Kevin looked so pleased that Karen felt she should know what he was talking about. But for the life of her his meaning eluded her, unless he meant…

Of course, that was what he meant.

Just in case Karen had missed his meaning, Kevin spelled it out for her. "We can have breakfast together and then go back to bed until I have to go to work. Or better yet, we can have breakfast in bed."

"I'm not sure that's a good idea."

Kevin looked confused. "I don't get it. Don't you find me physically attractive?"

"Of course I do." Finding Kevin physically attractive had never been the issue. Karen had been attracted to him from the moment she first laid eyes on him. "It's just that…"

"What?"

"I hoped we would wait until we got married."

"Married?" Kevin's face registered his shock. Obviously, marriage was not in his game plan. "How can we even consider getting married if we don't know how we will get along? We talked about this before. I told you that we needed to find out if we're compatible and if we can live together before we discuss marriage. I thought you agreed with me."

"I guess I did back when we talked. But I've been having second thoughts. The Bible teaches that sex is only for marriage."

"What is it with you and the Bible all of the sudden?" Kevin slammed his fist on the table. "I don't mind you going to church but don't bring religion into our relationship."

"It's not just religion. It's about having a relationship with God. I've been working on making my relationship with God my number one priority."

"What about our relationship? Our relationship is supposed to be your number one priority."

"It's not your top priority, so why should it be mine?" If Kevin was going to attack her, Karen would attack right back.

"What does that mean?"

"Your job. You prioritize your job above our relationship. And poker night. It comes before us. You only see me when it fits into your schedule."

Kevin's eyes narrowed. "That's because you refuse to take the relationship to the next level. I made my priorities clear before we started dating. If we were having a physical relationship, you would move up my priority scale in a hurry."

Kevin's intentions were becoming clear to Karen. "So, this is primarily about your wanting to be intimate. It's not about us having a closer relationship at all."

"Being intimate is how we will have a closer relationship. That's what intimacy means, after all."

"I don't think so. I believe that sex outside of marriage is immoral, and I really want to wait to have sex until we get married...*if* we get married." There. Karen had said it. There was no going back now.

"You certainly didn't seem to think it was immoral when you were sleeping with that slime ball Mike Sloan."

Ouch. That remark hit Karen like a slap in the face, but she knew Kevin had a point. "You're right," she admitted. "I was messed up when I was seeing Mike. I made a lot of mistakes that I am trying not to repeat."

"So I am paying the price for Mike's sins, is that it? I'm outta here. Call me when you're sane again." With that Kevin stood up and walked away. He made it halfway to the door before turning around and coming back to the table.

Maybe he's having second thoughts. Karen heart was in her throat as she tried to think of a way to make things better between them.

He stopped at the table and reached behind him for his wallet. He pulled several twenties out of it and laid them on the table. "That should cover the meal and the tip. I wasn't going to stick you with paying the check." He turned to leave, then pivoted toward her once more. He snatched the jewelry box off the table. "I think I'll hold on to Grandmother's pearls."

⌘ ⌘ ⌘

The third time Kevin walked away from the table, he exited the restaurant without ever looking back. When Karen had made the decision to stick to her values, she had done so with the knowledge that Kevin's breaking up with her was the mostly likely outcome. She had tried to steel herself for that eventuality. Yet tears trickled down her face as she stared at the entrance of the restaurant, hoping against hope that he might get to the parking lot and change his mind. Hoping that he might decide she was worth waiting for. After a few minutes had passed, she knew it was futile to sit there any longer. She paid the check with the money Kevin had left and headed home.

A glow from the living room alerted Karen that Chad was still awake. She sat down beside him on the couch and put her head on his shoulder. He embraced her tightly and stroked her head as the tears began to flow in earnest. He held on until the sobs subsided, then released her and handed her a tissue.

"Tell me all about it," he said gently.

27

Friday morning, Kevin was back at work for the first time in more than two weeks. He rose early and was at the dealership when it opened for business. A couple smart-alecks looked at their watches and pantomimed having heart failure from the shock of seeing Kevin at work at such an early hour. He ignored them. Most of his coworkers offered their condolences and welcomed him back warmly. After such a long absence, it felt good to back in his normal environment. However, he couldn't deny that he arrived several hours earlier than he had hoped. If he'd had his way, he would have been consummating his relationship with Karen about now, but there was no sense in beating that bush.

Josh approached Kevin with two cups of coffee in hand. He handed one to Kevin. "So, how are you doing?"

Kevin took a sip of the black liquid. "Tired, but otherwise fine. It was a rough two weeks, to be sure."

"How old was your grandmother?"

"Eighty-four. She'd lived a long life. It was her time to go. The hard part was going through her stuff and trying to decide what to do with it all."

Josh shook his head in empathy. "I lost my grandmother last year. Sorting through her personal belongings felt like an invasion of her privacy."

Kevin knew exactly what Josh meant. "Grandma held onto so much stuff. We threw away boxes and boxes of things that she had probably treasured, but it had no meaning to us. It was weird."

"Did you keep some things for yourself?"

"Sure, but I couldn't bring much back on the plane. I shipped my grandfather's golf clubs back here. He's been dead for six years. I don't know why my grandmother hung on to them all these years. I kept a few photos and a few pieces of her jewelry. And a few trinkets; nothing of much value or consequence."

Patrick, one of the younger salesmen, walked by and interrupted their conversation. "I bet Karen will be happy to see you. After two weeks, she's probably anxious for you to take care of business, if you catch my drift." He snickered and nudged Kevin in the side with his elbow.

"I already saw her—last night. We took care of business."

Patrick laughed and slapped him on the back before walking away. "That's my man. Sorry about your grandmother. "

Josh looked at him skeptically.

Kevin shrugged. "It's none of his business. I'm simply letting him think what he wants to think."

Josh was the only salesman at Wilson Chevrolet with whom Kevin had been honest about his relationship with Karen. The rest had assumed the couple was sleeping together by Thanksgiving, or Christmas at the latest, and Kevin had done nothing to correct their assumptions. If they knew the truth, they would make his life miserable with their teasing. Most of the single guys made it abundantly clear that they hoped to have sex by the third date, and they considered themselves quite the gentleman to wait as long as a month. It was unthinkable, in their minds, that any virile man would be celibate for six months, particularly when he was in a steady relationship.

"What did happen last night?" Josh asked discretely when they were alone.

"She told me she wants to get married first."

"Married? Have you proposed?"

"No. We haven't even talked about it."

"Do you want to marry her?"

"I don't know," Kevin answered wearily. "She's a wonderful lady, and I enjoy being with her. But she has three children. I'm not ready for that. Then there's the issue of Mike Sloan."

"That's right. She slept with him, but she refuses to sleep with you. I'd say that makes her a hypocrite."

"That's what I told her. She's gotten religious lately. I liked her better before she started going to church and reading the Bible. At first

I thought it was fine for her as long as she didn't try to involve me in it. But now it's changing her and affecting us. We had a fight. I walked out on her at the restaurant. I think we broke up."

"I think that's for the best. It doesn't sound like you two are compatible anymore."

"It may be for the best, but it sure does hurt. I miss her already."

Several times during the day, Kevin picked up the phone to call Karen, but each time he hung up the receiver without dialing her number. He had no idea what to say to her. One moment he thought he should apologize for pressuring her to compromise her values, and the next he was angry and frustrated with her for being so inconsiderate of his needs. He finally decided that the best course of action was to do nothing for a few days. He would reassess his feelings next week. If he still missed her, he would try to make amends.

⌘ ⌘ ⌘

When Karen awoke on Friday morning, it was still dark. Her heart was pounding, and her body was drenched in sweat. Another nightmare! It had been more than a week since the last one, and Karen had prayed that they had stopped for good. Obviously, that was not the case. She supposed it was brought on by the stressful encounter with Kevin the previous night.

There does seem to be a pattern of having nightmares when I'm upset about my relationship with Kevin.

Karen stretched and rose from the bed. *5:15. Too early to go down stairs. I don't want to wake Chad.* Karen headed for the shower. By the time she was done and had taken a few minutes for her morning devotion, she heard Chad walking around the kitchen.

Chad offered to drop Austin and Kyle off at school on his way to yet another meeting with the project architect. He took all his belongings with him when they left, as he would be returning to Chester after the meeting.

"I have about ten days' worth of work on a basement I'm refinishing," Chad told Karen over breakfast. "Then I'll be moving up here. I've rented an apartment as of May first."

The boys cheered loudly. They were as excited as Karen to have him close by.

Chad winked. "You'll see me so much that you'll get sick of me."

Karen hoped that they would see him often, but between his work and Emily Clark, with whom he was totally infatuated, she doubted very much that he would wear out his welcome.

Karen's plan for Friday included continuing her work on the sofa table and meeting with Pastor Vinson for another counseling session. She was rubbing tung oil into the bare wood when the ringing of the telephone interrupted her work.

"Hey, Sis. It's Chad. I have a job proposal for you." Static on the line made it tough for Karen to hear him clearly.

"Chad. I can't hear you very well. It sounded like you said you have a job proposal for me."

"That's right. A paying job. Mr. Stevens has several antique pieces that are in pretty rough shape. He's willing to pay top dollar to have them restored. I told him about your work, and he wanted me to ask you if you'd be interested."

"I'd be interested in looking at them and figuring out if I'm up to the job."

"Great. I'll set up a meeting for the first Friday after I get back. He wants the restoration to be authentic, so you'll probably have to do some research. They are from the late 1800s."

Karen hugged herself with excitement and pumped her fist in the air. "A paying job. I'm going to get paid to do what I love best."

⌘ ⌘ ⌘

Pastor Mark Vinson began the counseling session by asking Karen how her week had gone.

"Good and bad. It was very eventful. It's hard to know where to start."

"Why don't you start with something good? What is most on your mind right now?"

"I may have a job refinishing antique furniture." Karen's face lit up as she revealed this tidbit of information.

"Would that mean you wouldn't work for Greg Marshall any longer?" Greg had shared with Mark what a valuable addition to his staff Karen Harper was. As a matter of fact, Greg had mentioned her frequently in their conversation of late.

"No. It would be a side job, although eventually I might like to have my own furniture restoration business." Karen went on to tell him about her brother's impending move to Fredericksburg and his business restoring old houses.

"That's wonderful." Mark sincerely meant it. "Let's move on. Have you had any more nightmares?"

"None until last night."

"Did something happen that might have triggered a nightmare?"

"I had a disagreement with Kevin, the guy I'm dating. At least I was dating him until last night. I think he broke up with me."

"We didn't talk about Kevin last session, did we? I don't have any mention of him in my notes."

"I don't think so. I've been seeing Kevin for about six months. Between our work schedule and family obligations, we only see each other once or twice a week. Trevor doesn't like him."

"I only have one question about Kevin. Is he a Christian?"

"No."

"Second Corinthians 6:14 says, 'Do not be yoked together with unbelievers.' That's pretty cut and dried. You've invested a lot of time into a relationship that has no future, if you are going to live according to God's word. Kevin is not who God wants you to spend your life with."

Karen screwed up her mouth and looked like she might cry, but she nodded to let Mark know that she agreed with him. She had wasted a lot of time on the wrong man.

When Karen didn't speak, Mark continued, "You said you think he broke up with you. If he did, you need to let him go. If he didn't, well, I think you know that you need to end this relationship. Your relationship with Trevor might improve when Kevin is out of your life for good." Mark let his words sink in, before taking the conversation in a new direction. "Were there any other significant events you want to talk about?"

"I saw my father-in-law. I didn't mean to. We both showed up at my parents' house at the same time."

"Let me get this straight. Seeing your father-in-law was a bad thing?"

"Yes. Well, it was uncomfortable. I don't get along with Jeff's parents."

"They are your children's grandparents and their link to their father. It's not acceptable for you to not get along with them. You need to work on restoring this relationship for your sake and the sake of your children."

"They don't like me. They blame me for Jeff's death."

"I thought alcohol caused his death."

"It did. But, if he had been happy, he wouldn't have been drinking. If I'd been a better wife, he would have been happy. I didn't make him happy, so he drank too much and now he's dead."

"Were you happy before his sister got sick?"

"Yes. We were very happy. We had a great marriage until he got angry with God. Then everything fell apart."

"Do they know about the drugs and the other women?"

"I'm not sure. It was fairly common knowledge around town. I didn't want them to know, so I never said anything about it to them. I assumed they would blame that on me, too. He wouldn't need other women if he were happy at home. No matter what he did, they could blame it on me for not meeting his needs."

"How does their blame affect you?"

Karen shuddered and tears splashed down her cheeks. "After the funeral, they called social services and said I was an unfit mother. They wanted to get custody of the boys. I was investigated. I had to have my friends and family testify that I took good care of the boys. The social services worker concluded that the charge was completely unjustified."

Mark handed her a tissue.

Karen blew her nose before adding, "It was horrible. I had just lost Jeff, and they were trying to take my boys away from me."

"How often do they see the children?" Mark asked.

"Whenever I visit my parents, my mother arranges for the boys to spend some time with the Harpers. They saw them at Thanksgiving and

Christmas, and they spent four days with them last week. The boys will spend two weeks with them in July. I don't want to have anything to do with them, but I don't keep the boys away from them."

Mark leaned forward. "Have you forgiven them?"

Karen looked surprised, then almost angry. "No," she cried out. "How can I forgive them after what they tried to do?"

In his gentlest voice, he asked, "Who are you hurting by not forgiving them?"

Karen's expression changed from one of anger to one of contemplation. Mark gave her a few moments to think about it. "Forgiving them doesn't imply they weren't wrong or they didn't sin. It simply means you are not going to hold their sin against them. Christ tells us that we must forgive others if we are to receive forgiveness." Mark picked up the well-used Bible from his desk and opened it. Handing it to her, he pointed to Matthew 6. "Read verses 14 and 15."

Karen took the Bible from him and focused her eyes to where Mark pointed. "For if you forgive men when they sin against you, your heavenly Father will also forgive you. But if you do not forgive men their sins, your Father will not forgive your sins."

Her mother had said the same thing to her only a few days earlier. It seemed that God was not going to let Karen hold onto her unforgiving spirit.

Before she left his office, Pastor Vinson led Karen in a prayer forgiving her in-laws of their actions against her. He suggested that Karen write a letter to them, telling them she forgave them and asking for their forgiveness in return. "I'll help," he kindly offered, pulling a sheet of stationery from the box on his desk.

28

After spending the weekend missing Karen terribly and feeling like a heel, Kevin called Karen Sunday evening.

"Hi. It's me." Kevin half expected Karen to slam the phone in his ear. He breathed a sigh of relief when she didn't.

Karen had resigned herself to never hearing from him again, so his familiar voice on the other end of the line caught her completely off guard. Her heart raced furiously and her pulse quickened. All of her resolve to end the relationship flew out the window.

"Hello." Karen tried desperately to sound nonchalant but knew she failed miserably. The single word came out breathlessly, as if she'd been sitting by the phone for days waiting for his call.

"I called to say I'm sorry. I was kind of rough on you Thursday. Blame it on fatigue, stress, sexual frustration. I don't know. Bottom line—I'm sorry."

He sounded sorry, and Karen realized she'd missed him even more than she had expected.

"Apology accepted." She said the words almost before Kevin finished his apology. *Too eager. Exhibit some self-control.*

"Can I take you dinner Tuesday?" Kevin asked tentatively.

"Do we have to wait that long? I'm free tomorrow night." *So much for self-control. Don't you have any self-respect, girl?*

"Monday's poker night." *Ouch.* That statement brought Karen back to reality. Would Kevin ever put her ahead of poker night? "Right. I forgot." Her voice was flat and devoid of emotion. To his credit, Kevin caught on to the change in her tone.

"You *are* more important to me than poker. But I've missed two weeks, and the guys will kill me if I miss again. Plus, I need to spend some time with these guys. They're my best friends. I need guy time after all I've been through."

Karen wasn't completely satisfied but decided to not fight this particular battle now. "Of course. I was being selfish. I'll see you on Tuesday."

⌘ ⌘ ⌘

Robin was back at work on Monday morning. Karen was glad to see her friend and lunch companion. Greg had eaten with her a few times, but many of her lunch hours had been spent alone.

To say Robin was a proud grandmother would have been a major understatement. Already three framed photos of Nicole sat on her desk and others were tucked onto her bulletin board. Karen stopped at Robin's desk to ooh and aah over the precious little girl.

"Congratulations, Grandma. She's beautiful."

"I know." Robin beamed. "She's a wonderful baby. I am so thankful that she's healthy and that God allowed her to be part of our lives. Hannah's husband e-mailed me some more pictures. You have to see the one of Nicole in the yellow polka dot dress you sent her."

Karen peered over Robin's shoulder. "Precious. Absolutely precious."

"I want to use one of them as my screen saver. I was thinking about this one." Robin clicked on the frame to enlarge the photo. In it, Hannah was cradling baby Nicole in her arms, while Robin stood behind them encircling both of them in hers.

Karen agreed that it was perfect. "Three generations of Jennings women all together. I'd better get to work now, but I want to hear more about your darling granddaughter at lunch."

At lunch, Karen heard all there was to hear about baby Nicole. Then she filled Robin in on her very eventful couple of weeks. Robin was surprised to learn that Greg and Karen had dined alone on two occasions, but she covered her shock well. She was, however, wondering if there was more going on between the two of them than either would admit. Karen also shared with Robin that she had been to counseling.

"Talking to Mark has been very helpful. He thinks I should not be dating Kevin, since Kevin is not a Christian."

"I would have to agree with him." Robin had been tempted to offer the same opinion whenever the subject came up, but she hadn't felt it was her place to do so. Now that Karen had broached the subject, she considered the door to open for her to speak freely. "From everything you have told me about Kevin, I don't believe he is the man God has for you. He doesn't share your faith, and he doesn't seem interested in being a father to your boys. I would advise you to pray very seriously about taking Mark's suggestion. You should terminate your relationship with Kevin."

Karen examined the sandwich in her hand. Finally, she spoke in a small voice. "I know I should, but I don't think I'm strong enough to do that."

"Then I will pray that Kevin breaks it off with you," Robin said firmly but gently.

⌘ ⌘ ⌘

If Kevin had any inkling of the storm that was brewing in the Harper house, he would never have rung the bell on Tuesday evening.

Austin greeted him at the door. "Momma isn't ready yet. She said for you to wait for her in the living room."

Kevin took a seat on the couch. He had only sat in this room a couple of times, but he didn't remember the couch facing the window. Had Karen rearranged the furniture while he was gone?

Kevin heard the front door open and close. Trevor poked his head in the living room as he walked by.

"Hi, Trevor." Kevin did his best to sound friendly.

No response. Trevor kept walking.

"Trevor." Kevin rose from his seat and walked to the entryway. "Trevor, I'd like to speak to you."

Trevor stopped with his back to Kevin. He exhaled deeply a couple of times before turning around and following Kevin back into the living room. He stood facing Kevin, his arms planted firmly on his hips.

"So what's the problem, Trevor?" Kevin asked him, trying to sound casual. "Why don't you like me? I've never done anything to deserve your animosity."

Trevor looked Kevin in the eye. Kevin could see the anger brewing there. "You are a jerk." Trevor spoke the words slowly and deliberately.

"That may be true, but you don't know me well enough to say that."

"I know a jerk when I see one. You aren't the first jerk she's dated."

Kevin was puzzled. Could Trevor be talking about Mike Sloan? Surely Karen hadn't introduced Mike to her children. He was still trying to decide how to respond when Trevor continued.

"You remind me of him."

"In what way?"

"You look like him." No one would confuse Mike with Kevin. Mike's hair was considerably darker than Kevin's, and he was several inches shorter and probably 30 pounds heavier than Kevin. Trevor must be talking about some other jerk.

"I look like who?"

"The guy from the hospital. Danny."

"Never heard of him. Does he live around here?"

"No. He lives in Chester. My mom was dating him before my dad died."

"Before your father died?" Kevin was certain he must have heard wrong. "Did you say she was dating him before your father died?"

"Yes. I didn't like him, and I don't like you." Saying that, Trevor turned and walked away, leaving a speechless Kevin in his wake.

Kevin paced around the room. *Karen cheated on her husband.* This was too much for him to handle. No wonder Karen never wanted to talk about her past. What else had she not told him? Did he really know this woman at all?

Horrible words kept running through his mind. He wanted to scream, "You slut! You are just like Christine."

⌘⌘⌘

"Hi, Kevin." Karen stopped abruptly as she entered the living room. Something was wrong, but she wasn't sure what it was. She had passed Trevor exiting the living room as she entered. She looked at Kevin and then behind her in the direction Trevor had headed. Something had transpired between the two of them. What was it?

"Kevin, are you all right?" Karen had never seen Kevin like this. His face was taut. He looked angry. Angrier than she'd ever seen him.

"No, I am definitely not all right." He spoke in a careful, controlled tempo. "Trevor and I have just been having a chat. Tell me about Danny." It was an order, not a request.

Karen knew the time had come to spill the secrets she had tried so desperately to hide.

She took a deep breath, exhaled slowly, and began. "I worked part-time at the hospital, in admissions. Danny was a security guard there. My desk was close to his post. He would stop by and make small talk during his breaks, and sometimes we would eat lunch together. He was married but unhappy. My marriage was falling apart. We had a lot in common. At first we were merely two friends commiserating with one another about our problems. He was the only person I knew who really understood what I was going through in my marriage. After a while, we became more than friends."

Karen waited for some kind of reaction from Kevin.

He stood with his arms crossed over his chest, his eyes condemning her.

Karen wanted him to understand her side. "I wasn't looking to have an affair. I was just lonely and needed a friend. Jeff ignored me. He didn't want me, but he didn't want a divorce either. I felt trapped. Danny paid attention to me. He listened to me. He told me I was beautiful. He was like a soothing balm for my aching heart. I'm sorry it happened, but Jeff was as much to blame as I was. He cheated on me and ignored me long before I met Danny."

Kevin remained stone-faced. "Did you engage in this affair while your husband was dying of cancer?"

"Cancer? Jeff didn't have cancer." Karen was puzzled. What made Kevin think that Jeff had died of cancer?

As if reading her mind, Kevin answered her unspoken question. "I read his obituary. You wouldn't tell me anything about yourself, so I searched on the Internet for information. I found Jeff's obituary. It asked for donations to be made to the American Cancer Association. I assumed he had cancer."

"His sister, Jessica, had cancer. She died a couple years before Jeff.'"

"How did Jeff die?"

"You really don't want to know."

"You're right. I don't want to know anything else about you. I know enough already to know you are not the woman I thought you were. I'm through, Karen."

Karen's heart was breaking. *It's not fair!* she screamed inside. *You didn't even listen to my side of the story.*

But she didn't utter those words. She knew that God had answered Robin's prayer for her. Kevin was breaking up with her for good.

She simply said, "Good-bye, Kevin. You're a good man, and I hope you find someone who will make you happy."

Kevin left without responding.

29

Karen sat nervously in the church lobby waiting for her counseling session with Pastor Vinson. Since her last session, the pastor had met with Trevor. Trevor refused to discuss the session with Karen, but Karen sensed a softening in Trevor's demeanor towards her.

"Karen." She turned as the pastor called her name. "Come on back. I'm sorry to have kept you waiting."

She settled herself in the comfortable brown swivel chair across from Mark, who sat behind his desk. Unable to hold it in any longer, she blurted, "Kevin and I have ended our relationship."

"I think that is for the best. How are you handling the breakup?"

"I'm sad and lonely. I miss him."

Mark didn't appear surprised by her words. "It's only natural. Give it a little time. Keep in mind that God has a wonderful plan for your life. He wants what is best for you. I think you will be amazed to look back on this time in a few years and see how much God has done in your life and how far He has taken you. I assure you that you will not regret the breakup or the pain you are experiencing right now."

Karen pulled a tissue from the box on the corner of Mark's desk and dabbed her eyes. "I know you are right, but it still hurts."

Mark moved from behind his desk and sat in the chair next to Karen's. He held out his hands. "Let's begin this session with prayer."

Karen allowed him to hold her hands as he prayed for healing for Karen's heart, for patience as she waited for God's plan to unfold, and for wisdom for himself as he sought to counsel her.

"My session with Trevor was rather enlightening," Mark began, his tone serious. "He exhibited a great deal of anger toward his father for dying. He also expressed anger at you, but he wouldn't elaborate. Can you shed some light on Trevor's feelings?"

Karen had vowed never to discuss the events of the night of Jeff's death, but she knew now that she had to, if she was going to help Trevor get over them. She took a deep breath and exhaled before answering. "The day before his death, Jeff and I took off from work and went to Virginia Beach. We walked on the beach and talked more than we had in years. For the first time in a very long time, he talked about his hopes and plans for the future. We ate lunch at a seafood restaurant on the beach. Jeff ordered two bowls of she-crab soup." Karen smiled at the memory. "Jeff loved she-crab soup. I had clam chowder. It was a great day."

Mark smiled with her. "It sounds like it. It might help Trevor if you share happy memories with him. He needs to know that you loved his father."

Karen knew he was right. Trevor had heard the fights, but he didn't know about the ways they had been working to improve their marriage. "The next day was Saturday. Jeff worked in the yard and around the house all day. After dinner, he sorted through the mail and began paying bills." Karen turned to look at Mark. "That's when he saw the cell phone bill. We had a big fight. Jeff said terrible things."

"You fought about the cell phone bill?" Mark questioned.

"Jeff got angry when he saw that I had made a lot of calls to Danny."

"Who's Danny?"

"I was having an affair with Danny. I loved him. That's why I asked Jeff for the divorce. After Jeff rededicated his life to the Lord and started trying to repair our marriage, I quit seeing Danny."

"Did Jeff know about Danny?"

"Yes. I told him when we discussed getting divorced. He was shocked and upset, even though he admitted to having been with several women in the past three years. I think the affair is what got Jeff's attention. He had never considered that another man might find me attractive or interesting."

"If he knew about you and Danny, why was he so upset about the calls?"

Karen grimaced. "I didn't stop calling him. I didn't see him again, but he had become my closest friend. I needed to keep him in my life.

171

We talked three or four times a day. In an effort to improve our marriage, Jeff and I started "dating" again. We spent a weekend in Williamsburg and bought season passes to King's Dominion. What really angered Jeff was that I called Danny while we were in Williamsburg together."

"I see." Mark was beginning to get a better picture of the issues Jeff and Karen had faced and the damage they had each done to their marriage. "Okay. You two fought. Then what happened?"

Karen stood up and walked over to the window. She stared out the window for several minutes. "Jeff left for a few hours. It was pretty late when he returned, but I was up waiting for him. I smelled the alcohol as soon as he opened the door."

Karen began to pace around the office. "I walked into the kitchen, bracing myself for another fight. He looked at me with his bloodshot eyes and said in the saddest voice I have ever heard, 'I've lost you, haven't I?' In that moment I wanted to hurt him the way he had hurt me for so long. So I simply said 'Yes.'"

Karen shivered. Tears welled in her eyes. "If I'd known it was the last time I would speak to him, I would have told him that I loved him and that the marriage wasn't over. That would have been the truth. But I had endured so much pain that I struck back. Jeff hung his head like a condemned man. He went back outside, and I went to the bedroom. I heard the door open again. I listened for footsteps, but I didn't hear any. What I had heard was Trevor leaving the house, not Jeff returning. After a minute or so, the silence was broken by a loud, sharp sound. I thought it sounded like a gun going off."

Karen looked away again and paused. In a very small voice, she said, "It was a gun going off. Then I heard Trevor scream. By the time I got outside, Trevor was running toward the house. 'Call 911!' he screamed. Tears streamed down his face. I knew Jeff was dead. He had shot himself in the head."

Mark grabbed a handful of tissues and walked over to Karen. He handed her the tissues and gathered her in his arms. All of her pent-up emotions poured out. She blubbered into Mark's shoulders until her tears were all spent. She turned a tear-stained face to look at Mark as she stepped out of his embrace. "If only I had swallowed my pride and told Jeff I loved him, he would still be alive. My boys would still have a daddy. Trevor is right to blame me."

"I can understand why you feel that way. Certainly, I cannot condone your actions, but much of the blame rests on Jeff's shoulders. You are not responsible for your husband's actions. He alone made the decision to end his life. He turned his back on God and ruined his life and your marriage with alcohol. You didn't cause your husband's suicide, but you are not innocent, either.

"Karen, it's not my place to condemn you. Neither does God condemn you. He wants you to repent and allow Him to forgive you. First John 1:9 says, 'If we confess our sins, He is faithful and just and will forgive us our sins and purify us from all unrighteousness.' Have you confessed this sin, Karen?"

She shook her head no.

"Would you like to now?" Mark asked.

"Yes."

Mark led Karen in a prayer of repentance. "You've asked Him to forgive you. Do you believe that He has?"

Karen nodded affirmatively.

"Now you also have to forgive yourself. That's the hard part."

"I don't know how. I don't think I can."

Mark paused for a moment, and his eyes closed, as if he were whispering a prayer for guidance. Then he spoke. "Karen, you've mentioned a couple of times that you restore damaged wood furniture. I'd like to hear a bit about the process."

Karen was relieved to change the subject to something she truly enjoyed talking about. "Okay. I begin by removing the old finish." Her voice gained strength as she talked about the familiar process. "I remove stain using steel wool and wood stripper. I rub the wool gently over the wood until the stain is lifted. Removing paint is more difficult. I brush stripper onto the wood and allow it to set. Then I scrape away the paint using a putty knife. After that, the wood is prepared to receive the stain. The residue is removed, and the wood is sanded smooth. Then the new finish is applied. The final step is to seal the finish to protect it."

Mark rubbed his chin. "Very interesting. So you can't do it all in one session, can you?"

"Oh, no." Karen shook her head. "It is a time-consuming process. Some projects go faster than others, but they all require multiple sessions over several days."

"What are the most time-consuming projects?"

"Pieces that have several coats of paint. I recently refinished a dining room table. The table had been painted three times, without removing the old paint. I had to scrap off the layers one at a time. It required a great deal of time and effort."

"Was the effort worth it?"

"Absolutely. It had been white, but the paint was chipped and discolored. It was really ugly. Underneath all the paint, I found beautiful wood in great condition. When I stained it, it was gorgeous. It's in my dining room now. My brother says that I can look at an ugly or damaged piece of furniture and see the potential in it. I guess he's right."

Mark smiled. "That's a lot like the way God sees people. We all come to him damaged. We've been marred. Some of us have harmed ourselves through sin and bad choices. Others have been hurt by others or by the circumstances of their lives. No matter how we got damaged, we are all in need of restoration. When we come to God, He peels off the layers of hurt, pain, guilt, and sorrow. The process isn't quick, and it isn't painless, but it is necessary. Jeremiah talked about this process in terms of a potter reforming a clay pot."

Mark reached for the Bible lying on his desk and opened it to Jeremiah 18. "In verses 3 and 4, Jeremiah writes, 'So I went down to the potter's house, and I saw him working at the wheel. But the pot he was shaping from the clay was marred in his hands; so the potter formed it into another pot, shaping it as seemed best to him.' You've been marred by hurt and betrayal and also by your own sin. But God looks at you and He sees your inner beauty and your potential. God wants to scrap away the layers of hurt and reshape your life in the way that seems best to Him. As you let Him have His way, I think you will start to see the Karen that God sees and forgiving yourself will be easier."

Karen sniffled. Mark handed her another tissue.

This time her tears were not of sorrow, but of hope.

30

Karen ran to the mailbox as soon as she parked the car in the driveway. "Please, please, let it be here." She knew that it wasn't the second she opened the box. The package would be bulky. All she saw were envelopes and flyers. "Maybe it wouldn't fit in the mailbox." She ran to the front porch. "Yes!" She pumped her fist in glee. Propped up against door was a brown, padded envelope. It had to be the package she was expecting.

Karen whistled as she wrapped the two gifts. Then she tucked them into the large gift bags that held the other presents for Bethany and Brittany. Today was the Marshall twins' ninth birthday. Greg had invited the entire staff and their families, as well as some other friends, to a barbecue at his home.

"Let's go, boys. We don't want to be late." Karen waited impatiently by the front door, presents in one hand and the car keys in the other.

"I'm starving," Austin called out from the kitchen, his head in the refrigerator.

"All the more reason to get going," Karen called back. "Don't eat anything. Dr. Marshall will be feeding us dinner very soon."

Austin closed the refrigerator and ran out the front door as Trevor came down the stairs. Kyle was already waiting for them in the car. Karen had feared that Trevor would think the birthday party too childish for him. She had been pleasantly surprised when he not only agreed to accompany the family but also seemed to be looking forward to it. Karen supposed Greg was responsible for Trevor's positive attitude. The two Saturdays they had spent together had done wonders for Trevor.

Karen recognized also that the changes in her own life were having a positive impact on Trevor. A few weeks had passed since her breakup with Kevin. Already her heart had mended, although she missed his companionship. She grudgingly admitted to herself that she liked being part of a couple and she missed that feeling more than she missed Kevin per se.

Pastor Vinson had cautioned her to avoid jumping straight into another relationship. "Focus your attention on God and your family for now. Let God send you the right man in His time."

God was helping her to forgive herself and to leave the guilt and hurt behind. The nightmares ceased after her confession to Pastor Vinson of her role in Jeff's death. She and Trevor had a tearful but healing conversation, and she had asked for Trevor's forgiveness. When he gave it, it was wholehearted and complete.

"There's a million cars here," Kyle announced as Karen turned onto the street where the Marshall family lived.

"I don't think there's quite a million," Karen laughed, "but you're right that there are quite a few. I wonder where I can park." Cars lined both sides of the street, but there was room in the driveway. Karen pulled in, and the family piled out of the car.

"There's a note on the door," Austin yelled as he ran ahead of the rest of the family. "It say's 'Party Guests—Come around to the backyard.'"

As they entered the yard through the gate, Karen spied Greg at the grill. Gretchen sat in a reclining chair in the shade. Robin was at the patio table with a pile of brag books, showing off the latest pictures of Nicole. There were several people Karen recognized from church but to whom she hadn't been introduced. A dozen children played on the jungle gym. The man pushing Brittany on the swing looked exactly like Chad. On closer inspection, Karen realized it was, indeed, her brother.

"I wonder what Chad is doing here?" Although she had introduced him to Greg, the two men barely knew each other. Chad leaned over and whispered something into the ear of the lady pushing Bethany's swing. It was Emily Clark. *Things must be heating up between those two*, Karen thought.

Greg waved Karen over to himself. "I'm glad you're here. Gretchen was going to play hostess, but she threw her back out. I was hoping you would take over that role." Greg flipped burgers as he talked.

"Of course. What do you want me to do?" Karen could see that he was also grilling hot dogs and sausages.

"The meat will be ready soon. I need you to bring out the dishes from the kitchen. Everything is ready in the refrigerator. Also, if you could bring out the condiments, it would be a big help."

Karen opened the refrigerator and easily spotted the food Greg had purchased. She carried out a bowl of potato salad and another of broccoli salad, a platter of fresh sliced tomatoes and onions, a plate of cheese slices, and another holding lettuce leaves and pickles. Chad spotted her and came to help. He grabbed the mustard, mayo, and ketchup, as well as the chips and salsa.

Greg blessed the meal. In short order, each of the guests had fixed a plate and scattered across the yard to one of the many tables that had been set up. Karen found herself seated beside Greg; Chad and Emily also sat at their table. Karen had barely seen her brother since he moved into his new apartment. Chad devoted long hours to his work, but he apparently was making time for a social life. Trevor joined them at the table as well.

"I was thinking of doing a bit of crabbing on Saturday, Trevor," Greg said between bites of hot dog. "Are you free to go with me?"

"Sure. Can I, Mom?" Trevor looked pleadingly at Karen.

"May I?" Karen corrected. "Yes, of course."

"Is it okay if Uncle Chad comes, too?"

Chad looked surprised but pleased that Trevor had thought to include him. "Sorry, pal. I have plans." He fixed his gaze on Karen, sitting across the table from him. "I'm taking Emily to Chester to meet the folks."

Karen nearly choked on the piece of broccoli she was chewing. She thumped her chest and coughed. Greg pounded her on the back. "Are you all right?" His concern was touching.

"I'm fine. Really." She rolled her eyes at her brother in mock surprise. "Will wonders never cease?" To Emily, she said, "Chad's *never* brought a girl home to meet Mom and Dad."

A roguish smile played on Chad's lips. "That's because I've never met a girl as special as Emily."

Karen's heart skipped a beat. *My little brother is in love. Finally!*

"So, Trevor, I guess it's you and me on Saturday." Greg turned to Karen. "Would it be all right if Trevor spent the night here tomorrow? That way we can get an early start. The girls are staying with Gretchen. They're going to a ladies' tea at church on Saturday."

Karen agreed to Greg's plan.

"Greg, where's Sandy?" a man Karen didn't recognize called out from the next table.

"She went to Baltimore to visit her parents," Greg replied casually. If he was bothered by her absence, no one could tell it from his attitude.

"She told me she was coming to the party and leaving tomorrow." That comment came from Gretchen, who made no effort to hide her displeasure.

Greg wiped hamburger juice from his chin before replying. "Something came up. She had to leave today. Girls, are you ready to open your presents?" Greg's change of subject let everyone know that he had no further interest in discussing Sandy's early departure for her hometown.

Brittany and Bethany gladly began unwrapping the huge pile of gifts. They were well trained to open one gift at a time, properly examine it, and then thank the giver before moving on to the next present. Most guests had purchased the same item for each girl. They received the usual assortment of books, games, and toys. Tom and Gretchen gave each girl an American Girl doll. Bethany and Brittany squealed with delight and declared that the dolls were what they had been praying for.

Sandy had stopped by Tidewater Orthodontics and dropped off presents for the girls before leaving town. The girls opened the large boxes to find stuffed bears. Each bear was gaily dressed and when you pressed its heart, it played "Happy Birthday." Everyone exclaimed how cute the bears were. Karen felt a twinge of jealousy, although she knew it was silly. There was a strong possibility that Sandy would one day be the girls' new mother. It was only right that she should give them special gifts like the bears.

By happenstance, the girls opened Karen's gifts last. Careful to not ruin each other's surprise, they both pulled out the large, rectangular gift first. "It looks like a book," Bethany declared. They ripped off the paper to find that they each received a children's cookbook. The books were similar but not identical. "Cool," Brittany exclaimed. "Now, we can learn to cook."

Karen noticed a strange expression on Greg's face. She couldn't decide what it meant. She turned her attention back to the twins as they withdrew two long, slender packages, which turned out to be cooking spoons. The last present in each bag was smaller and squishier than the others. The girls unwrapped them and held up identical, handmade aprons. Each girl's name was embroidered on her apron, along with the command, 'Kiss the Cook.'

"They are so cute."

"Where did you find them?"

"Did you make them?"

It seemed as if all the ladies were asking questions of Karen at the same time. When Karen managed to get a word in, she told them that a friend had made them. Kim had come up the previous Friday, and the two friends had shopped for upholstery fabric. Karen told to Kim about the upcoming birthday party and confided that she needed something else to make her gifts as special as she wanted them to be.

"Aprons would be nice," Kim suggested.

"I thought about aprons. I looked in a few stores, but I haven't found anything girlish enough. It's hard to find a 'cute' apron."

"I could make them," Kim had said.

Karen looked at her askance.

"Really," Kim insisted, "it would be easy, and I would like to."

Karen hesitated. "Well, if you're sure. I need them next Thursday."

"I'll sew them this weekend and put them in the mail on Monday. You should have them by Thursday."

Karen loved the idea. They picked out the fabric while they were shopping. Karen had feared they wouldn't arrive in time, but Kim was true to her word. Karen couldn't have been more pleased. At least until she saw the frown on Greg's face as he hurried past her and into the house.

She quickly found Robin. "Greg seems upset. Did I get them something I shouldn't have?"

179

Robin didn't have an answer for her, but Gretchen did. "No, sweetie," she said softly as she gave her a squeeze. "You misunderstood Greg's reaction. He was touched by your gifts. You gave them what Cindy would have given them, if she were here."

Karen helped with cleaning up before she left. She didn't get another chance to speak with Greg. Trevor informed her on the way home that Greg would pick up him after school the next day. "He's going to take me out to dinner."

⌘⌘⌘

The next day Greg arrived at the house promptly at 5. Karen was in the midst of dinner preparations.

"May I speak to you for a moment?" he asked politely.

Karen made certain that the food on the stove would be fine for a few minutes and joined him in the living room.

"The sofa table looks great. I passed you downtown the day you bought it. I honked, but you were busy tying it to the top of your van."

Karen was positive that Greg didn't come in to discuss her furniture. She waited for him to get to the point.

"I wanted to talk to you about yesterday. To explain my reaction." Greg twiddled his thumbs. Karen had never known Greg to be shy or nervous. "I've never told anybody this, and I'm sure the girls don't remember it. They were too small." Greg chewed on his lower lip.

"The last Christmas Cindy was alive the girls were five. They loved to bake cookies and help Cindy in the kitchen. But, of course, they slowed the process down considerably. Cindy shooed them from the kitchen when she got ready to cook Christmas dinner. I was in the den, and the girls crawled up in my laps looking heartbroken. 'What's the matter with my princesses?' I asked them. 'We're too young to help Mommy cook,' Bethany said. Then Brittany added, 'Mom says we can learn to cook when we turn nine.'"

Karen felt her breath escaping from her as if she'd been punched in the stomach. "I had no idea. I remembered how much I liked to cook with my mother at their age. Cooking together bonded us. Even when I was a rebellious teenager, my mother and I could always get along in the kitchen. I wanted them to have happy memories of cooking with their grandmother, or perhaps, if you marry…"

Somehow Karen couldn't say "Sandy." While Sandy was a wonderful lady, Karen could not envision the nurse cooking with the Marshall twins.

"It was the perfect gift. Thank you." Greg gently kissed her cheek.

31

Sandy opened the door wearing a paint-spattered T-shirt and jeans with torn knees. Greg had told her to dress casually for their date, but this was taking casual way too far.

"Oh, hi, Greg. Come in." Sandy seemed surprised to see Greg, but she opened the door and gave him entrance into her living room. "Can I get you a soda?"

"Okay. Sure." Sandy left a rather confused Greg standing in the doorway and went to the kitchen. He had planned to take her out for barbeque and a movie. Now he was wondering if they had gotten their signals crossed.

"Are you painting?" Greg asked as he accepted the drink and took a seat on her couch.

"Yes. I'm putting the condo on the market next week. It's needed a new coat of paint for ages. I have a few repairs that need to be made, also. Then I think it will be ready for sale." Sandy opened her drink but did not sit. Then her eyes widened. "Oh, my gosh, I've been so busy painting that I totally forgot about our date tonight. I'm so sorry."

Greg had never seen Sandy so flustered. "Don't worry about it. I can wait for you to change." Sandy's frown alerted Greg to switch gears. "Or better yet, I'll help you paint." Sandy's expression perked up, and the decision to forego the date in favor of painting was made. "The important thing is for us to spend time together." Uh-oh, the frown was back.

"Actually, Greg, I've been meaning to talk to you since I got back from Baltimore." Sandy's weekend trip to celebrate Mother's Day with her parents in Baltimore had been extended on both ends to almost a full week. She had returned on Wednesday, but this was the first time Greg had seen her in more than a week. She had said little during their two phone calls. Greg steeled himself to hear what Sandy had to say.

"Let me start at the beginning." Sandy spread a towel and sat down in the chair opposite the couch. "For quite some time I have felt God impressing upon me to move closer to my family. I guess it started after my father's stroke last fall. A few months ago, before we started dating, I mailed out some resumes and started making inquiries about obtaining a position at a hospital in Baltimore. When I didn't get any responses, I assumed I'd be staying here. Then last week, I received a call from Baltimore General. They asked me to come in for an interview on Thursday."

"That's why you missed the girls' birthday party," Greg interposed.

"Yes. I'm sorry about that, but it was the only time they could schedule the interview, and Baltimore General was my first choice. I went back for a second interview on Monday and was offered the job on Tuesday. It was exactly what I've been looking for. I accepted it on the spot." Sandy's joy was evident in her face and her voice.

"Let me see if I've got this straight." Greg set the soda can on the coffee table and leaned forward, elbows on his knees and head propped on his hands. "You're selling the condo and moving back to Baltimore." Greg, to his utter amazement, found his reaction to be one of happiness for his friend. *His friend.* In all these weeks of dating, he finally acknowledged to himself that Sandy had become a good friend and nothing more.

"Yes, isn't it wonderful?" she bubbled. Then her joy dimmed a bit. "Well, not for us, I guess, but it's what I really want. All my family is there. My brother and sister live close to my parents. I want a chance to watch their children grow up and be involved in their lives."

"Of course, it's wonderful." Greg stood and walked over to Sandy with his arms wide open. "Congratulations on the new job. I'm happy for you." Sandy stood and allowed Greg to give her a big bear hug. Greg didn't feel any regrets about Sandy's news. He had enjoyed her company and had hoped that special feelings would emerge, but they hadn't and he was honestly happy for her.

"Please don't be upset with me. Spending time with you has been great, and all, but..." Sandy seemed to struggle for the right words.

"But there was no spark," Greg finished for her, as he again took his seat, as she had.

"You felt it, too. I thought it was only me." Sandy breathed a sigh of relief.

"You are such a godly woman, Sandy, and you will make someone an excellent wife. I kept hoping that passion would kick in."

"I know what you mean. The day we went hiking was the first and, now that I think about it, the only time that you kissed me. It felt like I was kissing my brother."

Greg chuckled. "That's exactly what I thought. I guess that's why I never felt inclined to try again."

An uncomfortable silence fell between them. They both sipped their soft drinks as they pondered their next moves.

"The offer to help paint still stands."

"Really? I could use the help. I've never painted before."

"We still need to eat, though. I'm starving. What do you want on your pizza?" Greg was already reaching for the phone. "I'll have it delivered so we don't waste any time. We've got a lot of work ahead of us if you're going to have the condo ready to be shown next week."

Greg stayed until midnight. They managed to get the bedrooms and the hall done.

He came back on Saturday with the girls and Trevor. Greg and Trevor finished painting, and the girls helped Sandy put up some new curtains. Greg repaired a leaky faucet and hung new blinds in the kitchen. Trevor replaced the toilet seats. The girls washed the windows inside and out. With the exception of the worn flooring, the condo looked almost brand new. A handyman would be there on Monday replace the vinyl in the kitchen and bathrooms. New carpet would be installed midweek. The condo would be ready for the Open House scheduled for the next weekend.

"I can't thank you enough," Sandy told the work crew as they were leaving. "You girls did a great job. Trevor, you and Greg make a great team."

32

It was the last Friday before school let out for the summer. While the end of the school year signaled freedom for the boys, it meant a loss of freedom to Karen. Instead of having an entire day for herself each week, Karen would now be occupied doing things with and for her sons. Not that she spent her Fridays pampering herself or lying about idling. In fact, Friday was typically her busiest day of the week. It was the day she devoted to shopping, running errands, scheduling doctor and dentist appointments, as well as cleaning the house and working on her refinishing projects. Fridays had been even busier since she started on the refinishing projects for Mr. Stevens, her first paying customer. She'd spent a few mornings at the library doing research so she could replicate the original style before beginning work on a Victorian armoire. Lately, she had also made time for a few girls' lunches out with Emily; Karen had a sneaking suspicion that they would be related soon and wanted to get to know Emily better.

Karen was, of course, looking forward to having more time for the boys. She had already planned a trip to Virginia Beach and had promised Kyle that they would visit the Zoo. Austin had announced last Saturday that he was writing a book and needed his mother's help; Karen knew nothing about writing books, but she loved to read and would willingly lend a hand to help Austin in this endeavor.

But, right now, she had a dozen things she wanted to accomplish on her last free day. Regretfully, she would get none of them done this day. On Monday, Greg had reminded her that she was to accompany him to Richmond for a meeting of the Virginia Orthodontic Association. Fortunately, the conference was only scheduled for the morning. They would attend sessions until noon, then head back to Fredericksburg, stopping along the way for lunch. With a bit of luck, Karen would have a couple of hours to shop for groceries and vacuum before she had to pick up the boys from school.

"You're quiet over there." Greg's sudden comment after a long silence startled Karen. She jumped in her seat.

⌘ ⌘ ⌘

Greg chuckled at Karen's surprised face, which was quickly turning the color of a ripe tomato.

"I was just thinking about what I'm going to do with the boys all summer."

Karen's voice was tender. Greg had noticed that it always took on that quality when she spoke of her sons. The realization had warmed his heart. Too many parents, in Greg's opinion, griped about the time and energy it took to raise children, as if children were nuisances. Greg firmly believed that children are gifts from God, and he was learning that Karen's heart agreed with his own in that regard.

"Tell me what you have planned." Greg found that he looked forward to the hearing about her plans.

"We have so many ideas, I don't know if we will be able to work them all in. I think we'll start with a trip to the zoo, probably next Friday. The boys went to a petting zoo at the fair a couple years ago, but they've never been to a real zoo. Kyle was so small that he doesn't remember the petting zoo. He's my true animal lover. So that's my top priority."

"The National Zoo or the Virginia Zoo?"

"The one in D.C."

"That's the National Zoo. It's owned and operated by the Smithsonian."

"I didn't know there was a Virginia Zoo."

"Yes, it's quite nice. It's down in Norfolk. Gretchen and Tom took the girls there last summer. We took them to the National Zoo several years ago, but I doubt they remember."

"Maybe we should go to the Virginia Zoo." Karen had seemed so confident about her plans just moments ago, but now Greg heard the hesitation in her voice. "I'm really nervous about driving in all the Washington traffic and trying to find the zoo on my own."

"Well, it's a toss-up as to whether the traffic is worse in D.C. or in Norfolk. They can both be nightmares during rush hour, which is something of a misnomer. Rush hour in D.C. is officially four hours long, morning and afternoon."

Karen winced.

"Your best bet is to drive to Springfield and take the subway," he advised. "It will drop you a couple blocks from the zoo. Have you ever taken the subway into D.C.?"

"No, I've never even been to D.C."

Greg had been trying to help, but Karen sounded even more alarmed.

"Hey!" Greg had a sudden inspiration. "Why don't I go with you? I mean we—me and the girls. The girls would love it. I could drive. We can pile everyone into my Suburban. There's plenty of room for all of us."

"Are you sure you don't mind? Trevor would probably agree to go, if you were going with us."

"Mind? I'd love to go. What do you think? Do we have a date for next Friday?"

"Sure! Why not?" Though she tried hard to sound nonchalant, Greg detected the excitement in her voice.

"By the way, I've been meaning to thank you for all you're doing for Trevor. I means a lot to him, and to me."

"You're welcome, but no thanks are necessary. I'm doing it as much for my sake as Trevor's."

"We went to Chester for Memorial Day. He told the whole family about the crabbing expedition."

Greg pretended to look chagrined. "I hope he didn't tell them everything."

Karen laughed aloud.

"What's so funny?" Greg questioned her.

"I was just picturing you with a crab hanging off your chin."

Greg groaned.

"When Trevor told that story, we laughed until our sides hurt."

Greg feigned indignation. "You think it's funny that I was mortally wounded?"

187

"You don't seem any worse for wear. I wish Trevor had taken a picture of you."

Greg gave up acting offended and laughed along with Karen.

"Fortunately, there was no one nearby with a camera or a video recorder. I was hopping from one foot to the other, yelling at Trevor to pull the critter off, and Trevor was rolling on the dock howling with laughter. That crab was holding on for dear life. Finally, I managed to swat it, and it let go."

"It's too bad someone didn't get it on tape. We could have sent it in to *America's Funniest Videos*. It would have won, for sure."

The rest of the trip was spent in easy banter. Greg asked Karen about her plans for summer vacation. Each year, Greg closed the office for two weeks in July and took his family to the Outer Banks. Karen told him of her plans to spend a week at Virginia Beach and a week in Chester.

"Will your parents join you at the beach?" Greg inquired.

"Yes, and Jeff's parents. I think Chad and Emily will come, too."

"Did I hear you correctly? Jeff's parents are going on vacation with you?"

"Yes, you heard correctly. Actually, they are taking us on vacation and paying for everything for me and the boys."

"That's wonderful. You have to tell me how that transpired." Karen had shared with Greg that she wasn't on speaking terms with Jeff's parents, but she hadn't elaborated on the cause of their estrangement.

"Mark, I mean Pastor Vinson, helped me see that I needed to forgive them and ask their forgiveness for things we said and did after Jeff died. Mark helped me see that they reacted out of their pain and that forgiving them didn't make their behavior, or my own, right. It only meant that I wouldn't hold it against them any longer. He helped me write them a letter. They'd been wanting to heal the relationship as well, but they didn't know how to bridge the gap."

"That's great news. God is in the healing business."

"Yes, he is. The Harpers invited us for a cookout on Memorial Day. While we were there, they offered to take us to the beach and invited Mom and Dad to come along."

"What will you do with the boys while you work?"

"Austin and Kyle will go to day camps and vacation Bible schools. Trevor has a job working with Chad. What about your girls? How will they spend the time when you are working?"

"Most of the time, they will stay with Gretchen and Tom. They, too, are signed up for VBS at practically every church in town. The first thing the girls want to do is see the newest Disney movie. They are begging me to take them this weekend, and frankly, I'm just not up to it. I was wondering…"

"I'd be glad to take them," Karen interjected. "I'll be going anyway."

Greg chuckled. "How about tomorrow night? There's a new action movie opening this weekend that I'd love to see. Do you think Trevor would want to watch it with me, while you take the younger children to their movie?"

"I'm sure he would. I know he wants to see it. I think I got the short end of this deal." Karen giggled. "You get Trevor, and I get four elementary school kids."

"I'll sweeten the pot. How about we go to a matinee, around 4 or so, then I'll take everyone out for pizza afterwards?"

"You've got a deal."

⌘ ⌘ ⌘

The conference was as long and tiring as Karen had expected it to be, but it did not live up to her expectations on one count—it was not boring. She had dreaded sitting in an uncomfortable chair for three hours listening to a speaker drone on about the newest software for managing a professional orthodontic office. She had been surprised that each participant was seated in front of a computer monitor and got to experience the new software firsthand. Rather than hearing about how much better it was, Karen saw the improvements for herself.

By the time the session ended at quarter till twelve, Karen had made up her mind that she was not leaving the convention center without her own copy. She found Greg and insisted that he purchase a copy on the spot. After listening to her enthusiastic assessment of how much it would improve her work life, he pulled out his credit card.

Greg's first session had dealt with the latest breakthroughs in bracket technology. Manufacturers were consistently experimenting with making brackets more effective and less intrusive. Greg was pleased with the newest developments. He had also been to a session designed to increase awareness of the possible hazards of his profession. No healthcare professional, particularly one who had his hands in patients' mouths all day, could afford to be careless about preventing the spread of germs from patient to patient or from patient to doctor. All in all, Greg decided that it had been a very educational morning.

"I thought we would get out of the city before we stop for lunch. Is that all right with you?" Greg asked Karen as he eased out of the parking space in the garage adjacent to the convention center.

"Fine. They fed us bagels and coffee at ten, so I'm not starved by any means."

⌘⌘⌘

Karen was enjoying listening to Greg share what he had learned at the conference when she noticed that he was exiting I-95 at Ashland. A knot formed in the pit of her stomach. Of course, there were several restaurants within a very short distance of the exit. She would let Greg choose; odds were he wouldn't pick *that* restaurant.

"There's a Big Boy here. How does that sound?"

The knot got bigger. "Great," she heard herself say.

"Hey there. We haven't seen you around here in quite awhile." The waitress, whose nametag read *Sheila,* addressed her comments to Karen. Karen recognized her from her many visits here with Mike. "I'll seat you in my station. It'll give us a chance to catch up while you eat." She laid two menus on the table and walked off.

Great. The knot was so big that Karen didn't think she would be able to eat a single bite of lunch. *Just what I want to do—catch up with some waitress I barely know. She probably thinks Greg is Mike.*

Greg lifted an eyebrow but didn't comment on the waitress's overly friendly behavior.

Sheila returned with two glasses of ice water and utensils. She took her order pad from one of the large pockets of the black apron tied around her waist. "Ya'll want the usual, or you want a minute to look at the menu?"

"The usual?"

Sheila caught the question in Greg's voice. "Hey, you're not the same guy. What happened to that other guy you used to come in here with?" Sheila mouthed "Sorry" to Karen and shrugged.

"I'm not seeing Mike anymore." Karen decided to let it go at that. The less said, the better in circumstances like this.

"What was that all about?" Greg asked after Sheila left to turn their order into the kitchen.

While Greg was ordering, Karen had worked out a truthful but vague response. "Awhile back I was dating a guy named Mike from Fredericksburg. I still lived in Chester. This was a good place for us to meet. We would have lunch here, and sometimes we would go to King's Dominion." *And sometimes we would not go to King's Dominion.* "We broke up about a year ago—soon after I moved to Fredericksburg." She took a sip of water, hoping that would signal Greg to change the subject.

He didn't take the hint. "Did you move to Fredericksburg to be closer to Mike?"

"Yes and no. Mostly yes. But I did need a change. There were too many painful memories in Chester. I wanted a new start. I thought I would have it with Mike. I guess that was not what he had in mind."

Karen hoped that Greg would leave it at that. She was grateful when he did.

"You'll never believe what I let Robin and Gretchen talk me into doing tonight," he said.

Karen declined to guess.

"I'm going on a blind date."

"A blind date?" This came from Sheila, who had just returned with their food. "Aren't you dating her?" She nodded in Karen's direction as she set a chicken Caesar salad in front of Karen.

"No," Greg and Karen answered Sheila's question in unison. They both started laughing.

Sheila set Greg's plate down and walked away shaking her head.

"A blind date? Seriously?" Karen knew that the two women had been anxious to get Greg back in the saddle, so to speak, after their attempt to pair him with Sandy failed. She did not know, however, what had transpired between Greg and Sandy to end their relationship.

"Yes." Greg had the look of a condemned man resigned to his fate. He picked up his grilled chicken sandwich, then put it back down. "I'm so rattled I almost forgot to say grace before eating."

Greg reached over and took Karen's hands as he offered thanks for their meals.

"How in the world did they ever talk you into that?" Karen asked as soon as Greg said "amen."

"I suppose you know that they've been playing matchmaker for a few months now."

Karen's mouth was full of salad, so she nodded affirmatively. Robin didn't participate much in office gossip, but she'd let the matchmaking scheme slip out one day at lunch.

Greg took a bite of his sandwich before continuing. "After two failed attempts with women from church, they decided to take a new approach. This new lady works in Tom's office. They're not telling me much about her. They want me to go into this with an open mind."

"What happened with you and Sandy?" Karen hoped she wasn't being too forward, but Greg had brought up the subject of his dating.

"She's moving to Baltimore to be closer to her family." Greg reached for his water.

"Are you okay with that? I thought you two were getting along pretty well."

"I'm fine. It was always more of a friendship than a romance, anyway. She was very nice and we enjoyed each other's company, but there was no romantic attraction on either side. She was offered a job in Baltimore, and she jumped on it. As a matter of fact, there's a farewell reception Sunday after the morning service so everyone can say goodbye and wish her well."

Despite the fact that he had done most of the talking, Greg had finished his sandwich while Karen still had nearly half of her salad left. He excused himself and sought out the restroom.

Sheila laid the check on the table. "That other guy, Mike, was in here last week with his wife." She watched Karen for a reaction.

Karen kept chewing and ignored her.

"So this guy is your new 'friend.' He seems a bit old for you."

"Actually, he's my boss. We're on our way back from a conference." Karen didn't know why she was even bothering to respond to Sheila. With some luck, she'd never run into her again.

"Conferences can be fun, if you get my drift."

"He's a friend."

"Yeah, a friend with benefits, I bet."

Karen started to answer but noticed that Greg had walked up.

"I'll pay for the check while you finish up," Greg said.

"I'm done." Karen could not get out of there soon enough.

They were a few miles down the road before Greg asked the question Karen knew was coming.

"What is a 'friend with benefits'?" He looked over at Karen, but she refused to meet his eyes.

Staring straight ahead, she decided to be honest. "It's a term for friends who sleep together. Often they aren't dating. They sleep together to meet each other's, uh, needs."

"That sounds risky."

"I guess it is."

Greg didn't say anything for several minutes. He seemed to be mulling things over. The silence was deafening, but it sure was better than having to answer the question she knew Greg was pondering. She stared at the floor and twisted her hands.

Greg cleared his throat. *Here it comes.* "Did Mike get benefits?" His voice was gentle and devoid of judgment.

"That was different. We were dating. I thought I loved him. I thought we were going to get married." Karen's words came out in a hurry, defensively. Her voice shook, and she struggled to keep a tear from escaping. She was afraid if that first one fell, she would cry the rest of the way home. She didn't want to ruin Greg's opinion of her and jeopardize their friendship.

"So it's okay to sleep with someone if you think you're in love. Is that what you believe?"

"No. But I believed it at the time. Or at least that's what I told myself," she murmured.

"So you've changed your beliefs since." It was more of a question than a statement.

"Yes." Karen spoke with more conviction now. "Since I started going back to church, I've realized that God's way is the best way. He gives us boundaries for our protection. If I'd done things God's way, I would have saved myself a lot of heartache and guilt." Karen took a deep breath and looked directly at Greg. "I've repented of the mistakes I made with Mike and Danny. I know God has forgiven me, and I'm committed to living a pure life."

"That's what I wanted to hear."

Karen was relieved. Greg seemed truly happy to hear of her renewed commitment to Christ and Christian values.

"I should probably tell you that Trevor spoke to me about his father's death and about Danny. I know it wasn't any of my business, but it was important for Trevor to have someone to listen to him. I'm truly glad that you have your life back on track."

Karen heard no condemnation in Greg's voice. She was thankful he was willing to let her past be in the past. Neither of them could think of anything else to say, so they rode in silence for many miles.

As they neared Thornburg, Greg cleared his throat. "God's been working overtime on you lately, hasn't He?"

"He certainly has."

⌘ ⌘ ⌘

"Are we still on for tomorrow night?" Greg asked the question as Karen was climbing out of his car that was now parked in her driveway.

"Of course. I'm even going to let you pay for the movie and dinner."

"How kind of you."

"And I want to hear all about your blind date."

"Ah. Well, we'll see about that."

33

The kiddie movie had been even cheesier than Karen had expected, but the kids loved it. They had laughed at the dumbest things. Karen enjoyed watching them enjoy the film. Their laughter was the sweetest sound to her ears. Greg and Trevor had thoroughly enjoyed their "guy" movie. Everyone had eaten their fill of pizza, and the children had all disappeared to the arcade room. Karen had waited until now to ask the question she'd been dying to ask all evening.

"So, how was the date?" Her silly grin let Greg know she wanted all the gory details.

"It was an unqualified disaster." As Greg didn't seem particularly upset about it, Karen assumed he was joking and decided to press on.

"Was she old, bald, short, and fat?"

"No, no, no, and no. She was drop-dead gorgeous and even of an appropriate age. Did you know that the first date they fixed me up with was only 32? I was in high school when she was born." No, Karen had not known that. But she wasn't going to let Greg get away with changing the subject.

"You're not weaseling out of telling me about your date that easily," Karen chided. "Where did you take her?"

"I took her to Mario's Italian Restaurant. It was the worst evening of my life."

"It sounds terrible. Dinner at one of the finest restaurants in town with a gorgeous woman. I can certainly understand why the evening was so miserable." Karen didn't try to hide her sarcasm or her amusement. "I'll keep on pestering until you tell me the whole story. You might as well get started."

Seeing there was no getting out of it, Greg relented. "For starters, I bought a bouquet of flowers for her. It turns out that she's allergic to flowers. She tossed them in the garbage can as we walked to the car."

"She didn't!" Karen's mouth flew open; she couldn't imagine anyone being so calloused.

"She did," Greg assured her. "Then she proceeded to sneeze all the way to the restaurant. She blamed the sneezing on a reaction to the lingering smell of the flowers in the car." Greg rolled his eyes for effect. "I opened all the windows to give her some fresh air, but she complained about the wind messing up her hair. Plus, the traffic noise gave her a headache."

Karen was laughing aloud. "It sounds like you couldn't do anything right."

"It gets worse. I took her to a steakhouse."

"I thought you said you went to Mario's?" Karen interrupted.

"We wound up at Mario's eventually, but we started out at the new steakhouse in Southpoint. My date was not happy, as she doesn't eat red meat, and refused to get out of the car. I offered to go anywhere she wanted. She would only say that wherever I wanted to take her was fine. So I suggested Mexican. "Too spicy." Then I tried seafood. "Can't abide the smell." Finally, she conceded that she liked Italian food, so that's how we wound up at Mario's. By the time the hostess seated us, all I wanted to do was eat my meal as quickly as possible, so I could take her home and never see her again."

"I can certainly understand why." Karen was actually starting to feel a bit sorry for Greg, while at the same time thoroughly enjoying his misery. "Continue," she commanded.

"A quick meal was not to be." Greg sighed and rolled his eyes once again. "The hostess showed us to a booth, but my date wanted to sit at a table. Then we had to change tables twice. She was oh, so very polite as she demanded her own way. She put her hand on the hostess's arm and said as sweetly as she could, 'I believe I feel a draft. Would it be possible for us to move to another table?'"

As Greg said this, he gently placed his hand on Karen's arm and affected his best *I don't want to impose, but I really want my own way* voice. Greg's impression of his date's mannerism was priceless. Karen wished she had a video recorder.

"After we moved, she took the hostess's arm again. 'I'm afraid this table is too close to the kitchen. Could we possibly have that table over there in front of the window?' The hostess was exceedingly patient, but the frustration was evident in her eyes. I wanted to walk out and leave my date there on her own."

"But you didn't," Karen interjected. "You are too much of a gentleman, Greg."

Greg shrugged. "No, I didn't. We finally settled into our table and ordered. When the food came, she sent everything back. The chicken was too dry, the sauce too spicy. She even sent back the salad, claiming that the dressing was too sour. I didn't give her a chance to order dessert. She went to the restroom, and I called a cab to take her home. I told her I didn't want to risk her having another reaction to the lingering flower smell in my car."

Karen wiped tears from her eyes with the back of her hand. "That's the funniest story I've heard in a long time."

"I called Gretchen and told her no more matchmaking. I would rather be alone than go through all this. If God wants me to have another wife, He is perfectly capable of bringing her into my life without any help from Robin and Gretchen. I don't plan to do any dating for a while. I need lots of time to recuperate."

"I'm not dating right now, either. Mark Vinson counseled me to take a three-month hiatus from dating to get over Kevin and to grow closer to God."

"Good advice," Greg commented. "When will the three months be up?"

"July 25."

Karen was still laughing about Greg's date when the children returned. It seemed they were all in need of ice cream. Karen and Greg piled the kids into his Suburban and headed for Carl's, their favorite ice cream shop.

34

The ringing of the phone interrupted Karen's efforts at removing the original finish from the nightstand she was beginning to restore. Karen had delivered the fully restored Victorian armoire to Mr. Stevens last Saturday to rave reviews. Mr. Stevens had been so thrilled that he had paid her a 10 percent bonus over their agreed-upon price and had given her the two matching nightstands to begin work on.

Karen quickly laid aside the piece of steel wool in her hand, stripped off the protective yellow gloves she was wearing, and ran the 15 feet from the laundry room to the kitchen nook. She managed to grab the phone, and press the Talk button just before the answering machine picked up.

"Hello," she said quickly as she put the phone to her ear.

"Hello, yourself." Karen immediately recognized the caller's voice.

"Chad! Hi. What's going on?"

"I was checking to make sure you were home. I'm going to stop by in a few minutes. I have something I want to show you."

⌘⌘⌘

True to his word, Chad knocked on Karen's door about 15 minutes later. His hands were filled and wonderful smells emanated from him.

"Come in," Karen said holding the door for him. "What smells so good?"

"Allman's Barbeque. I brought lunch." Chad held up a brown paper sack as evidence.

"Great! I'm starved. What time is it, anyway?"

"Eleven-thirty. Do you need to be somewhere?" Chad asked, suddenly concerned that he might be interfering with his sister's plans.

"Not until one, so we're fine. Let's eat." Karen led the way into the kitchen.

"Kyle and Alex are at VBS at the Baptist church," she explained as she poured two tall glasses of sweetened iced tea. "Since it's the last day, they are having lunch and a party."

"What's Trevor up to on his day off?" Chad asked as Karen placed their drinks on the table and sat down. Trevor worked for Chad Monday through Thursday and had a three-day weekend, the same as Karen.

"Greg Marshall took him fishing," Karen answered. "His twins are at VBS also."

Chad offered the blessing, and the two siblings were silent for a few moments as they savored the delicious first bites of their sandwiches.

"Sooo," Chad began. Karen recognized the teasing that was coming her way from that single word. "I've noticed that you and Greg are becoming something of an item. It seems like every Friday you two are doing something together."

Karen feigned mock irritation. "Really, Chad, don't you have more important things to do than invent gossip?" Even as she protested, though, Karen realized that people were starting to get the mistaken impression that the two of them were a couple. She'd overheard Katie and Jenna whispering something similar just yesterday afternoon. "So, what if we took our kids on a family outing? We're friends, nothing more."

"A family outing. Didn't you go to King's Dominion together last Friday? And the Friday before that it was the zoo. I seem to recall you mentioned going to the movies and to dinner a couple of times."

"Well, okay, I guess we've taken several family outings. But it's not like we're a couple. Greg is a nice man and a friend. That's all. We've never even been on a date." *Not a real date, anyway,* she told herself. *The home-cooked dinners were merely two friends sharing a meal, and the trip to Richmond was strictly business. None of them could be considered dates. Could they?*

"Of course, you haven't. Forget I said anything."

Chad evidently decided he'd picked on Karen enough for one

morning and made a deliberate effort to change the subject. "I could use a cup of coffee. Do you have any made?"

"Actually, I put on a fresh pot when you called."

Karen busied herself for a few moments as she poured them each a cup of coffee, reached into the refrigerator for the French vanilla creamer, and grabbed the sugar bowl and two spoons. As she set the coffee on the table, she noticed the white, rectangular box Chad had placed on the table.

"What is this?" she asked Chad, eyeing him suspiciously.

Chad got up to retrieve the creamer from the kitchen counter. "Open it."

Karen took the lid off the box. It was filled with small, white cards. She lifted one from the box. "Olde Towne Renovations, LLC. Chad Butler, Owner. Specializing in the renovation of historic homes," she read off the card. "Your business cards! Chad, how exciting! It makes it official. You are your own boss now."

"Well, it was really official when I got my business license from the city and filed the papers with the state to set up my company. But the cards make it seem real, for sure." Chad was beaming, and Karen was truly delighted for her brother.

Chad reached into the manila file folder he had carried into the house with him and retrieved the single sheet it held. He slid the page across the table to Karen. Karen gasped when she glanced at it.

"Business cards for me?"

"I printed up this sheet for you on my computer. If you approve them, I will order a box for you. You are in business for yourself, too, you know."

"Well, I only have that one job for Mr. Stevens. I'm not sure that one client qualifies me as being in business."

"Sure, it does, Karen," Chad assured her. "Mr. Stevens is my only client so far, too. But soon we'll both have plenty more. Mr. Stevens has many contacts and will give us excellent referrals. I'm certain you could get enough jobs to quit working for Greg and make a living doing restorations."

"I'm not sure that I want to quit working for Greg. Besides the fact that I really like my job, Greg provides me with health insurance. With three boys, I need insurance, and there's no way I could afford to pay the premiums on my own."

"Of course, I hadn't thought about that. But didn't you tell me that you don't really have enough work to justify your hours since Greg bought you that new accounting software?" Karen nodded yes, wondering where Chad was headed. "Maybe you could cut back to three days a week and have an extra day to work on your restoration business."

"That might work. I'll have to give it some thought," Karen said quietly.

"Some prayer," Chad corrected. "Pray about it and listen to where God is leading you."

Later that night, after the younger boys were in bed, Karen sat in the den with her Bible in her lap. But she was actually staring at a small card lying on the page.

Trevor walked by and noticed the card. "What's that?" he asked his mother.

"A business card that Chad made," she replied, holding out the white card for Trevor's perusal. A few months ago, she wouldn't have shared the card, or the dreams it represented, with Trevor for fear the rebellious teenager would have mocked her. But their relationship had improved dramatically in the past six weeks. Karen had Pastor Vinson to thank for the new closeness the two were sharing. Karen realized that Trevor's opinion of the new venture was important to her.

Trevor read the card aloud: "Olde Towne Restorations, LLC. Karen Harper, Owner. Specializing in the restoration of antique furniture."

Karen held her breath for a long moment as Trevor took in the words.

When he looked up, unshed tears pooled in his eyes. He came to Karen and embraced her tightly. "I'm so proud of you, Mom," he said roughly. "Will you still work for Greg?"

Karen noticed a trace of anxiety as Trevor asked the question. It made her aware, once again, of how important Greg had become in Trevor's life.

"Yes, I'll still work for Greg. It won't be any different than what I'm doing now, only I'll officially be in business."

She decided then and there that she would have Chad order the business cards, even if she didn't change her hours.

Trevor headed upstairs to bed. As he reached the top, he turned and said, "If you want to get married again, it would be all right with me. So long as you marry Greg Marshall, that is."

35

Everyone was in the office bright and early the first day back from vacation. Greg had picked up doughnuts. It was an annual tradition to spend a few minutes eating doughnuts and catching up on each other's holidays. Katie was showing off the baby bump that had appeared over the break. Jenna filled everyone in on the plans for her wedding, only two months away. Robin had updates on Nicole, who was now rolling over. Karen and Greg both looked tan and relaxed from their separate beach vacations.

"In another month, I will have worked here a year," Karen announced as she looked at the calendar.

"You're still a newbie," Katie teased. "You haven't experienced the last week of July yet."

"What's so special about the last week of July?" Karen inquired.

"You'll find out," was all Katie would tell her.

Robin pulled Karen aside. "I just want to warn you, whatever you do, don't agree to…"

"Hey, Karen, the fair opens next week. How about I take you and the boys on Thursday?" Greg didn't seem to notice that he interrupted Robin.

"Sounds great." Karen answered before turning her attention back to Robin.

"Go to the fair with Greg." Robin finished her warning.

"What? You want me to go to the fair with Greg? I just told him I would." Robin wasn't making any sense to Karen this morning.

"Newbie," Katie said, shaking her head as she left the break room.

"Live and learn," Jenna added on her way out the door.

"I tried to warn you." Robin also seemed to think Karen had committed a major faux pas.

Greg popped back into the room. "Robin, you and Chris should come, too. It's going to be great!"

"No thanks. I'm still recovering from the last time."

"The last time was four years ago."

"I'm good for another six then. Once every ten years is my limit."

"Party pooper." Greg left.

Karen walked with Robin as she went to the lobby to unlock the door. "So what's the big deal about going to the fair with Greg?"

"You'll find out soon enough. Suffice to say that Greg LOVES the fair more than any adult I know. He loves everything about the fair—the rides, the food, the games, the shows, the food, even the smells, and especially the food."

"Okay, I get it. Greg loves the fair." *It might be fun to go to the fair with someone who really likes it,* Karen thought. "He loves the zoo, too, and we had a great time there."

"Greg's enthusiasm for the zoo pales in comparison to his passion for the fair. He'll be there waiting in line when it opens, and he won't leave until they shut it down for the night."

"Robin," Greg called out, "what does my schedule look like next Thursday afternoon?"

"You're booked straight through until five o'clock," she answered, after checking the appointment calendar on the computer.

"You'll have to reschedule some patients. No one after two-thirty. I need to be out of here by three. The fair opens at four."

Robin shot a knowing smile at Karen.

⌘ ⌘ ⌘

"You're in very good spirits today," Robin commented to Karen as they ate lunch later that day in the break room. "Did you have a great vacation?"

"I did. We spent a week with my parents and a week with Jeff's. Until Jeff's death, I had always been very close to his parents, especially his mother. I hadn't realized how much I missed having them in my life. It's wonderful how God has helped us to forgive and move on. But, that's not all. Tomorrow will be three months since Kevin and I broke up."

"Is that a good thing?" Robin asked. Inwardly, she was grateful that Karen was not nursing a broken heart.

"Tremendously. I've gone three months without a date, three months without a man in my life. Mark Vinson helped me to see that I was going from one relationship to another without a break in between. He advised me to wait three months before dating again. It seemed like such a long time, but I've made it. Of course, it may be much longer until I actually have another date. There are no prospects on the horizon. But that's okay. I'm not in a rush. And no more meeting men on the Internet. From now on, I'm waiting for God to bring the right man into my life."

Robin gave her friend a quick squeeze. "Good for you. You sound like Greg."

"Greg? In what way?"

"In your outlook on dating. He has forbidden Gretchen and I from finding him any more dates. At that disastrous blind date, we were fired." Robin put her head into her hands and feigned exaggerated distress over her dismissal from the business of finding a wife for Greg.

"He told me about it. It was the funniest thing I'd heard in a long, long time."

Karen proceeded to share with Robin the particulars of Greg's date. It was hard for Karen to tell the story because she was laughing so hard. Robin was nearly in tears by the time Karen finishing relating the story.

"Having a laugh at my expense?"

Karen sobered immediately upon hearing Greg's voice. *I wonder how long he was there and how much he heard.* She turned to apologize to her employer but quickly realized that he was teasing her. So instead she said pertly, "Laughter is good medicine."

Robin exited, leaving Greg and Karen alone in the break room. "Are you free tomorrow night?" Greg asked as nonchalantly as he could manage. "I've got tickets to the dinner theater. I was wondering if you would like to go with me."

"I'd love to."

"Great. It's a date. I'll pick you up at 6."

A date. Tomorrow. July 25. With Greg.

⌘ ⌘ ⌘

Greg finished with his last patient at five minutes before three. "I've gotta go. Katie, I need you and Jenna to finish up here for me." As he passed Karen's door, he saw she was still at her desk. "What are you still doing here? The fair opens in an hour. I'm picking you up in 45 minutes."

"I'll be ready," Karen called after him, as Greg was already going out the back door. "He certainly takes the fair seriously."

"You have no idea." This came from Jenna. "Have fun. Hope you survive."

⌘ ⌘ ⌘

Greg could hardly contain his excitement in the car. "Kids, you are going to the oldest fair in the country."

"It's old!" Austin whined. "I want to go on new rides."

Greg tried another approach to make his point. "The rides are new, but the fair is old. It was started in 1738. It's older than the United States."

"I don't want to go to an old fair," Kyle protested, following his brother's example.

"I'd give up, if I were you." Karen patted Greg's hand sympathetically. He looked a bit, well...Karen couldn't quite read his expression. "They aren't old enough to appreciate the history lesson."

⌘ ⌘ ⌘

Greg paid for parking and bought seven armbands. "We can ride every ride as many times as we want. Who's ready for an elephant ear?"

Austin pumped his fist. "Yeah. We get to eat a real elephant's ear."

"Well, not exactly." Greg shook his head in mock frustration and leaned close to Karen's ear. "You've been neglecting your children's education."

Karen jabbed him with her elbow.

Greg purchased two of the large, flat pastries—one sprinkled with powdered sugar and the other topped with strawberries. They disappeared in short order.

"What shall we ride first?"

"Bethany wants to ride the merry go round," Brittany announced.

Trevor asked and received permission to go off on his own. "Meet us at the barbecue stand for dinner at 7," Greg told him. "Before you go..." Greg handed Trevor a $20 bill. "You might want a snack or to play the arcades." Trevor sought his mother's eyes for her approval before accepting the money and disappearing to find Tim, who was also at the fair.

Greg and Karen waited for the kids as they played in the Alligator. Greg's hand rested on the small of her back. He had touched her similarly a number of times on their date to the dinner theater. Each time excitement coursed through her, though she told herself that his touches were merely incidental as he guided her through the theater. There was nothing incidental this time. Greg Marshall was deliberately touching her back. If she stepped closer to him, his arm would be around her. *Stop this foolishness, Karen. You're acting like a teenager.*

Karen's wayward thoughts were interrupted by shouts from the children that they were ready to ride the double Ferris wheel. "I think I'll sit this one out," Karen said rather nervously.

"Oh no. You're going, and that's final. I was planning to ride with Kyle since he's the youngest, but it looks like I'll have to ride with you so you won't be afraid."

Karen's children had inherited none of her fears of wild rides and were eager to ride the Ferris wheel. It was quickly decided that Kyle would ride with Austin, and Bethany would ride with Brittany. Greg took hold of Karen's hand to help her into their car. She shivered at his touch. Greg mistook her reaction as one of fear and wrapped his arm around her shoulders. "Don't be afraid. I'm right here."

Karen laid her head on Greg's shoulder and closed her eyes. She breathed in his scent. He smelled of after-shave and candied apples and elephant ears. Karen found herself relaxing in Greg's protective embrace and actually enjoyed the ride.

By eleven o'clock, the children were done in. They had ridden the Inverter, the Round Up, and the Star Ship each twice and been back to the Ferris wheel three more times. Greg bought lemonade and hot pretzels for everyone.

Kyle crawled up in Greg's lap and put his head on Greg's shoulder. Through a big yawn, he mumbled, "I'm tired, Daddy. Can we go home now?"

Karen tried hard not to react to the tender scene, but her heart skipped a beat. *Could Greg Marshall be part of God's plan for her life?* Looking around, the seven of them did look like one big, happy family.

Greg hugged the boy tightly to his chest. "Sure, son. Let's go home."

By the time Greg pulled the van into the Harpers' driveway, all of the children except Trevor were fast asleep. Austin woke up enough to walk into the house.

"I'll carry Kyle in and put him to bed," Trevor volunteered.

Greg walked to the front door with Karen.

"About Kyle's comment—" Karen began.

Greg put a finger to her lips to stop her from talking. "I'd like the job," he said simply.

Tears welled up in Karen's eyes. When Greg leaned in to kiss her, Karen knew that God had restored her heart.

About the Author

SUSAN ELIZABETH BALL is a small business counselor. She has been involved in the Girls Ministries program of the Assemblies of God for more than thirty years, working to instill in girls a love for God and a heart for service. "I'm passionate about teaching girls that God has a wonderful plan for their lives," Susan says. "I want them to know that they can find forgiveness and restoration if they have strayed from the path."

Susan has been married to her high school sweetheart, Steve, for 29 years. They have three grown sons and one grandchild. They spent 20 years in Gainesville, Florida, before returning home to Virginia. They currently reside in Fredericksburg, which provides the setting for *Restorations*.

You may write the author at: susan@susaneball.com.

www.susaneball.com
www.oaktara.com